THE WAY YOU DIE TONIGHT

The Rat Pack Mysteries from Robert J. Randisi

EVERYBODY KILLS SOMEBODY SOMETIME
LUCK BE A LADY, DON'T DIE
HEY THERE (YOU WITH THE GUN IN YOUR HAND)
YOU'RE NOBODY 'TIL SOMEBODY KILLS YOU
I'M A FOOL TO KILL YOU *
FLY ME TO THE MORGUE *
IT WAS A VERY BAD YEAR *
YOU MAKE ME FEEL SO DEAD *
THE WAY YOU DIE TONIGHT *

* available from Severn House

THE WAY YOU DIE TONIGHT

A 'Rat Pack' Mystery

Robert J. Randisi

Severn House Large Print
London & New York

This first large print edition published 2016
in Great Britain and the USA by
SEVERN HOUSE PUBLISHERS LTD of
19 Cedar Road, Sutton, Surrey, England, SM2 5DA.
First world regular print edition published 2013 by
Severn House Publishers Ltd.

British Library Cataloguing in Publication Data
A CIP catalogue record for this title is available from the British Library.

ISBN-13: 9780727894472

Severn House Publishers support the Forest Stewardship Council™
[FSC™], the leading international forest certification organisation. All
our titles that are printed on FSC certified paper carry the FSC logo.

MIX
Paper from
responsible sources
FSC   FSC® C013056
www.fsc.org

Typeset by Palimpsest Book Production Ltd.,
Falkirk, Stirlingshire, Scotland.
Printed and bound in Great Britain by
T J International, Padstow, Cornwall.

'The Way You Look Tonight'
Jerome Kern Lyrics by
Dorothy Fields

To Marthayn
I love the way you look every night!

PROLOGUE

December, 2007

'Where's your Messiah now?'

With all the gangster movies Edward G. Robinson made during his career it was this line, uttered in Cecil B. DeMille's *The Ten Commandments*, for which he is well known. For years comics would use it when impersonating Robinson. 'Dathan' was as famous a role for him as 'Rico' in *Little Caesar* and 'Rocco' in *Key Largo*.

I was at home in my living room, watching *The Ten Commandments* on Turner Classic Movies, as part of a birthday tribute to Edward G. Robinson, who had been born on December 12th, 1893. I had already seen *Key Largo* and *Little Caesar*, and next – after Heston was done chewing the scenery – they were going to finish the day with the movie he did with Frank Sinatra in 1959, *A Hole in the Head*. In it, Frank and Eddie play brothers who don't get along very well, even though they love each other. In point of fact, Frank and Edward G. were friends.

That wasn't the only movie they had made together, though. Eddie had also appeared briefly in *Robin and the 7 Hoods*, one of the Rat Pack movies that was released in 1964. He had an uncredited part as 'Big Jim Stevens', a part he played as a favor to Frank.

1

I was missing one, though, a film I thought they should surely have included, except at the time it hadn't been made as an Edward G. Robinson movie. *The Cincinnati Kid* was a Steve McQueen picture, but as far as I was concerned, Eddie stole that film as the old poker pro 'Lancey Howard'.

Frank Sinatra was the Chairman of the Board.

Steve McQueen was the King of Cool.

Edward G. Robinson was Little Caesar.

The three men were connected by celluloid.

Frank wrote Steve McQueen into his 1959 film *Never So Few* when, incensed over something Sammy Davis said in an interview, he wrote Sammy out. Sammy eventually earned Frank's forgiveness but the film had been McQueen's big break. Since then he had become a major star in films like *The Great Escape*, *Baby the Rain Must Fall* and *Love With the Proper Stranger*.

I had first met Edward G. Robinson in the Fall of 1964 when he was researching *The Cincinnati Kid* role. Frank had convinced him to come to Sin City to learn everything he could about poker, and to spend some relaxing time with Frank, Dino and Sammy. Because I was friends with the guys, and because Robinson and I shared an 'Eddie G.' persona, it was only natural that we would meet. Add to that Jack Entratter's determination to make sure Edward G. Robinson had everything he wanted, and the old master and I ended up spending some time together.

These days I spent a lot of time in my condo, which was furnished in what designers would call a spartan manner. I had an easy chair – *not*

2

a recliner – that I'd settle into, usually with a cup of tea, or something stronger, so I could watch some of my old friends on TCM.

I finished watching the DeMille masterpiece, and then had about fifteen minutes before the next movie started. My kitchen was the kind with 'ette' on the end of the word, with a small oven, a refrigerator, and a tiny counter. I got myself some crackers and cheese, and then tonight a small bourbon. One drink at night usually served to relax and help me sleep, when simple tea didn't do the job. (Octogenarians need help sleeping, sometimes.)

While I waited for the next film to start, I took the time to drift back and think about everything that had happened in that Fall of 1964 . . .

One

I was watching a high-stakes poker game that was going on in one of the Sands' large suites. Having put some of our 'whales' – our biggest and richest clients – together for this game, Entratter had assigned me to watch and keep the peace. This was not only a clash of bankrolls, it was a clash of egos, as well. According to Entratter, nobody handled big egos like I did. Faint praise.

I was standing off to one side, watching the five men at the poker table – six if you count the dealer. There wasn't a lot of talking during a game like this, not with thousands of dollars at stake.

Three of the players were regulars. The other two I'd found to round out the game. I hadn't wanted to bring them in, because I didn't know them, but Entratter wanted the game to come off, so reluctantly I recruited them.

I watched the two new players carefully for the first couple of hours. Everything seemed on the up-and-up. When the relief dealer came in – a pretty girl named Laura – the players continued to pay attention to their cards.

The regulars were Dan Roburt, a big time gambler in his fifties; Harry Devlin, about sixty,

4

a millionaire businessman who came to town twice a year to blow a bundle; William Landry, a hotshot producer from Hollywood, at the top of his game at forty, who came to Vegas to indulge all his vices: gambling and drinking. I heard he was never drunk when he was working, but it seemed to me he was always drinking when he gambled. And yet, when he lost it wasn't because of that. He was just a terrible poker player.

The newcomers were Sam Temple, in his forties, and Carl Butler, also in his forties. I didn't know much more about them, except that they played for high stakes. When I offered them a chance at a big game, they jumped at it. As far as I could tell, they had never previously met.

Aside from me and the dealer, the room had a bartender, and a security man named Kendrick. Entratter would drop in a time or two.

'I hear Edward G. Robinson and Steve McQueen are makin' a movie about poker,' Devlin said.

'That's what I hear,' Landry, the producer said, 'but how do you know that?'

'Easy,' Devlin said. 'They tried to recruit me as an investor.'

'No go?' Landry asked. 'Don't like investing in movies?'

'I don't mind that,' Devlin said, 'but I lose enough money at poker without investing in a poker movie.'

'Don't think it'll be any good?'

'Steve McQueen?' Devlin said. 'He's a punk. And Robinson is over the hill. That's got flop written all over it.'

I didn't agree, but I wasn't there to partake in

5

the conversation. Neither were they, for that matter. They got back to the game, and conversation was once again at a bare minimum, limited to 'open', 'raise' and 'fold'.

During hour four Entratter put in an appearance. He used a key to come in. If he'd knocked Kendrick would have gone to the door, answered it with his hand on his gun.

Entratter came over and stood next to me.

'How's it goin'?'

'The regulars are cleaning up,' I said. 'And by that I mean Devlin and Roburt. Landry's making his usual donation. Temple and Butler are being fleeced.'

'But is everybody happy?'

'Happy as they can be,' I said. 'Have you heard anything about a poker movie with Steve McQueen?'

'Yeah,' Jack said, '*The Cincinnati Kid*.'

'With Edward G. Robinson?'

'And Ann-Margret.'

'Well,' I said, 'she gets around.'

It had only been months since Ann-Margret was in Vegas with Elvis making *Viva Las Vegas*.

'She's movin' up,' Entratter said.

'McQueen is a step up from Elvis?'

'In the movies, yes.'

'Hmm.'

'They got along on *Never So Few*. And that movie gave him a big lift up. He got a three-picture deal after that.'

'So he owes Frank.'

'Lots of people owe Frank.'

6

'I know.'

'How's Kendrick?'

'Alert.'

'I'll send somebody up to relieve him in a couple of hours.'

'And me?'

'I want you here the whole time.'

'Then you better send up some coffee.'

'OK.'

He walked to the door and let himself out. Kendrick followed him and made sure the door was locked. He nodded to me and went back to his position. He had not had a drink since the game started. I'd had a Coke. I walked over and stood next to him.

'Entratter's going to send up some coffee and, in a couple of hours, some relief for you.'

'I could use both,' he admitted.

Kendrick had been working at the Sands for eight months. This was not the first time our jobs had crossed, but it wasn't a regular thing. We didn't know each other all that well.

I went back to my position.

Two

The coffee arrived within half an hour. Kendrick answered the knock on the door and allowed a waiter to wheel in a cart with an urn and enough cups for anyone interested. All of the players imbibed except for Landry, who kept drinking scotch. I had a cup, and so did Kendrick. The bartender eyed the urn, so I told him to have a cup, too.

When there was a knock on the door again, Kendrick assumed it was his relief. Either that or a waiter to remove the coffee urn. He walked to the door and put his hand on the knob. I wanted to be more careful, though.

'Wait a minute—' I said, but he didn't react. Instead, he opened the door.

'I'm here to relieve you,' a man said, entering the room.

'I don't know you—' Kendrick started to say, but suddenly the other man had a gun in his hand and he cold-cocked him.

Another man came into the room behind the first. It was the waiter who had brought the coffee. He was also holding a gun.

'Everybody relax,' the first man said, as Kendrick went down, 'and nobody will get hurt.'

I guess I should have relaxed, but instead I grabbed the coffee urn, yanked the top off and tossed the contents in the direction of the two gunmen. I did it without thinking, because if I had thought about it first, I probably wouldn't have done it.

There wasn't a lot of coffee left, but what there was of it was hot. It landed on the first man's face. He dropped his gun and screamed, clawing at his eyes.

The second man was only partially scalded on the arm, but he wasn't able to get out of the way of the urn. The big metal container slammed into him, driving him back several feet.

Before he could regain his balance I put my hands on the serving cart and ran at him. I drove it into him, driving him back even further, until he was pinned to the wall. His gun went flying and struck the floor. There was a metal tray on the table. I picked it up and slammed him on the head with it. His eyes rolled back and he slumped over the table.

The first man was still staggering around, his hand to his scorched face. His gun was also on the floor.

I ran over and bent down to pick up one of the guns.

'Don't!' somebody said.

The voice came from the poker table. I looked and saw one of the players pointing a small, nickel-plated gun at me. It was Landry, the producer.

'What the hell . . .' I said.

'Sorry, Eddie,' he said, 'but I needed the money.' He backed away from the table to cover the other players. 'Put all the money in the center.'

'How you plan to take the money out, Landry?' I asked. 'Your two partners aren't gonna be any help.'

'So I won't have to split with them, after all,' Landry said.

'What the hell?' Devlin said. 'I thought you were a big shot producer?'

'So did I,' Landry said. 'Turns out one bad movie can put your career in the crapper. You!' he shouted to the bartender.

'Me?'

'Yeah, you,' Landry said. 'Find something to put the money in and collect it all.'

The buy-in was a hundred grand. That meant there was half a million dollars in the room. But I was wondering where Landry had gotten his buy-in if he was broke enough to want to rob the game?

'Like what?' the bartender asked.

'A bag,' Landry said. 'A box. Something. Come on!'

'You can't do this,' Dan Roburt said. 'You'll never get away with it.'

'They were supposed to do it,' Landry said. 'I just told them about the game. But they blew it, so it's on me now.'

'But you didn't plan on this, Landry,' I said. 'Mr Roburt is right. You can't get away with this. This is the Sands, for Chrissake. You know who owns this casino.'

Landry was sweating, and fidgeting. He was starting to realize the position he was in.

'You'll never get out of the building,' I said. 'If you do, you'll never get out of Vegas.'

'Goddamnit!' he said through gritted teeth. 'This wasn't supposed to happen like this.'

The bartender had found a plastic bag, and had come out from behind the bar.

'You still want me to collect the money?' he asked.

Nobody answered.

I had the feeling Landry wanted a way out. I figured if I could give it to him, I wouldn't get shot.

'Landry.' He didn't hear me. He was looking inward at something only he could see. It was too far to make a grab for the gun, and the men at the table were too scared to do it.

10

'Landry!'

This time he looked at me.

'I have an idea.'

'What?' he asked.

'Put the gun down and walk out,' I said.

'What?'

'Just put it down and walk out. Go.'

Landry's eye flicked around the room.

'I can do that?'

'Sure,' I said.

'You won't try to stop me?'

'No,' I said. 'But you have to go without the money. And you have to leave Vegas. Go back to LA.'

'Back to work?'

'If that's what you want,' I said. 'Look, I'm trying to get all of us out of this room alive. That's what's important.'

He wiped his hand over his face. It was slick with perspiration.

'Back to work,' he said, again.

'That's what you really want to do, isn't it?' I asked. 'Work? You don't want to rob anybody, do you?'

'N-no.'

'Then put the gun down on the table and walk out.'

'OK,' he said, 'OK.' He started to put the gun down, stopped, then reached again and finally put it down. I watched the men at the table. Nobody wanted to pick it up.

Landry circled the table, then stopped.

'My money,' he said. 'The money I bought in with.'

'Pick it up at the cashier cage downstairs,' I said. 'I think the quicker you leave this room the better, don't you?'

'Yeah, sure,' he said. 'I get it.'

He looked at the men at the table, the men on the floor, and walked out the door.

'Jesus,' the bartender said.

'Kendrick!' I said, leaning over the security man. 'Wake up.'

'What?'

'Come on, get up,' I said, hauling him to his feet.

The two robbers were on the floor. One was still unconscious, the other was rocking back and forth, holding his burned face.

'Keep an eye on them,' I said. Still kind of stunned, he drew his gun and pointed it.

I walked to the phone.

'You really gonna let him leave Vegas?' Devlin asked.

'Hell, no!' I said. 'I'm gonna have his ass arrested when he gets to the cashier's cage downstairs.'

'You really think he'll stop there?' Sam Temple asked.

'Yeah,' I said, dialing Entratter's number, 'I really do.'

'Eddie,' Dan Roburt said, 'you must be a helluva poker player, because you sure bluffed the shit outta him!'

Three

When I got home that night I sat on my sofa and shook for a while. What was I thinking, going after two men with guns – and then talking Landry out of his? Who did I think I was, Jerry Epstein? Well, my big Brooklyn buddy probably would have gone after the first two the way I did, but he never would have dealt with Landry the same way. He would have taken it away for sure, probably breaking Landry's arm at the same time.

Jack Entratter called me into his office the next day.

'Are you crazy?' he demanded.

'What are you talking about?'

'You were there last night to keep the peace in the game,' Entratter said, 'not to go up against three hoods.'

'I don't know what I was thinking, but when I saw the security guy go down—'

'The bartender told me that Kendrick opened the door, and you tried to stop him.'

'That's true,' I said. 'I thought we should check who it was, first.'

'Well, at least that was good thinking,' Entratter said. 'Look, all the players were very impressed with you. They said you saved the game, saved all the money and – oh yeah, by the way – might have saved some lives.'

'I was an idiot.'

'No argument there,' Entratter said. 'I never said I pay you to get killed.'

'What happened to the gunmen? And Landry?'

'All under arrest,' Entratter said. 'And I fired Kendrick.'

'Can't say I'm sorry to hear that,' I said. 'He was useless.'

'That was quick thinking on your part, getting Landry to go to the cashier's cage.'

'He wasn't thinking straight,' I said. 'That was obvious. Who were the two guys with him?'

'Just two mugs he convinced to try to pull the job,' Entratter said. 'He promised 'em a cut.'

'Hollywood must've really chewed him up and spat him out,' I said.

'Looks that way,' Entratter said. 'His last three pictures tanked at the box office. No studio will work with him, anymore.'

'He shouldn't have come here to try and solve his problem.' I started to stand up. 'I'm going back to my pit.'

'Sit down,' Entratter said, 'I wanna talk to you about that.'

'About what?'

'Your job.'

I froze halfway out of my seat.

'Siddown, Eddie,' he said. 'I'm not firin' you.'

I sat down, relieved.

'But I am thinkin' about makin' a change.'

'What kind of change?'

'Somethin' that would free you up a little more for special jobs.'

'Are you taking me out of the pit?'

14

'Would that be so bad?' he asked.

'Kinda.' I had always liked my job.

'It seems like I need you more out of the pit than in it, these days,' Entratter said. 'For instance, you know this poker movie Steve McQueen's doin' with Eddie Robinson?'

'Yeah, they talked about it at the table last night.'

'Well, I heard from Frank,' he said. 'He'd like you to show Eddie around, and help him do some research into the poker playin' end of it.'

'When?'

'Later this week.'

'I can do that,' I said. 'I've never met him. That would be great.' Edward G. Robinson was one of the greatest actors of all time, as far as I was concerned. I wouldn't mind helping him research his role. 'But what's that got to do with taking me out of the pit?'

'I told you,' Jack said, 'it's just something I've been thinkin' about. Maybe we could create a new job title for you. You know, somethin' like . . . a freelancer. Or a . . . host.'

'Freelancer?' I said. 'Would that be a promotion? With a raise?'

'Well, I don't know,' Jack said. 'I'm just wingin' it here, Eddie.'

'Well, until you make up your mind can I go back to my pit?'

'Sure,' Entratter said. 'I'll confirm Robinson's arrival date and let you know.'

'OK.'

I stood up and this time he didn't stop me.

'Hey,' I said, 'what's wrong with your girl?'

15

'Whataya mean?'

'When I walked in she didn't look like she wanted to spit,' I said. 'In fact, she hardly looked at me at all.'

'I don't know,' Entratter said. 'She hasn't been herself lately. Might be that time of the month. She's doin' her job, though. That's all I care about.'

'Well,' I said, 'I'll go and do mine.'

Entratter waved me out and turned his attention to something on his desk.

When I got down to my pit I was only there an hour when one of the younger bell hops came over. His name tag said 'Bobby' but I didn't need that to identify him. I remembered his baby face.

The slot machines around us were 'dinging' as coins struck the coin trays and ladies screamed over their nickel hits. People nodded to me as they went by, some regular customers, others celebrities who came and went from month to month. On this night it was Jack Jones, who had completed his run at the Sands' Copa Room and was leaving the next day, and Steve & Eydie, who were coming in to replace him.

'Got a message for you, Eddie.'

'Thanks, Bobby.'

He handed me a message slip, gave me a salute and hurried back to the hotel. At that moment one of the dealers came over, reporting that a player wanted to raise his limit. I pocketed the message to read later.

16

Four

I had a typical day in the pit: okayed two players who wanted their limit raised, turned down another one who got nasty about it, so I had him escorted off the premises. I don't have to check with anyone before making a decision. It's my pit, and I usually know the players. If it's someone unfamiliar, I observe them for a while, see what kind of player they are. Find out if they're registered, maybe get some guidance from the hotel staff on what kind of money they're flashing.

I was finished with my shift before dinner, so I had the option of eating in the casino or heading out and getting something on the way home. I was single at that time, not seeing anyone in particular, so I had nobody else's wants or needs to consider. My friend Danny Bardini was out of town, and he was the only one I might have had dinner with. So I decided to head home, stop along the way for some Chinese take-out, and eat in my own kitchen.

Laying out containers on the table made me think of Jerry Epstein, my buddy from Brooklyn. I remembered having Chinese with him a time or two, and his share left less room on the table. Jerry's appetite was prodigious. While he was a big man, he managed to burn off most of what he ate and not get fat. I envied him that. I stayed in pretty good shape, but every once in a while

17

I'd have to change the size of my belt and have to start cutting back on the booze and burgers. A girl once told me that the size of a belt was determined by the middle hole, so I used that to gauge my weight. As long as I was in the middle, I was doing OK.

While I was eating out of the containers – instead of dirtying my plates – I emptied my pockets onto the table, and came across the message slip Bobby had given me. I washed down some pork lo mein with a sip of cold Piels and unfolded the slip so I could read it. It was a request for me to call someone named Robert Maheu. He'd left a phone number. At the bottom another word was written and underlined. It said, 'Personal'.

I put the slip down and picked up a spare rib. The name Maheu sounded familiar to me, but I just wasn't placing it. I was on my second rib when the phone rang. I wiped my hands on a napkin and answered it.

'Hey Eddie, what are you doin' home?' Danny asked.

'What are you doing callin' me if you didn't expect me to be here?'

'I called the Sands, they said you weren't there. I didn't know where else to call, even though you're hardly ever home.'

'That's why I decided to eat here,' I said.

'Whatayagot?'

'Chinks.'

'Enough for two?'

'You back?'

'Just got back.'

18

'Come on over, then. It'll keep in the containers. And bring some beer.'

'On my way . . .'

Danny Bardini had been my brother's friend when we were all kids in Brooklyn. After my brother was killed in a gang war, we became friends. And after I moved to Vegas, he followed, hung his PI shingle on Freemont Street, down from the Horseshoe.

He held up a six pack of Piels and said, 'Enough?'

'It'll do.'

He followed me into the kitchen, where we sat together and dug into the containers. This time I provided plates. We both used forks, never having mastered the art of chopsticks.

Danny told me about the case he'd settled in Los Angeles, and I told him about the robbery attempt at the poker game.

'Sounds like you made a pretty foolish move at the hold-up,' Danny said.

'I know,' I said, 'I wasn't thinking.'

He reached for a napkin, picked up the message slip instead, glanced at it.

'Maheu?'

'You know him?' I asked. 'The name's familiar, but I can't place it.'

'He's got a PI ticket, ran his own shop in LA until Howard Hughes hired him.'

I snapped my fingers as it came back to me.

'That's it! Hughes' right-hand man, right?'

'Right,' Danny said. 'When Maheu speaks, it's the same as Hughes speakin'. What's he want with you?'

19

'I don't know,' I said. 'I haven't had time to call him back.'

He frowned at the slip. 'No area code. Must be a local number. Call 'im,' he urged, holding the slip out to me. 'Let's find out.'

It was almost eight p.m., but time didn't mean much in Las Vegas.

I wiped my hands again and picked up the phone.

Five

I agreed to meet Maheu the next afternoon in a restaurant in Henderson, the next city over from Vegas, but I had to clear the decks first.

Danny wanted to come. He'd listened to my end of the conversation the night before, which hadn't gone on too long.

'I have some person business here in Vegas that I need some help with, Mr Gianelli, and I'm told you're the man to talk to.'

'Is this your business, Mr Maheu,' I'd asked, 'or Mr Hughes'?'

'There's really no difference, Mr Gianelli.'

Hughes had made his fortune as an aviator, aerospace engineer, and film-maker. Of late he hadn't been seen much in public, preferring to speak through Robert Maheu. I was curious about what he was doing in Vegas, so I agreed to meet.

I told Danny he couldn't come with me, but promised to tell him what it was all about. I called

Jack Entratter the next morning, finding a dried smear of rib sauce on the phone I must have left there the night before.

'Robert Maheu?' he said. 'What's he want?'

'Right now all I know is he wants to talk to me.'

'He's gotta be actin' for Hughes,' Entratter said. 'Find out what it's about, Eddie. We don't need Hughes stickin' his nose in Vegas.'

'OK,' I said, 'but I'll be in late.'

'I'll put somebody in to cover your pit,' he said. 'What else is new?'

As I hung up the irony of that comment was not lost on me, given the conversation we'd had the day before.

The restaurant Maheu had chosen turned out to be a greasy spoon. I guess he'd figured nobody would be looking for Howard Hughes' man in a place like that. Luckily, I liked greasy spoon food.

Our meet was set for eleven a.m. The breakfast crowd had cleared out and the lunch crowd hadn't come in yet. I picked Maheu out pretty easily, as he was wearing a suit that cost more than the clothes of everyone else in the place combined.

I walked to the booth he was seated in and said, 'Mr Maheu?'

'Mr Gianelli?'

He stood to shake hands, invited me to sit. I got the side of the booth with the cracked leather seat.

Maheu was unremarkable in appearance, mid-forties, with the look of a businessman – which

21

he basically was. According to Danny, though, a lot of that business had been dirty business in the past. He had done some work for both the FBI and CIA before hanging out his own shingle, and eventually going to work for Howard Hughes.

The safest thing to order in a greasy spoon was breakfast, so I had bacon and eggs and Maheu ordered a Spanish omelet. We both had coffee.

'You said this was personal,' I said, as we started to eat, 'but isn't everything Mr Hughes does business?'

'Mr Hughes doesn't differentiate between business and pleasure. It's all the same to him, so I was being only slightly disingenuous with my message in order to get you to call me back. I apologize.'

'Hey,' I said, 'I'm getting a free breakfast out of it, right?'

'Indeed.'

Maheu was dry, with no hint of humor. But with everything Danny had told me about him I was sure he'd lie, cheat or steal for Hughes.

'Why don't we get down to . . . it,' I said. I almost said 'business'. 'What do you need from me?'

'Actually,' Maheu said, 'my sole purpose for seeing you is to convince you to meet with Mr Hughes.'

That shocked me. Nobody got in to see Hughes. In fact, years later I discovered that in all the time Maheu worked for him, he never saw the man. All of their contact was through messages and telephone.

'Me? To see Mr Hughes?'

'That's right.'

'Where?'

'Right here, in Vegas.'

'When?'

'At your convenience.'

'Where is Mr Hughes staying?'

'That you will find out the day you see him,' Maheu said. 'We will send a car for you.'

'Do you know what this meeting is about?'

'Nobody knows everything Mr Hughes is thinking but Mr Hughes.'

I drank some coffee, lifted my cup to the waiter to indicate I wanted more. One thing about a greasy spoon, the waiter and waitress practically walk around with a coffee pot glued to their hands. Maheu also accepted a refill.

'How long has Mr Hughes been in Vegas?' I asked.

'Not very long.'

'Is Mrs Hughes with him?' Hughes was married to the actress Jean Peters at that time. She was one in a long line of beautiful women he'd been involved with, an impressive list that included Jane Russell, Terry Moore, and Ava Gardner, who I also had some history with.

'No, she chose to remain behind in Hollywood.'

I took a moment to pick my words carefully.

'What kind of shape is Mr Hughes in?' I asked. No, that didn't come out right. 'I mean, how is his health?'

'I think I know what you're asking, Mr Gianelli.'

'Please, just call me Eddie.'

'Eddie,' Maheu said, 'if and when you agree to see Mr Hughes, there will be some things

23

you'll need to know before you actually meet with him.'

'Well,' I said, pushing my empty plate away, 'maybe we should just get some more coffee and you can start telling me.' Or warning me.

'Does that mean you are agreeing to meet with him?' Maheu asked.

'Howard Hughes is the most notorious, the most enigmatic man in the country,' I said, 'and possibly the richest. Where is the down side to meeting with him?' Enigmatic? Where did I pull that word from?

'Very well,' Maheu said. 'Listen carefully.'

Six

I called Entratter when I got home and told him I wasn't coming to work that day.

'You meeting with him today?' he asked. 'Already?'

'Why wait?' I said. 'He's sending a car for me tonight.'

'You could leave from here, you know,' he suggested.

'Maheu and I have already arranged for the car to pick me up at my place.'

'OK,' Entratter said, 'just keep me informed. If a man like Hughes is planning to move in on Vegas, that's somethin' we should know about as soon as possible.' I knew by 'we' he didn't mean me and him.

24

I hung up and called Danny, flirted with his girl Penny, then told him about the meeting.

'Jesus, you're gonna get to see the great man himself?' he commented.

'Yeah,' I said, 'but this meeting came with a lot of warnings.'

'What kind of warnings?'

'The kind I'm not supposed to talk about,' I said.

'Maybe after?'

'Not even after.'

'You can't even tell me?'

'Danny,' I said, 'I signed a confidentiality agreement.'

'A what?'

'A contract, saying I wouldn't talk—'

'I know what a confidentiality agreement is,' he said, cutting me off. 'You mean he whipped one out right there and then?'

'Even got some egg on it,' I said.

'And you signed it?'

'Sure I did,' I said. 'It was the only way for me to find out what this is all about.'

'You know you're gonna tell me in the end, don't ya?' he said.

'Probably.'

'Well,' Danny said, 'if it's something you need help with you know where to find me.'

'I do,' I said. 'Thanks, Danny.'

After I hung up I did what any man who had an appointment with Howard Hughes would do – I took a nap.

When I woke up I took a shower and put on a suit. One of the things Maheu had told me was that although Hughes might greet me naked, he liked people around him to be properly dressed. But there'd be more about that later.

Maheu explained it to me very carefully. 'People think Mr Hughes is crazy when he sits around naked,' he explained, 'but the fact is he suffers from allodynia.'

'What's that?' I asked.

'It's a condition that makes it painful to be touched,' Maheu said. 'Wearing clothes and shoes sometimes aggravates it. So the only thing he can do is remain naked and distract himself from the pain by watching movies or television. Sometimes, he can't even brush his teeth because of the pain.'

'I never heard that before,' I said.

'He's also been in several plane crashes,' Maheu said, 'survived injuries that might have killed other men. He suffers from pain caused by those injuries, as well. Don't get me wrong,' Maheu said, 'he has his idiosyncrasies, but he's not crazy.'

'Well,' I said, 'I can see where people who don't know that would think he was crazy.' I was one of them. I felt small, at that moment, for judging a man I apparently knew so little about . . .

There was a knock at my door at seven p.m. sharp. I opened it, saw a man standing there dressed as a chauffeur.

'Mr Hughes' car, sir.'

'I'm ready.'

I stepped out onto the stoop and pulled the front door shut behind me, locking it.

When I was in the back of the limo and we

were underway, I asked, 'Where are we going?'

'My instructions are to drive you, sir, and not to answer any questions.'

'OK,' I said. 'I've got it.'

'Thank you, sir.'

There was a small bar in the back of the limo, and a phone. I didn't put either of them to use. Before long we were on the Strip, and then we were pulling in at the Wilbur Clark's Desert Inn.

Clark was a businessman who owned several properties in Las Vegas, the best known being the Desert Inn. At one time he also owned Havana Cuba's Casino Internacional. He was forced to sell it when the Nevada Gaming Commission ruled that no Nevada casino owner could also own a casino in Cuba. He sold it to Meyer Lansky.

In order to finish the casino, though, Clark had to sell 75 percent of it to members of the Mayfield Road Gang, bootleggers and gamblers from Cleveland. Despite not having controlling interest, though, Wilbur Clark was in total charge, and made sure his name appeared above the name of the hotel.

The limo left me in front and a valet opened the door for me before the driver could.

'Hey, Eddie G.,' the man said. 'What you doin' at the DI?'

'I've got an appointment, Sammy,' I said, slapping the man's palm.

'Excuse me,' the chauffeur said to Sammy.

'Sure, man,' Sammy said. 'Peace.'

'Mr Hughes is waiting, sir,' the chauffeur said to me.

'I'm on my way. What floor?'

'Top floor, sir.'

'What room?'

'The whole top floor.'

'Thanks.'

I walked through the lobby to the elevators, rode to the top floor alone. The only thing higher than this floor was the Sky Room, fashioned after San Francisco's Top of the Mark. When I got off, I was confronted by two beefy bodyguards.

'Sir,' one of them said, 'if you please, raise your arms.'

I obeyed and he frisked me down to my ankles.

'This way, sir,' the other one said.

I followed him to a door where we stopped.

'Inside,' he said.

'Just me?'

He nodded.

'Have you ever seen Mr Hughes?' I asked.

'No, sir,' he said. 'We were hired by Mr Maheu.'

'Shall I knock?'

'Knock and go in, sir.' He stepped to the side and positioned himself next to the door, hands folded in front of him. I guessed at the first sign or sound of trouble he'd rush into the room.

I knocked and went in.

Seven

The DI suites were huge.

I entered, found myself in an entry foyer with marble floors.

'Mr Gianelli!' a voice called from within the suite.

'Yes, sir?'

'Come in,' Hughes said.

I advanced into the suite, found myself in the living room. The curtains were drawn and the lights were on. The TV was going, but the volume was low. The flickering light from the screen threw shadows into the room.

There was a man on the sofa. As I was warned, he was naked, with a tissue spread over his genitals. Around him were many more boxes of tissues. Hughes preferred to pick things up with tissue, very mindful of possible germs. Again, the sign of a careful man, possibly an eccentric man – but not a crazy man. Also, there were no empty plates or glasses anywhere. Someone who was concerned with germs, I was sure he'd have those removed as soon as he was finished with them.

'Have a seat,' Hughes said. 'Don't be offended if I don't rise and shake hands.'

'I won't be,' I promised.

He waved me to an armchair and I sat in it.

I was not shocked that he was naked, but I was taken aback by his appearance, otherwise. His hair had not been cut in some time and hung to his shoulders, he hadn't shaved in several days so there was significant stubble, and his fingernails were long, almost talon-like. I knew he was sixty years old or so, but he looked a lot older than that. Photos I had seen of him in the past had shown a healthy, handsome, well-built man. This man was scrawny, at best.

'I know,' Hughes said to me, 'I look like shit, but don't worry, I clean up good.' I knew he was from Southern Texas, but there was only a slight accent. I'd heard recordings of his voice, seen him in newsreels. There was a time his voice was strong and clear. The voice I was hearing now was a little shaky.

'I'm sure you do, sir.'

'Never mind,' he said. 'It doesn't matter how I look – or smell.'

I hadn't noticed until he mentioned it but there was an . . . unpleasant musk in the air.

'Thank you for coming to see me,' Hughes said. 'You'll be wanting to know why, I'm sure.'

'I'm curious, yeah,' I said. 'Mr Maheu wasn't very . . . informative.'

'That's because Maheu doesn't know why I wanted to see you,' Hughes said. 'He only knows what I want him to know, and what I want him to tell the public.'

'I see.'

'Eddie – can I call you Eddie?'

'Sure, why not?'

'Eddie, I need your help.'

'What makes you think I can help you?'

'Vegas is your town,' Hughes said. 'I need somebody who knows this town in and out. That's you.'

'Is that what you've been told?'

'It's what I know from all the information I've gathered,' Hughes said.

I turned my head and looked at the television screen. There was a game show on, one I didn't recognize.

'What have you found out, exactly?'

'So you want a brief history?' he asked. 'About Brooklyn, your brother . . . your father?'

'We can skip all that,' I said. 'Why don't you start with when I got to Vegas.'

'There's no need to go that far back, either,' he said. 'You're the man everyone comes to when they need something in Vegas. The mob, Hollywood, gamblers, they all know who Eddie G. is.'

'I think you're giving me more credit than I deserve?' I said.

'Not when Momo Giancana and Frank Sinatra consider you a vital . . . friend. Not to mention the Kennedy clan.'

I almost said, 'I see,' again, but instead I kept quiet. Let the billionaire naked man come to the point on his own, I thought.

'Not that I am friends with either of them,' he went on, 'but no matter. Their opinions matter to me – at least in this instance.'

'And what instance would that be?'

'I'm thinking of coming into Vegas in a big way.'

'A big way?'

'Yes,' Hughes said, 'I want to buy some casinos.'

'Which ones did you have in mind?' I was hoping he wasn't going to say the Sands. Entratter would hit the ceiling with that news.

'That's where I need your help,' Hughes said.

'What can I tell you?'

'You can tell me which casinos are ripe to be taken over,' he said.

I laughed and said, 'How would I know that?'

'Don't be modest, Eddie,' Hughes said. 'When I check somebody out and decide that they're my man, I don't change my mind. I'll pay you well for the information, of course.'

'Let me get this straight,' I said. 'All you want me to do is tell you which casinos you should try to buy?'

'That's right,' Hughes said, 'and I understand how firmly entrenched the mob is in Vegas. I'm not trying to buck them. I'm just trying for a piece of the pie.'

And knowing what I knew about Howard Hughes, that would have to be a big fucking piece.

Eight

I sat quietly for a moment, mostly because I didn't know exactly what to say.

'Look,' Hughes said, 'I know you've heard a lot of stories about me. Some of them are true. And seeing me sitting here naked, you probably think the wrong ones are true.'

'I've heard you're a brilliant businessman,' I said. 'I've heard that you've been successful and made a fortune at everything you've ever tried. I assume those stories are true.'

'They are.'

'I've heard that you have a checkered past with women, and that you're very demanding in both your private and business life.'

'Again, all true.'

'I've heard that you're crazy.' I said that before I had a chance to change my mind.

'And I've heard that you speak your mind,' Hughes said. 'I'm glad to see that's true.'

I remained silent again.

'I'm not crazy,' he said.

'Glad to hear it.'

'Not all the time, anyway,' Hughes added. 'Like anyone else, I have my moments.'

'Of course.'

'Look,' he said, 'take some time. Think it over. Get back to me in . . . a few days.'

'You'll be here?'

'Right here,' he said.

'Not thinking about leaving the hotel?'

He smiled.

'Not planning on leaving this room, Eddie,' he said. 'Can we agree that you'll think about it?'

'I think I can agree to that.'

'Good, good,' Hughes said. 'I assume Maheu gave you his numbers?'

'He did.'

'Then you can call him when you want to see me again,' Hughes said. 'He'll arrange it.'

'All right.'

I stood up.

'Do you want any money?' he asked.

I wasn't sure I'd heard him right.

'What?'

'Money,' he said, 'like an advance? A retainer?'

'I'm not a private eye or a lawyer, Mr Hughes,' I said. 'No, I don't need any money. Not if all I'm going to do for now is think about your offer.'

33

'Fine,' Hughes said. 'I won't try to throw money at you, then. I'll wait to hear from you.'

'All right.'

I turned and headed for the door.

'Do me a favor, will you?' he asked.

'What's that?'

'Turn the volume up on the TV?'

I looked at him. For the first time since I'd entered the room he looked like he was in pain. If it hurt to be touched by his clothes or his shoes, I wondered how he withstood sitting on the leather sofa, or even walking on the rug?

I walked to the door, waited a moment to see if he wanted anything else, and then left.

'Done?' the bodyguard asked.

'For now.'

'Come on,' he said, 'I'll take you to the elevator.'

'I know the way.'

He waved for me to precede him.

'So,' he said, and I knew what was coming, 'what's he like?'

'What have you heard he's like?'

'Brilliant,' he said, 'and crazy.'

'One of those must be right,' I said.

Nine

Although I wasn't supposed to be working, I just naturally headed for the Sands. It was my home away from home. Actually, there were times it felt more like home than my house did. If I was ever driving and allowed my mind to wander, I automatically headed for the Sands.

I parked the Caddy, went in and took the elevator to Jack's floor. His girl wasn't sitting at her desk – which was odd – so I went right in.

'Where's the keeper of the gate?' I asked.

'Huh? What?' Entratter looked up from his desk. 'Oh, she still ain't out there? Damn it, I haven't seen her in hours. I don't know what's goin' on with her. She's been off lately.'

'Lately?' I sat across from him.

'What's on your mind?' he asked, then his eyebrows shot up. 'Wait. Did you see him? Hughes?'

'I did, this morning,' I said.

'What did he want?'

'"What did he want?" That's what you ask? Not what he's like, is he crazy, are the stories true?'

Entratter waved his hand and said, 'I know the answers to all those questions. Tell me what he wanted. Why is he in Vegas?'

'Well, this is really strange—' I started, but I was interrupted by somebody who ran into the room.

'Mr Entratter, y-you better come quick!' she said, her eyes wide. I stood up and looked at her. It was Marcia Clarkson, a pretty brunette who worked down the hall. We had gone out once, and had stayed friends. To me she was Marcy.

'Eddie! Jesus,' she said, when she saw me, 'y-you gotta come.'

'Where?'

35

She waved at us and said, 'Come on, come on . . .'

I looked at Entratter, who got up from his desk, and we followed her out of the room and down the hall.

'There,' she said, pointing to the ladies' room. 'I-in there.'

I looked at Jack, who looked at me, and then I pushed the door open and went in.

She was hanging from a pipe in the ceiling, by a belt that had been looped around her neck.

'Oh my God!' Marcy said, covering her face and turning away.

Jack Entratter said, 'Shit.'

It was his girl.

'Helen,' he said.

I think that might have been the first time I ever heard her name.

Ten

We had no choice but to call the police.

'This ain't somethin' we can handle ourselves,' Jack said.

Jack went to his office to make the call. I took Marcy back to her office and sat her down at her desk. She was shaking, and I got her a glass of water. Whiskey probably would have been better.

'What happened?' I asked.

'I don't know,' she said. 'I had to go to the bathroom. When I unlocked the door and went in, she was there. Hanging like that.'

'You unlocked the door?'

'Yes, we keep it locked. I have a key in my drawer, and she has one in hers. If anyone else wants to use the bathroom they come to one of us for the key.'

'So her key must be on her,' I said.

'I guess.'

'Give me your key, Marcy.'

'Why?'

'I better lock that door. We don't want anyone else going in til the cops get here.'

'Oh,' she said. 'All right.' She put her hand in the pocket of her jacket and came out with a key.

'Stay here,' I said. 'I'll be right back.'

I went down the hall to the ladies' room, started to lock the door, then stopped. I looked around, saw that I was alone in the hallway. Instead of locking the door, I went inside.

Helen was hanging from the pipe, swaying only slightly. The pipe was only exposed because the ceiling was being worked on by workmen. Any other time it couldn't have been done without breaking through the ceiling tiles. Like Marcy, she was wearing a jacket. I steeled myself, and went through the pockets.

No key.

I looked around to see if she had set it down on a sink, or if it had fallen to the floor. There was no key, anywhere.

How had she gotten in?

I went back into the hall, locked the door and returned to Marcy's office. She was sitting with her head down on her desk. When I walked in she looked up at me with tear-stained eyes, magnified by her glasses.

'What happened, Eddie?' she asked. 'Why would she do that?'

'You think she hung herself?'

'Well . . . what else could have happened?'

'Did you and she talk much, Marcy?' I asked.

'N-no, not really,' Marcy said.

'Jack said she hadn't been herself lately,' I said. 'Did you notice anything wrong?'

'No,' she said. 'Even when we were in the bathroom at the same time we just sort of said hello. E-Eddie, do you think . . . can I go home now?'

'I'm sorry, Marcy,' I said. 'The cops are gonna want to talk to you.'

She hugged herself, as if she was cold. Jack came into the room.

'Cops are on the way,' he said.

'I locked the bathroom door.' I showed him the key, then put it in Marcy's top drawer. 'Why don't you stay here with Marcy?'

'Where are you goin'?'

'I want to check on something.'

I left the office and walked down the hall to Entratter's. When I got to Helen's desk I opened her top drawer – the same one Marcia used for her key. There was no key there. I sat at the desk and opened the drawer to the right. Still nothing.

How had she gotten into the bathroom without the key?

I was still thinking about that when two uniformed police arrived.

Eleven

The policemen took a look at the scene, asked a few questions and then called for the detectives. I knew when the call came in, and they saw the address, who would take the call.

Hargrove.

'Well, well,' Detective Hargrove said, as he entered Jack's office. 'Little trouble at the Sands?'

'If you call the death of an innocent woman "a little trouble", detective,' Entratter said.

Hargrove looked at me.

'What's your involvement, Eddie?'

'I just happened to be in the neighborhood.'

Behind Hargrove came his partner, Martin. He looked unhappy, probably because he was still partnered with Hargrove.

'Well,' Hargrove said, 'we better take a look at the scene.'

'I'll take you—' Entratter said, starting to get up.

'No,' Hargrove interrupted. 'I want Eddie to show us.'

'Why?' Jack asked.

Hargrove smiled and said, 'Because I'm in charge, Mr Entratter.'

'It's OK, Jack,' I said, standing up. 'I'll show him.'

We left Jack's office and I stopped at Helen's desk.

39

'What are you doing?' Hargrove asked.

'We'll need this,' I said, opening the drawer and taking out the key. 'I locked the bathroom so nobody else would go in.'

As we walked down the hall, he asked, 'Who found the body?'

'One of the girls who works here. She's down the hall at her desk with one of your cops.' The other uniform was standing in front of the bathroom door.

'Detective,' he said. 'We had him –' he nodded to me '– lock the door again after we took a look.'

'That's fine,' Hargrove said. 'Open it, Eddie.'

I unlocked it, went to open the door, but Hargrove grabbed my arm.

'That's good enough. You can go back to your boss. We'll be along after we're done.'

'There's something you should know—'

'There's a lot we should know,' Hargrove said, 'and we'll find it all out, don't you worry. Now run along.'

I handed him the key and said, 'Suit yourself.'

As I re-entered Jack's office he asked. 'What are they doin'?'

'Taking a look.' I sat down again.

'I knew somethin' was wrong with her,' he said, shaking his head, 'but not this.'

'Not what, Jack?'

'Suicide?' He shook his head again. 'Why didn't she talk to me first?'

'Did you and she talk a lot about your private lives?' I asked.

'No,' he said, 'not at all.'

'Then why would she confide in you?' I said,
'I don't think it matters much, anyway.'

'What do you mean?'

'I don't think she killed herself.'

'What are you talkin' about?'

'Her bathroom key was still in her desk,' I said.
'I used it to lock the door after we found her.'

'Then how did she get in?'

'That's the question.'

'Maybe Marcy—'

'She still has her key, Jack,' I said. 'Look, I
better go and see how she is, and stay with her
while the detectives question her. She's ready to
fall apart.'

'Eddie,' Entratter said, 'are you sayin' somebody
came into my hotel and killed my secretary?'

'I don't know what else to say, Jack.'

'She could've done it herself,' he said. 'Maybe
the door was left unlocked, maybe—'

'What did she stand on?'

'What?'

'To tie the belt around the pipe and then hang
herself,' I said, 'what did she stand on? There's
no chair, no ladder—'

'The trash can?'

'Not big enough.'

'Maybe she stood on the edge of a sink—'

'She could've done that, and jumped off,' I
said, 'but still . . . how did she reach the pipe to
tie off the other end of the belt? And we don't
even know if it was her belt?'

'Jesus . . . did you tell Hargrove this?'

'Oh no,' I said, 'Detective Hargrove wants to
find out the facts all by himself.'

41

'But you are gonna tell him, aren't you? Sometime?'

'Jack, if I figured it out, he should be able to figure it out, don't you think?'

'He's kind of an idiot, Eddie.'

'Yeah, well,' I said, 'maybe his partner will dope it out. He's kinda smart.'

'Jesus,' he said, 'murder. Man, I hope you're wrong, Eddie.'

'So do I, Jack.'

Twelve

The floor was closed off. Nobody allowed up, nobody allowed down. I sat in Entratter's office with him, trying to talk about something other than a possible murder.

The subject of Edward G. Robinson came up.

'Oh damn . . .' Jack said.

'What?'

'Eddie Robinson is comin' in tomorrow.'

'Well, that's tomorrow,' I said. 'The cops should be gone by then.'

'Let's just hope you're not in jail tomorrow.'

I sat up straight in my chair.

'Why would I be in jail?'

'Because Hargrove hates your guts,' Entratter said. 'If he can hang this on you, he will.'

'My experience with Hargrove tells me he's gonna call this a suicide.'

'Maybe it is.'

42

'She have any reason to kill herself?' I asked.

'Not that I know of.'

'And Marcy doesn't know. Is-was she close to anyone else?'

'Not that I know of,' Entratter said, 'but then I don't know who she's friends with.'

'She wasn't a very pleasant woman,' I said. 'Maybe she had no friends.'

'She wasn't pleasant to you,' he said. 'She didn't like you. That didn't extend to everyone.'

'Well,' I said, 'it'll be up to the cops to find all that out – if they bother to ask.'

Entratter frowned.

'Now, wait a minute,' he said. 'I wouldn't want this to be called a suicide if it's not.'

'That's gonna be up to Hargrove,' I said. 'He's the man in charge.'

'I was kiddin' you, Eddie,' he said. 'I don't expect him to arrest you, but I do expect him to investigate.'

'He will investigate,' I said, 'unless he calls it a suicide.'

Entratter sat back in his chair, looking unhappy.

'When does Robinson get in?'

'Tomorrow at noon.'

'And Frank?'

'He'll be here tomorrow around three.' He was still frowning.

'Am I supposed to take Mr Robinson to the tourist sights?'

'No,' Jack said, 'he wants to play poker.'

'In the casino.'

'No, the way they play it in the movie.'

43

'And how's that?'

'I don't know,' he said. 'You'll have to ask him that yourself.'

'I wish Frank was getting here before him,' I said. 'I'd like to talk to him first.'

'You could call him, but I don't know where he is. Just that he'll be here tomorrow. Look, about this . . . thing with Helen.'

'This thing?'

'Murder, suicide, whatever it is.'

'What about it?'

'Just what I said,' he answered. 'Murder or suicide. I want to know which it is.'

'And if it's murder?'

'Then I want the sonofabitch caught!'

'That's the police's job . . .'

'Yeah, you told me that, already,' Entratter growled.

'Look,' I said, 'why don't we wait and hear what Dick Tracy comes up with? Then you can blow up all you want.'

He pointed at me. 'If he says it's suicide, I'm gonna want you to look into it.'

'Me? I'll be busy with Edward G. Robinson. Besides, I'm not a detective.'

'You're as good as,' Entratter said. 'That's what they tell me.'

'They? Who are they?'

'Frank, Dino. Even your buddy, Bardini, says so, doesn't he? Put his life in your hands a few months ago, didn't he? In fact, he's done it more than once.'

'Jack—'

'There's no point in arguin' about it now,' he said. 'Let's wait and see what Hargrove says.'

44

'That's what I said.'

'And it's a good idea,' he said.

'Good, then we can stop arguing about it,' I said. 'How about a drink?'

'Don't mind if I do.'

He had poured two scotches and handed me one when Hargrove and Martin came into the office.

'We're movin' the body now,' he said. 'Is there family to be notified?'

'I don't know,' Jack said. 'I'll have to check with personnel.'

'Well, let me know as soon as you can.'

'So what's the call?' Entratter asked.

'The call?'

'Was she . . . murdered?'

'Oh, I doubt it,' Hargrove said. 'Looks like she strung herself up.'

'What did she stand on?' I asked.

'What?'

'What did she stand on to get the job done?' I asked again, without turning in my seat.

'Probably the sink,' Hargrove said.

'You said looks like she did it herself,' Entratter said. 'You're not callin' it that yet?'

'Not yet,' Hargrove said. 'Not til the ME does his thing.'

'We've talked to the other people on this floor, gotten all their names and addresses,' Martin said. 'You can open the elevators up again.'

'Thank you.'

'Don't leave town,' Hargrove said. 'Either of you. Just in case we need you.'

'We're not goin' anywhere,' Entratter said.

'So long, Eddie,' Hargrove said to my back. 'See you in jail.'

As they left I looked at Entratter and said, 'Funny man.'

Thirteen

I left Entratter's office and walked toward the elevators. All of the offices on the floor along the way were empty. Jack had said he was allowing anyone who was upset by the incident to go home. That appeared to be everyone. No doubt somebody had used it as an excuse to simply go home, but I hoped most of them had left because they were unnerved.

I know I was.

But I wasn't going home.

I stopped at the elevator, turned and walked back. The personnel office was empty. I went to the file cabinets and looked for Helen's file. The problem was I didn't know her name, but since she was Jack Entratter's secretary, I thought the file would be prominent. Luckily, it was right there in front of the top drawer.

Her name was Helen Simms. According to her file she was single, just turned forty, had an apartment in a quiet neighborhood off the strip, which was only a few blocks away from being in Henderson.

There was more, but I decided to take the file with me. If the cops hadn't taken it by now, maybe they wouldn't be looking for it. Especially if they were going to call it a suicide.

I tucked the file underneath my arm and walked to the elevator.

When I got home I dropped the file on the kitchen table. I'd stopped at a chicken place for take-out. I got a beer out of the fridge, knife and fork from a drawer and pried the top off my meal. While I ate I went through the file thoroughly. She had no family – or none that was in the file. She'd had nothing but good work reviews from Jack. And she got a good raise every year for the past eight years.

That was all there was. If I wanted to ease my curiosity any further I'd have to go to her home. Did I want to do that? And take a chance of running into the cops?

And why should I do it when I knew a perfectly good detective?

I tossed my trash, washed my silverware, opened another beer, and called Danny.

'Sounds like you want to hire me to investigate this woman's death,' Danny said.

'Well, I was thinking of it as more of a favor,' I said, 'but if it comes to that, I suppose I could worm a fee out of Entratter.'

'And why would it come to that?'

'I think if the police call it a suicide, Jack's not going to be happy.'

'So why not wait?'

'Because I'm curious,' I said. 'I've read her file. I think the only other way to learn anything is to go to her home.'

'Take a look around, talk to the neighbors,' he said.

'Exactly.'

'That idiot Hargrove is bound to call it a suicide,' Danny said. 'To label it anything else would mean more work for him.'

'Look, I'm not asking for a lot of time,' I said. 'Just have a look around.'

'Yeah, I can do that for a buddy,' Danny said.

'And get back to me as soon as you can.'

'You tellin' Entratter about this?'

'I will, but not yet.'

'And what about Edward G.?'

'He'll be here tomorrow,' I said. 'So will Frank.'

'Your ol' buddy Frank.'

Danny liked Dean, but he wasn't crazy about Frank. There wasn't much I could do about that, so I didn't say anything.

'OK,' Danny said, 'what will you be doing tomorrow while I'm checkin' on Jack's girl?'

'I'll be with Robinson, I guess,' I said. 'Right now that's my primary job.'

'Why are you messin' with this other thing, then?' Danny asked. 'Just curiosity?'

'Yeah,' I said. 'But Entratter said if the cops called it suicide, he wanted to know for sure. He wants somebody lookin' into it.'

'And he picked you.'

'I think he did that because he knew I'd ask you for help,' I said.

'What about the big guy?'

'Jerry? There's no reason to bring him in. Don't even know if Jack would go for it.'

48

'OK,' Danny said, 'but as soon as somebody's arm needs to be twisted, or a leg has to be broken, I say bring in the big guy.'

'I'll go along with that, Danny.'

'OK. I'll call you tomorrow. Home or work?'

'Try both,' I said. 'I'm not sure where I'll be.'

'Gotcha. Do me a favor?'

'Sure.'

In the worse Edward G. Robinson impersonation ever, he said, 'Ask Mr Robinson to say "where's your Messiah now?" for me.'

Fourteen

The next day I was in the Sands at noon, when Edward G. Robinson was supposed to arrive. I didn't greet him in the lobby, though. I wanted to give him time to get settled, and I didn't want to seem too eager to meet him. So I sat at the bar in the lounge and had a drink.

While I was there Julius LaRosa walked in. LaRosa had risen to fame as a singer on the Arthur Godfrey show, and had a short-run TV series a few years back. Frank was his idol. He was a handsome kid with a big smile, and he was turning the full wattage on me.

'Hey, Eddie!'

'Hello, Juley,' I said. 'Drink?' I signaled to the bartender.

'I'll have a martini,' Juley told him.

He accepted the drink and remained standing.

49

'Eddie,' he said, 'can you get me a couple of tickets for a show?'

'Here at the Sands?'

'No, the Golden Nugget. It's sold out and I need two tickets.'

I didn't ask who the second ticket would be for. At that time I didn't know if LaRosa was married or not.

'I can make a phone call.'

'Will you?' He sipped the drink and set it on the bar. 'Thanks.'

'Are you staying here?' I asked.

'Yeah, I got a room.' But I knew he wasn't performing at the Sands. He was doing a stint in the lounge at the Riviera, up the strip.

'I'll have the tickets held for you.'

'I won't need to have 'em in my hand?'

'They'll be at the box office for you,' I promised. 'Guaranteed.'

He took my hand, pumped it enthusiastically and exclaimed, 'Thanks, Eddie. Thanks a lot. Frank's right. He always says you're the man.'

As he went out the door, I thought, Oh yeah, that's me. I'm the man.

'Can you bring me a phone?' I asked the bartender.

After I made the call I had two more people approach me to arrange something for them. One player wanted dinner at the Sahara, and another wanted an increase in his credit limit, even though he wasn't playing in my pit. I accomplished both with a phone call.

By the time I was finished I was thinking that

maybe Jack was right. Maybe I needed to come out of the pit and be some kind of . . . casino host. When I first met Frank and Dean, I had some contacts in Vegas. But during the intervening years, with people realizing that I had their ear, I became even more well known. I could pretty much get people what they needed with a well-placed call.

Casino host. A new job. Maybe even with a raise, if I could play Jack right.

I was giving the phone back to the bartender when it rang. He answered it, then held it out to me.

'Mr Entratter, for you.'

'Somebody told me you were down there,' Jack growled. 'What the hell are you doin', takin' it easy?'

'No, I'm—'

'Eddie Robinson is in his suite,' Jack said. 'He's waitin' for you.'

'I'm on my way.'

'Good,' he said, and slammed down the receiver.

I got out of there before somebody else came to me with a problem or a request.

Fifteen

I knocked on the door of Edward G. Robinson's suite. The last time I felt this nervous was when I met George Raft a few years back.

The door was opened by a young woman in a

51

business suit that did nothing to hide her curves. Not showgirl curves, but enough. The color of the suit was green, which worked well with her red hair. It was long, but at the moment was gathered into a bun at the nape of her neck. I imagined her removing the pin and shaking it out when she got home at night.

'Yes?' she said. 'Can I help you?' I realized she'd been waiting for me to say something.

'My name's Eddie Gianelli,' I said. 'I'm here to see Mr Robinson.'

'Oh,' she said, with just a slight widening of her green eyes, 'Eddie G., right?'

'That's right.'

'Well, come in,' she said, backing up a bit. 'Mr Robinson is waiting for you.'

'Sorry if I'm late,' I said, entering. I closed the door behind me. Robinson had the same kind of suite the Sands supplied for their top performers.

She stuck her hand out for me to shake. I guessed her to be about twenty-eight.

'My name is Gloria Benjamin,' she said. 'I work for the studio.'

'Hello. Are you a . . . chaperone?'

'I hardly think Mr Robinson needs a chaperone,' she said. 'He's a lovely old gentleman.' She suddenly turned and looked behind her, as if to be sure he hadn't heard her description of him.

'Don't worry,' I said, 'he's not there.'

'He's in the bedroom, unpacking,' she said. 'He insists on doing his own unpacking.'

She was a very serious young woman, probably charged with seeing that the movie star stayed happy.

52

At that moment the man himself came walking into the room, wiping his hands on a towel. He was in shirtsleeves and grey suit pants.

'Well, hello,' he said. 'Are you the famous Eddie G.?'

'I'm Eddie G.,' I said, 'but in your presence, Mr Robinson I'd hardly call myself famous.'

He finished drying his hands and then extended his right to me. I shook it. I knew he was over seventy, but he had a nice firm grip.

'Honey, can you give me and Eddie G., here, some time together? Go check out your room.'

'All right, sir, but you have that interview later today . . .'

'I'll be ready,' he said. 'You come and get me and I'll be ready.'

'All right, Mr Robinson.' She turned to me. 'Goodbye, Mr Gianelli.'

'Goodbye, Miss Benjamin,' I said. 'I hope I see you again.'

Robinson opened the door for her and then closed it behind her.

'A lovely girl,' he said, 'she's just a bit . . .'

'Intense?'

'Yes,' he said. 'Intense. How about a drink?' he asked.

'It's a little early for me.'

'Me, too,' he said. 'Can we get some coffee sent up?'

'Sure, I'll take care of it.'

'I'll just finish cleaning up,' he said. He started for the bedroom, then turned and said, 'We're going to have to come up with something to call each other, since we're both Eddie.'

'And we're both Eddie G.,' I added.

He laughed and went into the bedroom. I called for the coffee and told them to rush it. It was there by the time Robinson came out. He'd changed into a fresh shirt and pair of pants. He had chin whiskers, but I wasn't sure if he was growing some kind of beard or just hadn't had a shave.

'Wow,' he said, 'I've never gotten room service that fast before.'

'You've never stayed at the Sands before.'

The tray with coffee and cups was on the table in front of the sofa. We both sat in front of it and I poured out two cups.

'I wasn't sure if you were hungry,' I said.

'I am,' he admitted, 'but I'd rather go out and eat. Can we arrange that?'

'We can.'

'Without the intense Miss Benjamin?'

'I'll bet we can sneak out.'

'Frank told you why I'm here?'

'I heard from Jack Entratter,' I said. 'Frank will be here later today.'

'I'm supposed to play this legendary poker player opposite Steve McQueen in the film *The Cincinnati Kid*. Those are the kind of roles I get now . . . old.' He touched his chin. 'I'm trying to grow a goatee to see if it makes me look rakish.'

'I'm sure it will, sir.'

'Oh, no, don't call me sir, Eddie,' he said. 'Say, why don't you just call me Eddie, and I'll call you Eddie G. How's that? Or you could call me . . . Manny.'

54

'Manny?'

'My real name is Emmanuel.'

'I think I'll go with Eddie, si – I mean, Eddie.'

'OK, Eddie G.,' he said. 'How about some lunch?'

'Where would you like to go?' I asked. 'There are several really good places off the strip.'

His bushy eyebrows went up.

'Why would I want to eat off the strip?' he asked. 'Let's eat somewhere in the building, to start. I want to see the Sands.'

'Well, I can certainly show it to you, Eddie.'

He smiled, and damned if he didn't look a bit rakish.

Sixteen

I took Edward G. Robinson to the Garden Room. I asked the waitress for a particular booth. It was one I knew could not be seen from the door. I didn't want people bothering Robinson for his autograph while he was eating.

We ordered and Robinson told me about his role as Lancey 'the man' Howard. Set during the Depression, the film featured Steve McQueen as the young poker player trying to beat the best, who was Lancey Howard.

'So you're Minnesota Fats,' I said.

He pointed at me and smiled. When he did that his eyes twinkled.

'That's what I equated it to,' he said. 'It's the

55

poker version of *The Hustler*. My role was supposed to be played by Spence Tracy, but he had to bow out because of his health. When they offered it to me I jumped at it.'

'Where'd the story come from?'

'A novel by a writer named Richard Jessup. The book came out in 1963.'

'Did you read it?'

'I did,' Robinson said. 'I enjoyed it, and I really enjoyed the script. I'm going to have fun playing this character, but I need some practical experience playing the game.'

'Have you ever played poker before?' I asked.

'Oh yes, I have, but not the way the men in the book played it. I need to adapt that outlook of the game. You know, that the game is everything.'

'Well,' I said, 'you'll sure as hell get that feeling here.'

A waitress named Nell came over and her eyes widened when she saw Robinson. Working in Vegas you come across a lot of celebrities, but Edward G. Robinson was a bona fide movie star, and a legend, to boot.

'Hi, Eddie,' she said, but she was looking at him.

'Hey, Nell,' I said. 'Meet Mr Edward G. Robinson. Eddie, this is Nell.'

'Well,' Robinson said, 'I've certainly heard about Las Vegas' beautiful women.'

'Oh,' Nell – who was very pretty – said, 'those are the showgirls, Mr Robinson, not the waitresses.'

'You mean the showgirls are prettier than you?' he asked. 'I find that hard to believe.'

The old charmer had her blushing. Because he didn't want a huge lunch – he was looking forward to going out to dinner later – we ordered, on my recommendation, turkey sandwiches and French fries. I had mine on white, and he had rye. We both had iced tea.

'I'll get that right out,' she said, and flounced away. She had probably been on her feet since the early breakfast rush, but suddenly she had new spring in her step.

Robinson sat back and smiled at me. He looked pleased about something.

'Eddie G.,' he said. 'You now –' he pointed his finger at me and closed one eye – 'you're the legend in this town.'

'Oh, I don't think so.'

'Hey,' he said, 'they call me a legend, so I guess that qualifies me to make the judgment. I've heard all about you from Frank and Dino – especially Frank. They value your friendship.'

'And I value theirs,' I said. 'Now *they're* the Vegas legends, not me.'

'Oh yes,' he said, waving a hand, 'on the stage, of course it's them, but in town – in the casino and on the streets – it's you, my friend. I'm quite pleased to meet you.'

'Well . . .' I said, surprised at how embarrassed I felt, 'I appreciate it.' Was the old gent trying to charm me the way he had charmed Nell?

'Frank said something about us all having dinner together tonight,' he went on.

57

'I can arrange that. Frank should be in his suite in a couple of hours.'

'Then we have time to eat our lunch at our leisure,' he said.

I started to say yes, but Nell suddenly appeared with a phone.

'It's for you, Eddie,' she said. 'Mr Entratter.'

She plugged it in beneath the table and I grabbed the receiver.

'Excuse me,' I said to Robinson. 'Jack?'

'Where are you?'

'At lunch with Eddie,' I said.

'Ain't that gonna get confusing?' he asked. 'Callin' him Eddie?'

'He's Eddie, I'm Eddie G.'

'Yeah, whatever,' he said.

'What's got you so happy?' I asked

'I heard from your friend Hargrove.'

'Already?'

'Yeah,' he said. 'He's callin' Helen's death a suicide.'

'Oh.'

'Yeah, oh,' he said. 'The man's an idiot. Look, Eddie, I need you to see to Eddie while he's here, but I also need you to do what you can to find out what happened to Helen.'

'I understand, Jack.'

'I know I'm puttin' pressure on you, but I'm gonna make it worth your while. You know that new job we talked about?'

'Yeah.'

'Well, think about it,' he said. 'We'll structure it any way you want. You want out of your pit? You got it. You wanna spend some time in the pit, OK.'

58

'This host thing, Jack,' I said, 'you'd be sort of inventing a new job, wouldn't you?'

'Yeah, whatever,' he said, sourly. 'Listen, go ahead and use that PI buddy of yours, if you want.'

'Will you pay him?'

'Yeah, whatever his fee is,' Jack sad. 'Eddie, I want the answers, here. Maybe you didn't like Helen, but she was a good kid.'

'Hey,' I said, 'she's the one who didn't like m—' but he'd hung up on me.

I hung up and Eddie asked, 'Trouble?'

'Nothing you have to worry about, Eddie,' I assured him.

'Well, we can talk about it, can't we?' he asked. 'While we eat?'

I thought a moment, then said, 'Yeah, sure, why not?'

Nell came with the iced teas and asked, 'You done with the phone, Eddie?'

'No,' I said, making a sudden decision. 'While I've got it here I'm gonna make a call.'

'OK,' she said, 'let me know.'

'Excuse me one more time?' I asked Robinson. 'And then I'll explain everything.'

He took a sip of his tea and said, 'Go ahead, don't let me stop you. I'll enjoy watching the legend at work.' There was no hint of humor in his remark. He meant it.

I dialed a long distance number and when it was answered, I said, 'Hey, Jerry, how'd you like to meet Edward G. Robinson?'

'I'll be on the next plane, Mr G.'

Seventeen

Over our sandwiches I told Robinson what had been happening.

'The poor woman,' he said, shaking his head.

'Jack finds it hard to believe she committed suicide,' I said. 'I do, too, having witnessed the scene myself.'

'It's a terrible thing, either way,' he commented. 'What did you see that leads you to believe it's murder?'

'Two things,' I said. 'One, the only way she could have hung herself was to stand on a sink – only the sink was too far away. And two, you need a key to get into the ladies' room, and she didn't have one on her.'

'Could it have been on the floor?' Robinson asked.

'I looked,' I said. 'It was nowhere in the room.'

'Perhaps,' Robinson said, 'it was flushed down the toilet or washed down the sink drain.'

'Why would somebody do that?'

'I don't know,' he said, 'I was just suggesting a way the key could have vanished.'

They were valid suggestions, two ways that a key could have been disposed of, but why? And by who?

'Who is Jerry?' he asked, picking up the second half of his sandwich. He paused a moment to lick mayo off his thumb.

'Jerry Epstein's a friend of mine from Brooklyn, where I grew up,' I said. 'When I need help, he's usually the one I call. He and my friend, Danny Bardini, who is a private eye here in town.'

'And Jerry? Is he a private detective, as well?'

'Uh, no,' I said, 'Jerry sort of comes from the other side of the tracks.'

'A gangster?'

'I wouldn't call him that to his face.'

'And yet you and he and the private eye, you work together?' he asked.

'We're all from Brooklyn,' I said, 'and we work together well.'

'So you're all friends?'

'They're my friends,' I said, 'and they get along.'

'So you're going to find out what happened to this poor unfortunate girl?'

'I'm gonna give it a try.'

'What about the police?'

'The police and I don't get along,' I said. 'Specifically, the detective who was assigned to this case. I think he's calling it a suicide to get my goat. Or Jack Entratter's.'

'He doesn't sound very good at his job.'

'He lets his personal feelings get in the way.'

'I see. Can't you simply go to his superiors?' Robinson asked.

'That's not the way things are done in Vegas, Eddie,' I said. 'There's no way to be sure who to trust in the police department. I have to stick with the people I know are on the level.'

'Like your friends.'

'And Jack Entratter.'

61

'Isn't he your friend?'

'He's my boss before he's my friend,' I said. I checked my watch. 'Frank should be here soon. Do you want to go back to your room until he gets here?'

'I would like to get some rest before dinner,' he said. 'Why don't you and Frank just come and get me when you're ready to go?'

'And for dinner, you want to stay on the strip?'

'Well, of course,' he said, spreading his arms expansively. 'I'm in Vegas, I want to see the lights.'

'OK, then,' I said. 'I'll show you back to your roo—'

'I can find my way to the elevator, Eddie G.,' he said. 'You probably have some plans to make.'

'Yeah, I do.'

He stood up and said, 'I'll see you later. Is this . . .' he waved at the table.

'On the Sands,' I said. 'You bet. You're our guest.'

He laughed, patted me on the arm and said, 'See you later, my boy.'

Nell came rushing over, looking disappointed.

'I waited too long,' she said, pushing out her cute lower lip.

'For what?'

'I was gonna ask for his autograph.'

'Don't worry, sweetie,' I said, 'he's gonna be around for a while.'

'He's a real charmer,' she said. 'Not at all like he is in the movies.'

'You like older men?' I asked. She was in her

mid-twenties, which put her right on the edge of being too young for me.

She poked me in the chest and said, '*Charming* older men, Eddie.'

Once again she flounced away, fully aware that I was watching. But I couldn't watch for long, because I had things to do. Frank was coming in, Jerry would probably be in tomorrow, and I had to find out if Danny had learned anything.

Eighteen

As I got out of the elevator on Frank's floor I saw him come out of his suite and turn my way.

'Frank—'

'Eddie, baby,' he said, spreading his arms expansively. The famous smile lit up his face. 'Come on, we gotta go.'

'Go? Where?'

'I was just comin' to find you,' he said. 'We're goin' to the Sahara.'

'Frank, if you wanna eat—'

'I do, but not here,' he said, hustling me down the hall. 'You got your Caddy?'

'Yeah, but—'

'Never mind,' he said, as the elevator doors closed. 'It's stupid to drive your car to the Sahara. We could walk there.'

'Yeah, but Frank—'

'I know, I'll be recognized. But you can get us a limo, right?'

'Well, yeah, right, but—'

'Then let's do it, pally!' he said. 'We can talk on the way.'

In the lobby I grabbed a valet named Tommy and told him I needed a limo fast.

'Sure, Eddie,' he said. 'Comin' up.'

'Are we running from somebody, Frank?' I asked.

'No, no,' he said, 'nothing like that. Did Eddie get in? Hey, that's right, he's Eddie and so are you. And Eddie G.—'

'He and I went through that already,' I said. 'Yeah, he's here and we got acquainted over lunch.'

'Good, good,' he said. 'What's the plan?'

'Dinner tonight, the three of us,' I said. 'Somewhere on the strip.'

'OK, good,' Frank said. 'I'll let you set it up.'

'Only not the Sahara, if we're going there now.'

'Right, right, not the Sahara. Man, I need a drink.'

'What's going on, Frank?'

'Nothin', nothin',' he said. 'Take it easy. All is well.'

I knew Frank had his manic moments – probably more so since last year, when Frank Jr had been kidnapped and JFK killed – but since I wasn't a doctor I didn't know if this was an example of a high, or if it was actually a low.

'Car's out front, Eddie,' the valet said.

'Thanks, Tommy.'

'Let's go, kid,' Frank said.

He hurried across the lobby with me running after him . . .

*　*　*

When we got to the Sahara we were let off in the back, in front of the restaurant. There was a well-cared for lawn there ringed by over 200 motel rooms.

We went in and were immediately shown to Frank's table, which was always held for him.

Once we were seated, Frank ordered a martini, and I had a beer. After he sipped the drink he seemed to settle down a bit.

'What's goin' on, Frank?' I asked again.

'Nothin', Eddie,' he said. 'I've been on edge a little lately, that's all.'

'You want something to eat?'

'Maybe an appetizer,' he said, 'nothing much. We're gonna have dinner with Eddie.' He waved to the waiter and ordered an antipasto.

Then he sat back and took a deep breath before lighting a cigarette and taking another sip of his martini. Suddenly, he seemed calm.

'So what's goin' on with you?'

I told Frank about my lunch with Robinson.

'I like him,' I ended with. 'He seems like a cool old guy.'

'He's a legend in this business, Eddie,' Frank said. 'I'm proud that I got to do two movies with him, especially *Hole in the Head*. That was some experience.'

Our antipasto came and we began to pick at it, after ordering two more drinks.

'You gonna get in trouble for bein' out of your pit?' Frank asked.

'Jack's thinkin' about creating a new job for me,' I said. 'Casino host or somethin' like that. Leave me free to do stuff for people.'

'What do you think of that?'

'I like bein' in the pit,' I said. 'We have to talk about it, after . . .'

'After what?' Frank asked. 'Somethin' else goin' on? Come on, kid, spill. Tell your Uncle Frank everything.'

So I did . . .

By the time I was done, so was the antipasto. Frank had a third martini, but I nursed my second beer along.

'So, the cops are sayin' she killed herself, but you and Jack don't believe it.'

'Jack doesn't want to,' I said. 'I just don't see how she could've.'

'Because of the sink and the key.'

'Right.'

'Sounds like you know what you're doin', Eddie,' Frank said. 'You gonna be able to work on that while you're dealin' with Eddie? Or should we get somebody else to show him the ropes?'

'No, no,' I said, 'I wanna do that, Frank. I've already got Danny looking around at Helen's apartment, asking some questions of her neighbors.'

'And what about bringin' Jerry in?'

I smiled and said, 'The big guy's on his way. He's gettin' the first available flight.'

'I'll foot the bills, Eddie G.'

'You don't have to—'

'Listen,' he said, 'you're doin' a lot, for me, for Eddie, and for Jack. It's the least I can do.'

'OK,' I said. 'I won't argue with you.'

He checked his watch, then downed the last of his martini.

'I gotta get back and sleep off these martinis,' he said. 'You set up dinner tonight with Eddie, anywhere you want, and let me know.'

'OK.'

'How'd you leave it with him?'

'That we'd pick him up from his suite.'

'What floor's he on?'

'Two below you.'

'OK.' We stood up. 'You go out and get the limo and I'll settle up.'

There wasn't much to getting the limo, but I got the feeling Frank didn't want me to see him settle up. I went outside, found the driver leaning against the car.

'Where to, Eddie?'

I looked at him. More and more lately it seemed that people knew me, even when I didn't know them. Or maybe I just didn't remember.

'What's your name?'

'Lou.'

'We're headin' back to the Sands, Lou, as soon as Frank comes out.'

'Right. Should I open the door for him?'

'Naw, just get behind the wheel. I'll get the door.

'Right, boss.'

As Lou slid behind the wheel, Frank came out and I opened the door for him. He slid into the back, I got in next to him and slammed the door.

'Home, Lou.'

Nineteen

On the way back to the Sands, Frank got quiet. Not depressed again, just quiet. When we got out of the car in front of the hotel he said, 'I'm gonna go see Jack. Pick me up at my suite for dinner, and then we'll get Eddie. OK, pally?'

'OK.'

Inside we split up. He went to see Jack, I went to my car. Driving to my house I tried to compartmentalize my thoughts, my tasks. I had to take care of Edward G. Robinson and help him with his research for *The Cincinnati Kid*; and I had to find out if Helen had killed herself or not. If not, did Jack also expect me to find her killer? And then, of course, there was Howard Hughes.

When I got home I showered and was picking out a suit for dinner when the phone rang.

'Eddie?'

'Yeah, Danny? What's up?'

'I found something,' Danny said. 'We need to talk.'

'When?'

'Now.'

'I'm getting dressed to go eat with Frank and Edward G. Robinson.'

'Do you know how incredibly pretentious that sounds?' he asked.

'Fuck you, come on over.'

'Got beer?'

'Some,' I said. 'Bring more.'

I had finished dressing by the time he arrived. He carried a large paper bag, stowed two six packs of Ballantine in the fridge, pulled out two Piels.

'OK,' I said, sitting on the sofa holding a bottle of beer in my hand, 'what've you got?'

He sat down in the armchair across from me . . .

Danny took me back to the day before, after we hung up. Actually, it was the next morning when he went into his office – the day after Helen's death.

He walked in and stopped at the desk in the outer office, where Penny sat. Penny was his girl Friday, but she'd always wanted to be more. For one thing, she wanted to be a PI. For another, she wanted to be his girlfriend. Well, recently they had taken steps to establish her as the latter, but she was still pushing for the former.

'I have to go out, doll.'

'Where?'

'On a case.'

'We got a client? When did that happen?'

'Just now, on the phone.'

'Danny,' she said, 'you've got to tell me these things, so I can start a file.'

'Well, don't start one yet,' he said. 'I'm doin' this as a favor for Eddie, but if he gets Entratter to pay us, then you can start a file.'

'OK,' she said, 'what's the favor?'

He told her about the woman found hanging in a bathroom at the Sands.

'That poor girl,' she said. 'What must have been happening in her life to make her do that?'

'Well, Eddie doesn't think she offed herself,' Danny said. 'So she must've had help.'

'What does he want you to do?'

'Ask questions.'

'You think Eddie knows enough to make that assumption?' she asked.

'Eddie's sharp,' Danny said. 'If he saw something that makes him think she didn't kill herself, that's good enough for me.'

'Then me, too.'

'I'm going to check out her place,' he said, 'ask some questions, talk to her neighbors.'

'What should I do?'

'What you always do, doll,' he said on the way out the door. 'Man the phones.'

'Woman!' she shouted after him. 'In case you ain't noticed, I'm a female. Get it?'

Oh, he got it.

Danny was driving a '63 Chevy Sting Ray at the time. He drove it to Helen Simms' address, a high-rise apartment building off the strip, in Green Valley.

He parked in the parking lot behind, entered through a back door, made his way to the lobby, where the occupants' names appeared on a board on the wall. There was no door man, no security. Expensive, yes, but not top of the line. As far as Danny knew, Helen was a secretary. He didn't know how much Entratter paid her, but it must have been good money.

He checked the board. Helen Simms lived on the eighth floor, apartment 803. On the first floor

70

there was an apartment for the manager. That's where Danny went.

He knocked and a man in a T-shirt opened the door.

'Lookin' for an apartment?' he asked. 'We're all full.'

'Not so much,' Danny said. 'Helen Simms, she died yesterday.'

'No foolin'?'

'I need to get inside her apartment.'

'You got a badge?'

Danny took out a twenty.

'If I show you my badge, I have to put this away,' he said.

The man considered, then took the twenty. 'Wait here.' He went inside, returned with a key. 'Make sure you bring it back.'

'No problem.'

Danny took the elevator to the eighth floor, fitted the key into the door of 803 and entered. He hadn't really impersonated a cop. Not really.

The apartment was small, a living room, bedroom, and kitchenette. He spent most of his time in her bedroom, and bathroom. The usual in her medicine cabinet: aspirin, Midol, cough syrup, eye drops, a couple of prescription bottles that he put in his pocket. He'd find out what they were for later.

There was a small writing desk in one corner of the bedroom. He went to it, checked all the drawers, the blotter on top. Then he went to her dressing mirror. People often left messages clipped to their mirror. No such luck. So he checked her refrigerator. The inside was almost empty, except for the remnants of a take-home salad, and a half bottle of white wine.

He hoped he'd find out more from the neighbors than he had from her apartment.

Twenty

He tried several of the other apartments on the floor, but the tenants were either at work or not answering. He'd have to try in the afternoon, when people came home from work.

However, he did get an answer when he knocked on the door of 805, which was directly across from Helen.

The door opened a couple of inches and a woman's eye looked out. There were enough wrinkles around it to tell him she was elderly.

'Yes? What do you want?' a tremulous voice asked.

'Ma'am, I'm sorry to bother you, but I'd like to ask you some questions about your neighbor across the hall? Miss Simms?'

'Helen? She's a lovely girl. Why are you asking? Why should I talk to you?'

'Ma'am, I'm sorry to tell you . . . Helen is dead.'

'What? That can't be, young man. I saw her yesterday morning, when she left for work.'

'And she didn't come home, did she?' he asked.

'Well, no . . .'

'That's because she's dead, ma'am.'

'Oh dear . . . are you the police?'

He decided not to lie.

'No, ma'am, but I'm assisting the police in their inquiries. Could I come in just for a few minutes and ask some questions?'

'I-I suppose so,' she said. She closed the door. He heard the chain lock slip off and then it reopened to reveal a tiny, old woman wearing a housecoat. 'Come in, young man.'

'Thank you, ma'am.'

He stepped inside and she closed the door. He immediately noticed the musty smell in the place. This was a woman who rarely opened her windows.

'Can I get you some tea or lemonade?' she asked.

'No, ma'am,' he said, 'I don't want to put you out. I just need to ask a few questions.'

'Well, please sit down, then.'

He looked around. The sofa and chairs were expensive, and they were covered with plastic. She sat down on the sofa, so he chose one of the chairs. The plastic creaked as he sat.

'How did she die?' the woman asked.

'That's what we're looking into,' he said. 'Someone may have killed her, or . . . she may have done it, herself.'

'Oh, no,' she said, shaking her head, 'that sweet child would never have done that.' She had bright blue eyes that looked out at him from a mass of wrinkles. Her mouth was set in a straight, disapproving line. 'No, no, never.'

'Then, ma'am—'

73

'My name is Miss Orchid,' she said. 'Or you may call me Martha.'

'All right, Martha,' he said, 'would you know of anyone who might want to hurt Helen?'

'Why, no,' she said. 'Everyone in the building who knows – knew her – liked her. I don't think you'll find anyone here who would hurt her. You should try that place.'

'What place?'

'That place where she works.'

'The Sands, you mean? The hotel?'

'Casino,' she said, slowly. Her tone was heavy with disapproval.

'You think someone at the casino wanted to hurt her?'

'I am saying that place is filled with evil people,' she said. 'This building is not.'

'Do you know if she had any . . . gentlemen friends?'

'Helen kept to herself,' Martha Orchid said. 'I never saw her go out after she came home from work.'

'What about something like grocery shopping?'

'She usually came home from work with a couple of bags of groceries. Sometimes she bought me a few things. I don't go out, you see.'

'I understand. So you've never known her to have an argument with anyone in the building?'

Miss Orchid hesitated.

'Martha?'

'Well,' she said, 'she did have cross words once or twice with Mr Hannigan.'

'And who is Mr Hannigan?'

74

'They call him the manager, but he's just a glorified super.'

'Oh, I spoke to him, briefly.'

'Well, perhaps you should speak to him more,' she suggested. 'Maybe you will learn something.'

'I'll do that,' Danny said. He had to return the key, anyway. 'Thank you for your time, Martha.'

He stood up. She rose to her feet more slowly and walked him to the door.

'How did she die?' she asked.

'That's not something you want to think about, ma'am.'

'I'm eighty-three years old, young man,' she said. 'Not much could shock me.'

He didn't believe her. A woman who thought casinos were evil would be shocked by a lot of things – least of all the way Helen Simms had died.

'Yes, ma'am,' he said, and left.

Twenty-One

He went back downstairs to the manager's apartment and rang the bell.

The man opened the door, chewing on something, and said, 'Got my key?'

'I'd like to come in and ask you some questions, Mr Hannigan.' He didn't hand the key back. Not yet.

'What about?'

'Helen Simms.'

75

'You said she's dead,' he replied. 'What's that got to do with me?'

'We need some information,' he said, knowing that the man would interpret the 'we' as being the police. He still hadn't claimed to be a cop, though.

'I'm eatin' my dinner.'

'I won't take long,' Danny said. 'I'll try not to upset your . . . family.'

The man scowled. 'Got no family. Just me. Yeah, OK, come on in.'

Danny went inside and closed the door. The apartment was similar to that of Martha Orchid's, but instead of smelling musty it just smelled stale – old food, sweat – and just plain dirty.

'OK, my dinner's on the table in the kitchen,' Hannigan said, turning to face Danny, 'so whatta ya want?'

'Do you know anybody in the building who might have had something against Helen Simms?'

'She was a stuck-up, snooty bitch but I don't think anybody wanted to kill 'er.'

'Stuck-up?'

'Too good for everybody else, ya know?'

'Everybody else, or you?'

Hannigan squinted at him.

'Whatta ya mean?'

'I heard you and she had words once or twice?'

'Who told you that?' Hannigan asked. 'The nosy old biddy across the hall?'

'Somebody.'

'Yeah, well, all I ever did was ask her out a couple of times,' Hannigan said. 'She got nasty and turned me down flat.'

76

'Nasty?'

'You know,' Hannigan said, 'one of those broads who can't just turn ya down, she's gotta shoot ya down, too. Ya know, make ya feel bad about yerself?'

'So she made you feel bad about yourself?'

'Hey, not me,' Hannigan said. 'I get plenty of broads. I ain't gonna break down and start cryin' just 'cause one don't like me. There's plenny of 'em out there. The bars are full of 'em.'

Danny studied the manager. Even if Hannigan had it in for Helen, he couldn't see the man going to the Sands unnoticed and killing her there. In fact, Mrs Orchid was probably right about that. For Helen to have been killed the way she was, where she was, it must have been somebody on the inside.

Jack Entratter wasn't going to be happy to hear that . . .

In fact, I wasn't happy to hear it, either.

'So that was it,' Danny said. 'I left him to his TV dinner.'

'And that's why you felt you had to come right over?' I asked. 'To tell me you think it was an inside job?'

'The more I thought about it, the more it made sense,' Danny said. 'Somebody on the outside would wait until she left the building. Why take a chance on trying to get in, maybe somebody seeing them where they didn't belong?'

'But somebody who already belonged wouldn't have to worry about that.'

'No,' Danny said, 'they'd just have to worry

77

about getting her alone – like in the ladies' room.'

'Makes sense. Will you come by tomorrow and snoop around?'

'On the payroll, right?'

'Right.'

'Hey,' Danny said, 'before I go, you never told me about your meeting with Hughes. How was he?'

'Naked.'

'For real?'

'Well, he had a tissue across his crotch, but yeah, pretty much.'

'So he's as crazy as they say?'

'Actually, I don't think so,' I said. 'He's got this disease that makes it hurt whenever anything touches his bare skin.'

'Anything?'

I nodded.

'Guess I'd sit around naked, too, if I had that,' Danny said.

'That's what I was thinkin'.'

'What about the floor?'

'What about it?'

'How's he walk in his bare feet?'

'I don't know,' I said. 'I was wondering how he even sat down.'

'I suppose he's got to,' Danny said.

'Yeah.'

'So what did he want?'

'He says he's looking to buy a casino.'

'And what's he want with you?'

'He says he's heard about me, wants my help in finding a place to buy.'

'You think he's after the Sands?'

78

'I don't know.'

'What did you tell him?'

'I said I'd think about it.'

'He offer you a lot of money?'

'Some.'

'He didn't find your price though, did he?'

'I've got to get to dinner, Danny,' I said. 'See you at the Sands tomorrow?'

'I'll be there, Eddie.'

'Let me get my jacket and I'll walk you out.'

I walked Danny to his car and watched him drive off. Then I got in the Caddy and drove to the Sands.

Twenty-Two

'Come on in,' Frank said. 'I'm almost ready.'

I stepped in and closed the door.

'I have to get my jacket, and my wallet,' Frank said. 'I'll be a second.'

He went into the bedroom, reappeared just seconds later, one hand in his pocket; I assumed tucking his wallet away. He put one arm into his jacket and said, 'OK, let's go.'

'How are you, Frank?'

'I'm good, kid.' He finished putting on his jacket, then slapped me on the arm, 'I'm good. Let's go show Eddie a good time, huh?'

We took the elevator to Robinson's floor and knocked on his door. When he answered and saw

Frank, his face became infused with genuine pleasure.

'Frank!' He grabbed him and they hugged each other. 'Good to see you.' He slapped Frank on the back.

'Hey, Eddie,' Frank said. 'Ready for a good dinner?'

'I'm ready.' Robinson was already wearing his suit, so he just stepped into the hall and pulled his door shut. He looked at me, smiled and said, 'Eddie G.'

'Hello, Eddie.'

'Where we goin', boys?' he asked, putting an arm around each of us as we walked to the elevator.

I decided to take Robinson to the steak house at The Golden Nugget. It was off the strip, but was still classic Las Vegas. I thought we could then check out the poker at Binion's Horseshoe.

Most of the conversation over dinner was between Frank and Robinson, catching up on each other's news.

At one point Robinson said, 'I'm so glad things worked out OK for you last year, Frank, when your boy was kidnapped. I tried to call, but I couldn't get through.'

'That's OK, Eddie,' Frank said. 'The cops and the FBI had my phones tapped, we were trying to leave them open for ransom calls.'

'Well, I'm glad he got home OK.'

'Much of that was due to this guy,' Frank said, slapping me on the back. 'Eddie G. was there for Junior at every turn. Don't know if we woulda got him back without him.'

80

'There were a lot of people in on that, Frank.'

He left his hand on my shoulder and squeezed.

'Eddie G.'s modest, Eddie,' he told Robinson. 'We can always count on him.'

'Well,' Robinson said, 'I counted on him for this meal and it was excellent. What's next, Eddie G.?'

'Next,' I said, 'is poker.'

We went over to the Horseshoe and watched a few hands of poker in the poker room. Having Frank Sinatra and Edward G. Robinson there at the same time created a bit of a stir, but poker players are a single-minded lot and eventually went back to their games.

'Eddie,' Pete Santos said, 'what are you tryin' to do to me?'

Santos ran the high-stakes poker room at the Horseshoe, and didn't like anything to disrupt things.

'Relax, Pete,' I said, 'Mr Robinson is doing research for a movie role. He just wants to observe. Besides, look at your players. They could care less.'

Frank and Robinson were standing off to one side, watching and speaking to each other in low tones, with their heads close together.

'They're not disrupting anything,' I said.

'Well, keep it that way, will ya?' Santos said. 'I don't need none of your celebrity friends messin' with my room.'

'Don't worry, they won't.'

'They better not, or Entratter will be hearin' from Mr Binion.'

81

He walked away, his shoulders hunched.

Frank and Robinson walked over to me.

'What's his beef?' Frank asked.

'He thinks we're distracting the players.'

'Are we?' Robinson said, looking over at the tables.

'Not anymore,' I said. 'Poker players can concentrate in a tornado.'

Robinson waved a finger and said, 'Now that's the kind of thing I need to learn.'

'I'll get you in to some private games soon,' I said, 'but for now you can watch here.'

'Good, good,' Robinson said. 'I'll just stroll around.'

He couldn't walk among the tables and watch, only the players were allowed near there. But he could circle around on the outside.

'Frank, can I ask you something?'

'Sure, pally,' he said. 'What's on your mind?'

'Have you talked to Howard Hughes about me?'

Frank looked away from the games at me.

'What makes you think I talk to Hughes about anything, let alone you?'

'I just . . .'

'What?'

'I had a conversation with him recently,' I said. 'He mentioned you.'

'Me? What did he say about me? And why were you talkin' to him?'

I decided to come clean.

'He's in Vegas, looking to buy. He thinks I can steer him toward a property.'

'Does he want to buy the Sands?'

'He didn't say. He just says he's looking to buy.'

82

'And how did I come up?'

'I just asked why he'd contacted me, and he said that you and Dean had confidence in me.'

'Well,' Frank said, 'I hate Hughes and the feeling is mutual. He didn't hear nothin' from me. And I doubt he heard it from Dino.'

I hesitated a moment, then said, 'Ava?'

'She hasn't spoken to him in years. No, I think maybe he was tellin' you what he thought you wanted to hear.'

'Maybe you're right.'

'You tell Jack about this?'

'Yeah,' I said. 'He's gonna see what he can find out, but he's kinda messed up about his girl getting killed.'

'Yeah, I can see that. How's that going?'

'I've got Danny lookin' into Helen's life to see what he can find out.'

'Your PI friend. He's a good guy.'

'Yeah, he is, and I've got Jerry comin' in tomorrow.'

'Sounds like you got everything under control, Eddie.'

'Yeah,' I said, 'sounds like it, don't it . . .'

Twenty-Three

Eddie Robinson turned in before Frank and I were ready. We offered to walk him to his room, but once we hit the lobby he said, 'I need you to show me around Vegas, Eddie, but I'm sure I

83

can find my way to my own room alone.' He said goodnight to us and went to the elevator.

'He's a nice man,' I said.

'He is that,' Frank said. 'Come on, I'll buy you a nightcap.'

We walked through the casino to the lounge. People nudged each other as Frank walked by, but nobody approached him. I figured once we were seated at a bar a few autograph hounds would get brave. In the casino environment, Frank didn't mind. But, when he was sitting with friends having dinner, he didn't like being bothered.

We sat at the bar and Frank ordered a martini. I settled for a beer.

'You want me to send a car to the airport to pick up Jerry tomorrow?' he asked.

'No, thanks. I told Jerry I'd pick him up. Besides, he likes to drive the Caddy from the airport.'

'How are you gonna divide up your time?' Frank asked.

'Not sure,' I said. 'I guess that'll depend on how much Danny finds out.'

'I could talk to Jack for you,' Frank offered, 'keep him off your back.'

'No, Frank, it's OK,' I said. 'I've got my own relationship with Jack. I can handle him. He's in a bad way, right now. I think he liked that girl more than I thought.'

'You mean . . .'

'No, no, nothing like that,' I said. 'She just worked for him for a long time.'

'What was she like?'

84

'Unpleasant,' I said, 'at least, to me. She didn't like me one bit.'

'Why not?'

'I don't know,' I said, 'and now I probably never will.'

'Lots of people don't like me,' Frank said, 'and I don't know all the reasons why. And I don't care.'

'That's because you're Frank Sinatra,' I said. 'The Chairman of the Board. I'm just Eddie.'

'Hey, man,' Frank said, 'you're Eddie G., the coolest cat in Vegas. Remember that, huh?'

'Yeah, sure.'

'And listen,' he said, 'be careful with Hughes. He's a snake.'

'I will.'

He finished his martini and slapped me on the back. 'I'll be around, pally, if you need help. Just call.'

'Thanks, Frank.'

He got off his stool, started away, then turned and said, 'Oh yeah, I meant to tell you. Dino's comin' to town. He's doin' his own show at the Sahara. I figured we'd go and see him.'

'Sure,' I said. 'That'll be good.'

He winked, smiled and left the lounge. Right outside the door two girls stopped him for his autograph. He signed, and laughed with them. When he was done he walked off with a jaunty step.

The girls came into the lounge, laughing and looking at his signature. They sat at the bar and ordered drinks. I had the feeling they were too young, but that wasn't my job.

I finished my beer and left the lounge. I was almost at the hotel lobby when a dealer caught up with me.

'Hey, Eddie?'

I turned and looked at him. His name was Patrick, and he'd been working at the Sands for a couple of years, but for six months in my pit.

'What's up, Pat?'

'Red Skelton wants to up his limit.'

I looked over at the table and Red waved to me and smiled. I waved back.

'Who's in my pit?' I asked.

'Henry Mills.'

'What'd he say?'

'He said no, but I told him Mr Skelton was a regular,' Pat said.

'Wait, Henry doesn't know who Red is?'

'I guess not.'

'Jesus,' I said. 'OK, I'll take care of it, Pat.'

'Thanks, Eddie.'

I walked back to the table with him, shook hands with Red, assured him it would only take a minute.

'Thanks, Eddie,' Red said, 'I knew I could count on you.'

'Are you playin' the strip?' I asked.

'No, downtown this time.'

'Well, sit tight.'

I went over to Henry Mills and told him it was OK to raise Red Skelton's limit.

'He's a star, and a friend of Jack Entratter's.'

'OK, Eddie,' Henry said, 'if you say so.'

'Hank, you gotta start recognizing these people.'

'I don't go to the movies much, Eddie.'

86

'Red's on TV.'

'Don't watch much TV, either.'

'Yeah, OK,' I said. 'But you gotta get a life, Hank.'

'Thanks, Eddie.'

No movies and TV, I thought, walking away. How the hell did the guy get hired? The Sands is a place where you had to recognize people. It was where the stars came to play.

Jesus, even in my head I sounded like a goddamn advertisement.

I left the building and drove home.

Twenty-Four

In the morning I got up early and drove to the airport. I was hungry, but waited to have breakfast with Jerry. He would have taken it as a personal affront if I hadn't.

'Mr G.!' He lifted me into a huge bear hug, which surprised me. In the past a handshake would do it, then a warm handshake. We had come a long way as friends.

'How you doin', big guy?'

'I'm good,' he said. 'I'm ready to help.'

He looked good, too. He was wearing a sports jacket and slacks and, thankfully, he had stayed away from the houndstooth jacket he'd worn last time he was in Vegas.

'Well, we're gonna be busy.'

I didn't bother trying to carry his bag for him.

I did that once, and almost dislocated a shoulder.

He tossed it into the back seat of the Caddy like a feather and got behind the wheel with a big smile on his face.

'Breakfast?' he asked.

'You bet,' I said.

I took him to a new place I had found off the strip, part diner, part mom-and-pop country cooking. It didn't matter to him, really, he went for a huge stack of pancakes and sausage. I went for scrambled eggs, bacon, potatoes, and toast. We both had coffee.

Over breakfast I told him everything that had happened, from Jack's girl to Howard Hughes to Edward G. Robinson.

'Howard Hughes,' he said, when I was done. 'Is he as crazy as they say?'

'Like a fox,' I said. 'I think he uses the rumors to his advantage, but he's definitely in his own world.'

'This broad that got hung,' Jerry said, 'she's the one that don't like you so much, right?'

'Didn't like me,' I said, 'right.'

'Guess you'll never know why, now,' Jerry said.

'Right now, we just have to be concerned with who killed her.'

'The cops ain't gonna like us steppin' on their toes.'

'Hargrove is callin' it a suicide,' I said, 'or he's telling Jack he's callin' it a suicide.'

'You think he's lyin'?'

'From the time he wakes up in the morning to the time he goes to bed at night,' I said, 'but in this instance, it may be strategic.'

'He's tryin' to put you off,' Jerry said. 'You think he figures somebody in the hotel killed the girl, and that makes you suspect?'

'Maybe,' I said. 'We know he's still wantin' to pin something on me.'

'And me, once he finds out I'm here.'

'Well, we'll keep that to ourselves as long as we can, although it won't be easy.'

'I can make myself smaller when I have to,' Jerry said.

'Yeah, right.'

After breakfast we jumped back in the Caddy and drove to the Sands. I took Jerry to his suite to drop off his bag, and then down to Entratter's office. I wanted to check in with Jack on everything.

'Jerry,' Entratter said with a nod as we entered.

'Hey, Mr Entratter.'

They were two big men who usually eyed each other warily. Jack thought that I got more reckless when I was paired with Jerry. He may have been right.

'Eddie, what's goin' on with Helen's case?'

Case? Like I was a detective?

'Danny's gonna be in here later to ask some questions, Jack,' I said. 'You've got to give him a big pass to go anywhere.'

'Yeah, OK,' Jack said. 'How does it look, so far?'

'Like an inside job,' I said. 'I mean, I can't be sure, but—'

Entratter spread his arms and said, 'Somebody I hired killed her?'

'Jack—'

'When I find out who it was—'

'Don't take it so personally,' I said, knowing that wasn't going to fly with him. 'Somebody could've got into the building . . .'

'You don't believe that,' Jack said. 'You think somebody who works for me killed her. Goddamnit! That's such a . . . a . . . betrayal!'

'Take it easy,' I said, 'we'll find out for sure.'

'Yeah,' he said, fuming, 'yeah, OK, I'll take it easy. What about Eddie?'

'I'm gonna get him into some private games so he can watch,' I said.

'Make sure nothing happens like the last time,' Jack said. 'We don't need Edward G. Robinson to be around when there's a hold up.'

I didn't mention that it was up to him to beef up security, not me.

'I'll talk to Billy about it,' he added. Billy Pulaski was an ex-Chicago cop Jack had hired several years ago to oversee security. After the hold-up he almost fired him, so I knew Billy would be putting the hammer down.

'I'll check in with him before I take Eddie anywhere,' I said.

'You call Mr Robinson "Eddie"?' Jerry asked, looking confused.

'I'll fill you in later,' I told him.

'Get out of here,' Jack said. 'Get it done.'

'Have you heard from Hargrove again?' I asked.

'No, not a word.'

I stood up. 'I can't believe he's really callin' it a suicide.'

'You think he's playin' us?'

'I do.'

'Then you better be careful,' Jack said. 'Don't step on his toes.'

'I'd like to step on his head,' Jerry said.

'And keep him under control.' Jack pointed at the big guy.

'I'm always in control,' Jerry said.

'Last time you were here you got arrested in the first hour,' Jack reminded him.

'Not my fault.'

'Go on,' Entratter said, 'go!'

Jerry and I started for the door.

'Hey, Eddie?'

'Yeah, Jack?'

'Have you heard from Hughes again?'

'No,' I said.

'Do you expect to?'

'Oh, yeah.'

'What're you gonna tell 'im?'

'I'll figure it out.'

'Let me know what happens.'

'I will.'

We left.

Twenty-Five

'I don't get myself in trouble,' Jerry grumbled in the elevator.

'Relax,' I said, 'he's stressed out.'

'Where we goin'?' he asked.

'We've got to meet Danny in the lobby.'

'Not at the Horseshoe?'

Jerry really liked the coffee shop at the Horseshoe, and I didn't blame him. It was probably the best one in town.

'No,' I said, 'Danny needs to get started here, askin' questions. Besides, we just had breakfast.'

'Like an hour ago,' he grumbled.

'Settle down.'

We exited the elevator just as Danny was coming through the front door. He waved, and when he reached us he and Jerry shook hands.

'You've got carte blanche to go anywhere,' I told Danny. 'Ask all the questions you need to.'

'What about Entratter?'

'What about him?'

'I've got to start with him, Eddie.'

'Why not start with me, then?'

'You didn't do it, brother.'

'Jack didn't do it, either, Danny.'

'But he may know somethin',' Danny said. 'Somethin' you don't know about the victim.'

'Yeah, OK,' I said. 'He's in his office now.'

'Where'll you be?'

'I'm gonna check with Eddie Robinson, see if he wants to do anything today. And I'm gonna try to get him into a private game tonight, which means I've got to check in with Billy Pulaski.'

'What about Howard Hughes?'

'I'm just waitin' for him to contact me again,' I said.

'What are you gonna tell 'im?'

'Still not sure,' I said. 'I'm thinkin' about it.'

'OK,' Danny said, 'well, I better get started.'

He headed for the elevator, then turned and said, 'I *am* gettin' paid, right?'

'Definitely,' I said, even though I'd forgotten to bring that up with Entratter, 'gettin' paid.'

He gave me a thumbs up and went to the elevators.

'Mr G.?' Jerry said.

'Yeah?'

'Remember what you said about keepin' the cops in the dark as long as we could about me bein' here?'

'Yeah,' I said, watching Danny get into an elevator, 'so?'

'That's gonna be harder than we thought.'

I turned and looked at him, then followed his hand to where he was pointing. Detective Hargrove had just come through the front doors and he was heading right for us.

Twenty-Six

'Well, well . . .' Hargrove said.

I wondered if he had also seen Danny coming into the hotel.

'Didn't take you long to send for the Brooklyn Bruiser, did it?'

'Hey,' Jerry said, 'I like that.'

'It wasn't a compliment,' Hargrove said.

'I know,' Jerry said, 'but I still like it.'

'Fine,' Hargrove said, 'use it with my blessing.' He turned to me. 'I was looking for you.'

'You found me.'

'Someplace we can talk?'

'Right here suits me.'

He looked around the lobby, off into the casino. There was a lot of activity, people coming and going, and nobody was paying any attention to us.

'OK,' Hargrove said, 'your buddy Bardini's been nosing around.'

'Isn't that his job?'

'Don't be a smart ass. He's been nosing around this case.'

'What case?'

'Come on, Eddie, don't play dumb.'

'What makes you think I'm playing?'

He poked me in the chest with his forefinger and said, 'I didn't come here to fence with you.'

'Hey!' Jerry said.

'What? Hargrove said.

'No poking.'

Hargrove took his finger off me, but left it extended.

'What are you gonna do about it, Epstein?'

'Well,' Jerry said, 'I could break it off. Wouldn't take much effort. But then I guess I'd get myself arrested.'

'Sure as hell would.'

'But you'd be missin' a finger,' Jerry said. 'It might be worth it.'

Abruptly, Hargrove's finger disappeared into a fist, which he then dropped to his side. Then he looked at me again.

'I checked Bardini's office and he isn't there,' he said. 'His secretary wouldn't give me anything.'

'She's a good girl,' Jerry said.

'But I wouldn't call her a secretary to her face,' I advised.

'You tell Bardini to stay out of my case,' Hargrove said, 'and if I catch him impersonating a cop it's gonna go bad for him.'

'You mean the case you're calling a suicide?' I asked. 'That case?'

'And he's probably poking around in it for you,' Hargrove went on. 'So call him off, Eddie, or it's both your asses.'

'You did say you were calling it a suicide, right?'

He looked at Jerry, stuck his hands in his pocket, then turned and walked out.

I looked at Jerry.

'You really could've snatched his finger off that easy?'

'Pops right off,' he said, 'at any joint.'

'That's interesting,' I said. 'What do we do now?'

'We're lucky Hargrove didn't go upstairs and catch Danny talking to staff,' I said. 'I better warn him.'

'We goin' back up?'

'I'll call Jack's office,' I said. 'Danny should still be there.'

He was, and Jack handed him the phone. I told him about Hargrove showing up, looking for him.

'Damn,' he said, 'somebody at Helen's building must've snitched.'

'You weren't impersonating a cop, were you?'

'I never tell anybody I'm a cop,' Danny said, firmly.

'Yeah, but you don't tell them you're not, either.'

'Well, now you're just quibbling.'

I let him hang up and get back to what he was doing.

'Now what?' Jerry asked.

I was about to answer when I saw a man come through the front doors.

'I don't think we're ever gonna get out of this lobby!'

'Who's that?'

'That's Robert Maheu, Howard Hughes' right-hand man, coming toward us.'

'No shit?' Jerry said. 'Howard Hughes?'

'Ah, Mr Gianelli,' Maheu said. 'I was, uh, looking for you.'

'You found me,' I said, telling him the same thing I had told Hargrove, but not with the attitude.

Maheu looked at Jerry.

'This is my friend, Jerry Epstein,' I said. 'Jerry, this is Robert Maheu.'

Maheu nodded at Jerry politely, but said to me, 'Can we talk?'

I was tempted to stay in the lobby, as we had with Hargrove, but decided Maheu didn't deserve the same treatment I gave the cop.

'Sure, but not here,' I said. 'Let's go next door and get a drink.'

'Next door?'

'The Flamingo.'

'Ah, yes . . . Bugsy's place.'

'Once upon a time,' I said. 'Is that all right with you, Mr Maheu?'

'That's fine.'

We started for the door, Jerry with us. Maheu stopped and looked pointedly at the big man.

'Oh, don't worry,' I said to Maheu, 'anything you have to say to me you can say in front of Jerry.'

Maheu looked at Jerry again, who said, 'I know how to keep my mouth shut.'

'I see,' Maheu said.

'So, we're still going?' I asked.

'Um, yes,' Maheu said, slightly unsure, 'to the Flamingo.'

Maheu went out the door and Jerry gave me a look behind his back.

Twenty-Seven

We got a table in the Driftwood Lounge. Since Morris Landsburgh sold the Flamingo in 1960 – a deal brokered by his friend Meyer Lansky – they had added 200 hotel rooms, and pretty much become a jazz destination. At any time you might find Lionel Hampton, Della Reese, Harry James, Fats Domino or Sarah Vaughan playing the lounge. (That said, don't ask me why Robert Goulet made his Vegas debut in 1963 at The Flamingo, right from his Broadway stint in 'Camelot.'). Just the previous year, much of the Elvis film *Viva Las Vegas* had been shot at the Flamingo, mostly exterior shots.

We settled in and ordered drinks from a

waitress. At that hour the lounge stage was empty, and it was fairly quiet.

'What's on your mind, Mr Maheu?' I asked.

'Mr Hughes was wondering what you had decided?'

'Well, to tell the truth, I've been a little busy,' I said. 'We had an employee murdered at the Sands.'

'Yes, I heard about that. Terrible thing. But I thought the woman hanged herself?'

'The police may think that,' I said, 'but those of us who knew her doubt it.' That was pushing it, but I figured I might as well let Maheu think we were all family at the Sands.

'Well,' Maheu said, looking around, 'I thought perhaps you had brought me here because you were going to recommend it to Mr Hughes as a place to purchase.'

'I doubt this would be available,' I said. 'It was bought only four years ago.'

'Then you have no suggestions as yet?'

'To tell you the truth, Mr Maheu,' I said, 'I don't think I'd be comfortable working for Mr Hughes.'

'And why is that?'

'Well, like I told you, I'm pretty busy. And, as part of the Vegas community, I'd feel pretty disloyal helping Hughes pick a place to take over.'

'Take over?'

'Isn't that what he does?' I asked.

'Sometimes,' Maheu said, 'but here in Vegas he's simply looking to make a reasonable offer to someone.'

I'd already learned from talking with Hughes that he wasn't quite what his reputation made him out to be, but still, it didn't seem to me he made reasonable purchases. I thought he was pretty ruthless when it came to getting what he wanted.

'Please pass along my regrets to Mr Hughes,' I said to Maheu.

'Are you sure?' he asked.

'Very sure.'

Maheu sat back.

'I don't think Mr Hughes will be very happy with that answer.'

'As I said,' I repeated, 'apologize for me.'

'I'm afraid that might be something you'll have to do yourself.'

'Well,' I said, 'I don't really have time—'

He cut me off by standing, doing up one button of his jacket, and saying, 'Good day.'

'I don't like that guy,' Jerry said, watching Maheu walk away.

'He used to work for the Feds.'

'That explains it, then. You really gonna turn down Howard Hughes?'

'I think I just did.'

'Didn't he offer you a buttload of money?'

'We didn't talk specifics,' I said, 'but I think a "buttload" was implied.'

'I gotta give you credit, Mr G.,' Jerry said. 'Don't know if I could turn that down.'

'Somehow I don't think you'd have a problem turning money down, Jerry,' I said. 'I don't think you do what you do strictly for money.'

'I do lots of things for money, Mr G.,' he said. 'But forget about that. It sure sounds like he don't think Hughes is gonna be real happy.'

'Fuck it,' I said, 'I've got too much to do to help him take over somebody's casino, because you know that's what he wants. He wants me to tell him what property is ripe for the pickin'. These people in Vegas are my friends, Jerry. Howard Hughes is nothing to me.'

'Well,' Jerry said, 'I just hope he takes your turn down in stride.'

'What's he gonna do, send some muscles to convince me?'

'I dunno, Mr G.,' Jerry said. 'Does Howard Hughes hire muscle?'

I shrugged.

'Well, then we better keep our eyes open,' he said. 'It's a good thing you called me.'

'Never mind Howard Hughes,' I said to him. 'How would you like to meet Edward G. Robinson?'

'I would love that,' he said, his eyes going wide. 'Him and Cagney – and Bogey, of course – they're the best!'

'OK, then,' I said, 'let's go and get that done right now.'

Twenty-Eight

'I thought we were gonna meet Mr Robinson,' Jerry said as we entered his suite.

'I've got to make some calls, first,' I said. 'I don't want to go to the fourth floor to use the phones, I don't want to use the phones in the lobby because it's too much like Grand Central Fucking Station, and I don't want to go home.

'I was just askin'.'

'It's OK,' I said.

He went to the bar and I went to the phone.

'I just have to set it up for Robinson to watch a poker game tonight.'

'That's what he's here for, right, just to watch?'

'Watch, observe, learn,' I said.

'A movie with him and Steve McQueen oughtta be real good,' Jerry said. 'Especially with Ann-Margret in it. Hey, is she gonna—'

'You met her last year,' I said. 'You're not gonna get that lucky two years in a row.'

'Just askin',' Jerry said, as I dialed. 'Want a drink?'

'Uh, yeah, I'll have a beer.'

Jerry brought me a bottle of Piels while I talked on the phone. I knew there was a high-stakes game in the hotel again that night. What I needed was permission to bring Edward G. Robinson up to watch. I started with Billy Pulaski, Jack's Head of Security.

'I don't know, Eddie,' he said. 'After what happened with Kendrick the other night—'

'What did happen with him?' I asked. 'I mean . . . did you fire him?'

'Oh yeah,' Pulaski said, 'so I'll be sittin' in on this game myself until I hire a new man.'

'Well, that's great, Billy,' I said. 'With you there we know things'll go OK.' I didn't mention the fact that it was me who kept the game from being robbed the other night.

'I think I gotta check with Jack, Eddie.'

'Sure, you do that.' I knew Jack would tell him to make it happen.

'And the players?'

'They wouldn't care as long as they get to play.'

'Do that, too, and I'll get back to you,' I said, and hung up.

'Problem?' Jerry asked. He was standing behind the bar with a bottle of beer in his big hand.

'Security,' I said. 'I told you about the attempted robbery. Pulaski is worried about it. He thinks bringing Robinson to the game might be a risk.'

'Ain't you his boss?'

'No,' I said. 'Jack's his boss. He'll call Jack, and Entratter will tell him it's OK. Then he has to check with the players.'

'Well, they won't say no to Edward G. Robinson, right?' Jerry asked. 'Rico?'

'I hope not,' I said.

'So what do we got to do until then?' Jerry asked. 'Get somethin' to eat?'

It had been a few hours since breakfast, so I said, 'Yeah, sure, let's go downstairs and get something to eat.'

He went to the Garden Café. I didn't want to leave the building until I talked to Billy again. Or maybe I should have called Jack and suggested that he call Billy. No, that might make Billy think I was going over his head.

He sat in a booth and Jerry started looking over the menu. It hadn't changed since the last time he'd eaten there, but I let him look.

'Hey, Eddie G.,' the waitress said. Her name was Lily, she'd been working there for about three months, which meant she'd never seen Jerry. 'Who's your big friend?'

'Jerry, meet Lily.'

'Hi,' Jerry said.

Lily was attractive, thirty-five or so, with red hair, green eyes and a very flirtatious manner. She turned up the heat on those eyes when she looked at Jerry.

'And what does Jerry want to drink?' she asked, smiling at him.

'Coffee,' he said. 'But I'll have a chocolate shake with my food.'

'OK,' she said, 'chocolate shake for the big guy.' She looked at me.

'Iced tea.'

'Comin' up.'

She walked away and Jerry watched her hips sway.

'You like redheads?' I asked.

'A lot.'

'She's single and, supposedly, kind of wild.'

'Naw,' Jerry said, turning his attention back to the menu. 'I like red-headed whores.'

'Jerry . . . have you ever had a girl? I mean, a regular girlfriend?'

'Of course,' he said. 'A few. But it never ended well. So I stopped. Started using only whores. It works out better that way.'

'OK,' I said. Far be it for me to try to change his mind from something that was working for him.

'How's the meat loaf?' he asked.

Twenty-Nine

We finished eating – Jerry went for the meat loaf and liked it, I had a burger and fries. I wasn't really hungry, and a burger was always my fall back meal. But we finished eating and I grew impatient, so I asked Lily to bring a phone to the table.

'I'm gonna call Billy now,' I said to Jerry, dialing.

'You got your way,' Billy said when he heard my voice. He wasn't happy. 'Entratter said to give you whatever you want.'

'Not me,' I said, 'Edward G. Robinson.'

'Whoever,' he said. He gave me the room number and the time that the game would start, and slammed the phone down.

'He sounded mad from here,' Jerry said.

'He'll get over it,' I said. 'He hasn't been working here that long.'

'Doesn't know that you're the man, huh?'

'You want dessert?' I asked.

'Pie,' he said.

I waved Lily over and we both had cherry pie.

'After this,' I said to him, 'we'll go up and see Mr Robinson.'

'That'll be great,' he said.

Edward G. Robinson answered the door to his suite himself.

'Oh, good, Eddie G.,' he said. 'I was afraid it was that annoying girl the studio stuck me with.'

'Eddie, this is my friend, Jerry. Jerry, meet Edward G. Robinson.'

'Wow,' Jerry said, 'this is a real honor, Mr Robinson.'

'Well,' Eddie Robinson said, shaking Jerry's big paw, 'you're a big one, aren't you? I could've used you in some of my earlier pictures.'

'Me? Really?'

'Come on in, both of you,' Robinson said. 'What's on the agenda for today, Eddie G.?'

'I've arranged for you to watch a private, high-stakes poker game,' I said, 'but it won't be until tonight.'

'What about the rest of today?' Robinson said. 'You can't leave me here. That girl will find me, I know she will.' He gave me a pleading look. 'You've got to hide me.'

'Do you want me to move you to another suite?' I asked.

'No, no, nothing as drastic as that,' he said. 'I don't want to get the poor girl fired. Just . . . let's do something.'

'Like what?'

'The Las Vegas Art League.'

'The what?'

'I want to go to the Las Vegas Art League,' Robinson said. 'Before coming here I checked to see if Las Vegas had an art museum.'

'It doesn't, that I know of.'

'Not strictly speaking, but the Art League has a space in a house at Lorenzi Park. Do you know where that is?'

'I have a general idea—'

'I have an address,' he said. 'That's where I want to go. And I'll buy dinner.' He looked at Jerry. 'How's that?'

'Works for me,' Jerry said.

I knew Robinson was an art collector. He had taken what used to be a badminton court at his Beverly Hills home and turned it into an art gallery.

I looked at Jerry and said, 'We're gonna go look at some art.'

'Let me change my clothes,' Eddie said, excitedly. He rushed into the bedroom.

'Art,' I said to Jerry, again.

'Don't forget,' he added, 'he said he's gonna buy dinner. Rico's gonna buy me dinner!'

'Yes, he is.'

I'd never seen Jerry so excited before, not even when he met Marilyn Monroe.

'Can we have Italian?' he asked.

Thirty

While Edward G. Robinson enjoyed viewing the art on exhibit at the Las Vegas Art League we found out that, in 1956, he had been forced to sell his personal art collection during the divorce from his wife. Nevertheless, he maintained his interest in art, and was even a painter himself.

It was interesting that he opened up to us about his interest in art, and the situation with his divorce. We did a lot of listening as he walked us past the various pieces.

As we drove away from Lorenzi Park – Jerry driving the Caddy, Robinson next to him and me in the back – Eddie said, 'Thank you boys for letting me go on and on about art this afternoon.'

'It was our pleasure, Eddie,' I said.

'Hey, I learned a lot, Mr R.,' Jerry said. 'I never knew nothin' about art before.'

'And what do you know now, big guy?' I asked from the back, slapping him on the shoulder.

'I learned I'm not the only one who has a blue period once in a while.'

'Oh, you're in the majority there, my boy,' Robinson said. 'There are lots of us who have blue periods.'

'What about you, Mr G.?' Jerry asked.

'Some of my blue periods go toward black,' I said.

'Where are we goin' to eat?' Jerry asked.

'Eddie, Jerry asked for Italian, so if you don't mind we're gonna go to one of Frank's favorite places, the Bootlegger.'

'The Bootlegger?' Robinson said. 'That's Italian?'

'Very,' I said.

Robinson put an affectionate hand on Jerry's arm and said, 'Well, if that's what Big Jerry wants, that's what we'll have.'

Eddie had started calling Jerry 'Big' Jerry early on, and I could tell the big guy liked it.

'I'll call Frank and have him meet us there. We've been there before, Jerry,' I said. 'Remember the way?'

107

'I got it, Mr G.,' he assured me, and gunned it.

The Bootlegger had the appearance of a speak-easy, but served some of the finest food in Las Vegas. Last year even mafia boss Sam Giancana had complimented Frank's choice of the Bootlegger for his go-to place in Vegas for Italian food.

Frank had to beg off. Something had come up, a problem with his schedule which he'd have to spend time on the phone sorting out.

'Tell Eddie I'll call him and we'll do somethin',' he told me.

So it was just the three of us.

Over dinner Jerry asked Robinson if he thought about collecting again.

'It's very hard,' Eddie said, 'when you've built up a collection and been forced to give it up, to try and start again. It's just too . . . heartbreaking.'

'I got ya,' Jerry said.

'So now I paint for myself,' Eddie went on. 'In fact, I'd love to paint you, Big Jerry.'

'Me?'

'Sure,' Eddie said, 'you'd make a wonderful subject.'

'Mr G.'s better lookn' than me,' Jerry said. 'Why don't you paint him?'

'Eddie G. is a very handsome specimen,' Eddie said with that twinkle in his eyes, 'but there's something special about you that I want to capture on canvas.'

'Wow,' Jerry said, 'ain't nobody ever said nothin' like that to me before, Mr R.'

108

'Well, I not only think you'd make a great subject for a painting, Jerry,' Eddie said, 'but I think you're a very fine young man.'

Jerry sat back in his chair and stared at the movie legend. I think he was stunned. And I knew he was thinking that Eddie Robinson still did not know exactly what Jerry did for a living. Would the older man feel the same if and when he did?

'Thanks,' Jerry said, finally. I'd seen Jerry become quiet and humble in front of women before – Marilyn and Ava Gardner – but never in front of a man.

But Robinson wasn't done. With a fatherly smile he added, 'I am a very good judge of character, Big Jerry. Believe me, after just this afternoon, I know you better than you know yourself.'

Jerry didn't know what to say to that, so he went to his fallback position, which was, 'Are we gonna have dessert?'

After three tiramisus we left the Bootlegger to head back to the Sands so Eddie Robinson could get himself ready for the poker game.

'What are you fellas going to do?' he asked.

'I've got some things to check on,' I said. 'Jerry'll probably come along with me.'

'Still looking into the death of that girl?'

'Yes.'

'Any leads?' he asked, then laughed. 'I've always wanted to say that in real life.'

Since he'd played so many gangster roles I doubted he'd even said it in the movies, but whatever made him happy was fine with me.

'Not yet,' I said, 'except that it still doesn't look like a suicide.'

'That can't make Jack very happy,' he said.

'No, it doesn't.'

'You know,' Robinson said, 'I'll understand if you guys have to spend more time on that and not so much with me. I mean, after all—'

'No, no,' I said, cutting him off, 'it's very important to Jack – and to us – that you get what you need from this trip.' Not to mention, important to Frank.

'Well, all right, then,' Robinson said.

We pulled up in front of the Sands and gave the Caddy to a valet. I told Robinson we'd come and get him later, and then Jerry walked his new friend to the elevator.

Thirty-One

I went to the front desk and asked, 'Any messages for me?'

'Got one, Eddie,' the girl said. Her name tag said: Candy. She handed me a pink message slip. The number on it was Danny's. Maybe he had some news after talking with Helen's co-workers.

'Can I use your phone?' I asked.

'Sure, Eddie.' She flipped it around for me. I dialed Danny's number. Penny answered.

'What's happening, Eddie?'

110

'I just had dinner with Edward G. Robinson, little girl. Who'd you eat with?'

'Eat? What's that? I've been working late.'

'I was trying to catch Danny in, returning his call.'

'He's not here. He might be home. This about the girl at the Sands?'

'That's right.'

'That was an awful thing. Can the police really be stupid enough to call it a suicide?'

'We're talking about Hargrove, Penny,' I said. 'I think he sits at his desk trying to come up with new ways to be stupid.'

'You're probably right.'

'OK, I'll try him at home,' I said. 'If you see him let him know I called. I'll be here at the Sands most of the night, and I'll keep checking my messages.'

'You got it, Eddie.'

'Goodbye, my love.'

'If only,' she said, giggled and hung up.

I turned just as Jerry came toward me.

'What's up?' he asked.

'Message from Danny, but I didn't catch him at his office. I'm gonna try him at home.'

I dialed Danny's home number from memory, let it ring ten times, then hung up.

'Not home?'

'Nope.'

'Then where is he?'

'I don't know.'

'Think he's in trouble?'

'I wouldn't have thought so,' I said. 'This case doesn't sound like the kind he could get in trouble with.'

'We're talkin' murder, right?'

'Well, yeah, but—'

'Murder's murder, Mr G.'

Jerry was speaking from strength, so I knew he had a point. I didn't like it, but I knew it.

'Let's face it, Mr G.,' Jerry said, 'guy in the shamus business, sometimes he gets into trouble.'

Yeah, I thought, especially when he does something for me. A couple of years ago he'd gone to LA for me and got kidnapped. Last year he was helping me and got arrested for murder.

I don't know why I thought this was an easy, simple case with no danger, just because it was Jack's girl who was killed, inside the Sands. Like Jerry said, murder was murder.

'All right,' I said, 'we've got time to kill before the poker game.'

'Then let's go find him,' Jerry said.

Thirty-Two

'Where do we start?' Jerry asked, as we walked through the lobby.

'Entratter,' I said. 'He's the first one Danny went to see.'

We found Jack still in his office. Helen's desk was very empty.

'Jack.'

He looked up as we entered.

'You know how much extra work there is when

112

you don't have a secretary?' he asked. 'If she did commit suicide she really screwed me.'

'But she didn't.'

'Still sure, huh?'

'I know what I saw, Jack.'

'Yeah, yeah . . . I heard all about it again from your buddy Bardini.'

'How long was he with you?' I asked.

'We talked for about twenty minutes,' Jack said. 'He's very thorough. I told him all I could about Helen, but I-I never realized how little I knew about her. I mean . . . her life outside of this office. I didn't know . . . anything.'

'And why should you?' I asked. 'She worked for you. You weren't friends. You didn't see each other away from work . . . did you?'

'What? No, no, I never did.'

'OK,' I said. 'Did Danny say where he was going next?'

'He was gonna to interview the rest of the office staff,' he said. 'And then some of the people in the hotel and casino, to see if they knew Helen.'

'Do you think they did?'

'Probably not.'

'What about lunch? Dinner? Did she ever eat at the Garden Café?'

'Probably . . . I don't know.'

'OK,' I said, 'OK.'

'What's wrong? Can't you find Bardini?'

'Not right now,' I said, 'but he might just be checking out a lead. We'll find him.'

'Yeah, OK.'

We turned to leave.

'What about Eddie Robinson? I got that call

113

from Billy. You got everything set for him?'

'I do,' I said. 'It's all set. But Billy was pissed.'

'I know,' Jack said. 'Fuck 'im. He'll get over it.'

'Yeah, OK,' I said. 'See you later, Jack.'

'Just let me know what's goin' on, Eddie,' Entratter said. 'Keep me in the loop.'

'Sure thing.'

I nodded to Jerry and we left the office.

'Where we goin'?' he asked.

'Just down the hall,' I said. 'I want to talk to Marcy. She found the body.'

He nodded and followed.

Thirty-Three

Marcy was seated at her desk, but she wasn't working. She was staring off into space. She probably should have gone home hours ago. There was a time she would have gone to the gym. Back when we had dated she had been in excellent shape, but I noticed lately she had packed a few extra pounds onto her five foot eight frame.

'Hey, Marcy,' I said, approaching her.

'Hmm? Huh? Oh, Eddie. Hi.'

'Are you OK?'

'Oh,' she said, sitting back in her chair, 'I just can't get the . . . sight of Helen . . . hanging there, out of my head. You know, I can't go into that bathroom. I go to the third floor.'

114

I put my hands on her shoulders and stood behind her.

'I understand, Marcy. Um, you remember Jerry, don't you? From his other visits?'

'Yes, I do,' she said. 'Hello, Jerry.'

'Ma'am.'

I couldn't remember if they had ever exchanged words before.

'Marcy, do you know of anybody on the Sands staff who didn't get along with Helen?'

'I talked to your friend, Danny,' she said. 'I told him she . . . wasn't very popular.'

'Did you give him some names?'

'Yes.'

'Can you give them to me, too?'

'Well, sure.'

'Good. And their addresses.'

'I made a list for him,' she said. 'I can duplicate it for you.'

'Great. Thanks, Marcy.'

Jerry and I stood aside while she wrote the list over again for us.

'You wanna dog the dick's trail?' he asked.

'I think it's the only way to find him,' I said, 'but I don't want to jump to any conclusions. Let's wait until tomorrow morning and see if we hear from him. I've got to get Eddie Robinson to that game, tonight.'

'I could start now,' he said, 'and visit some of these people.'

'It's getting late,' I said. 'Let's wait.'

'Sure thing, Mr G.'

'Here you go, Eddie,' Marcy said.

I went back to the desk and accepted the list

115

from her. There were eight names on it. I recognized five of them.

'All of these people didn't like her?'

'More than that, but these are the ones I know she had problems with.'

There were five women and three men.

'I thought I was the only one she didn't like.'

'You were,' she said. 'She didn't even notice these people, but they all . . . hated her for one reason or another. In fact, you were different.'

'In what way?'

'She noticed you,' she said. 'Everybody else she ignored. No, that's not right. She just didn't see them.'

'What about you?'

'We weren't friends,' she said, 'but we had to deal with each other every day. So we got along. We chatted in the . . . the ladies' room.'

'About what?'

She shrugged.

'I don't know. Nonsense. Who was playing the big room, who was laying the lounge. What was at the movies. Nothing deep.'

'So nobody knew her well?'

'Nobody.'

'OK.' I pocketed the list and headed for the door.

'I got a question,' Jerry said to her.

I stopped at the door and looked back.

'Yes, Jerry?'

'Why did Helen not like Mr G.?'

Marcy looked at me.

'You never asked her?'

'No,' I said. 'Would she have told me?'

'Maybe,' she said. 'I don't know.'

'Do you know?' Jerry asked.

'Well, one time in the ladies' room she was fuming about something,' she said. 'It turned out to be you.'

'Me? Why?'

'She didn't think you respected Jack Entratter,' she said. 'She thought you were . . . flippant, flaky.'

'Flaky? Me?'

'Why would she be mad that Mr G. didn't respect Mr Entratter?'

'Well . . .' she said, and then looked at me, 'she was in love with him.'

'But . . . he's married?'

'He doesn't talk about his wife much,' Marcy said. 'She's never around, really. They have a house. She stays there. She's never here – or hardly ever.'

I tried to remember if I had ever seen Jack's wife. I couldn't.

'Wait a minute,' I said. 'Helen was in love with Jack? She told you that?'

'She didn't have to,' Marcy said. 'I could tell.'

'Did Jack know?'

'I don't think so.'

'Did you tell this to Danny?'

'No,' she said.

'Why not?'

'It never came up,' she said. 'I only thought of it now because of Jerry's question.'

'So then Danny wouldn't have gone to see Jack's wife,' I said, mostly to myself.

'What?' Marcy said.

'Nothing,' I said. 'Why don't you take some time off, Marcy?'

'That comin' from you, Eddie, or Mr Entratter?'

'I'll square it with Jack,' I said. 'Go. Take a week, if you need it.'

'I can't take a week, I need my salary—'

'With pay.'

'You can do that?'

'I said I'd square it,' I repeated. I wasn't really positive I could, but I thought Jack would go along.

'Well, all right,' she said, and started opening her desk drawer. I assumed she was taking out her purse, preparing to go home, but Jerry and I left and walked to the elevator before I could be sure.

Thirty-Four

On the way down, Jerry said what I was thinking.

'Does this make Mr Entratter's wife a suspect?'

'I don't know,' I said. 'I don't think so. At least, not to the police. Not if they're calling it a suicide.'

'What about with you? And Danny?'

'Not Danny,' I said. 'He doesn't know about it.'

We reached the lobby and got out.

'When's the game?' Jerry asked.

'Four hours.'

'We could get a lot done.'

118

I checked my watch. It was almost eight. This was Vegas. It was still early enough to call on some people. But I wasn't yet ready to start going over ground already covered by Danny.

'We've got to talk to Danny first,' I said. 'He should be in his office in the morning.'

'Or home now,' Jerry said. 'If he's not missing.'

'OK,' I said, 'let's try him.'

This time I used a house phone to call Danny's home. No answer. Then I called Penny's home. No answer there, either. I called the office. She wasn't there.

'Whataya think?' Jerry asked.

'She could be out,' I said. 'She could be between the office and her home.'

'She could be missing.'

'I don't wanna get paranoid about this, Jerry.'

'I know, Mr G.,' Jerry said, 'but I could go out for something while you're taking Mr R. to the poker game.'

'Jerry, I don't need *you* to go missing.'

'Danny's not even been gone twenty-four hours,' Jerry said. 'Like you said, let's not get para . . . let's not jump to any conclusions.'

'OK, look,' I said. 'Just take the Caddy and find either Danny or Penny. Make sure they're all right.'

'You want me to ask the dick anythin'?'

'No – yeah – just bring him back here and then call me.'

'Where are you gonna be?'

'I'll leave a message for you at the desk telling you what room I'm in. Call me there.'

'OK, Mr G.'

119

'Hey, Jerry,' I called, as he started away.

'Yeah?'

'Are you heeled?'

'Not yet,' he said, and hurried away.

Thirty-Five

Robinson let me into his suite and asked, 'Where's Big Jerry?'

'He had some things to do.'

'Workin', huh?'

'He's helpin' me out with something.'

'Well, all right,' he said. 'Just let me get my jacket.'

He went into the bedroom. Came back with more than a jacket. He was wearing a tie, and a vest along with it. Very dapper.

'What do you think?' he asked. 'Is this Lancey Howard?'

'It works,' I said, and added what I had been thinking. 'Very dapper.'

'Yes, he is,' Robinson said. 'I'm thinking about adding a pinky ring.'

'I'd re-think that part,' I said. 'Ready to go?'

'I'm ready.'

We left the room and walked to the elevator.

'Listen, Eddie G.,' he said, as we rode up, 'I think I'm going to be playing a character tonight. I'll be trying Lancey Howard on, if you know what I mean.'

'I do,' I said. 'It'll be a privilege to watch you work.'

He took a cigar from his pocket and said, 'I brought a prop.'

'Light it up.'

He put it back in his pocket and said, 'I will, when we get there.'

All the players were seated at the table when Billy Pulaski let us in. I could see the gun beneath his jacket.

'Billy, meet Edward G. Robinson.'

'A pleasure, sir,' Billy said.

'The pleasure is mine,' Robinson said. 'I appreciate you letting me watch.'

'That was up to the players, really,' he said, 'and Jack Entratter.'

'Well, I thank you, anyway.'

'You're welcome, sir.'

I could see that Eddie had charmed Billy out of some of his snit.

'Billy, you want to introduce him to the players?' I asked.

'Why don't you do that,' Billy said. 'After all, you're Eddie G.'

OK, maybe he wasn't over his snit.

I knew all the players. None of them had been at the game the other night, the one that somebody had tried to rob. Also, the bartender was different.

I moved to the table, said hello to everyone, then said, 'Gents, meet Edward G. Robinson. He's doing research for his new movie, *The Cincinnati Kid*.'

'I read the book,' Herb Cowlan said. 'You playin' Lancey Howard?'

121

'That's right,' Robinson said, surprised.

'You're dressed the part,' Cowlan said. He was a businessman in his forties who came to the Sands several times a year with a million dollars in his pocket.

Of the six players, Cowlan was the most impressed with Robinson. Several of them knew him and said how good it was to meet him. At least two of them didn't seem impressed. They were the youngest, and maybe had not seen many of his early movies.

'All right,' I said, 'shuffle 'em and deal.'

That was Robinson's cue to take out his cigar and light it up.

Lancey Howard was in the house.

Robinson stood for a good portion of the time, but as a concession to his age he finally took a seat.

This game was a little different from the ones the actor would be playing in the movie. For one thing, in the book and the movie – he told me – the games have a dealer, while in this game the deal passed from player to player. This was the players' preference. The Sands did supply dealers for games, but in this case the players all wanted to pass the deal.

The game was not dealer's choice, though. They were playing five card stud, which *was* the game they'd be playing in the film.

Robinson caressed the cigar he was holding as he watched, and he kept silent the whole time.

After a couple of hours I started to wonder where Jerry was and when he'd call me.

Billy came over and said, 'You keep checkin'

your watch. You expectin' somethin' to happen?'

'Not like the other night, no,' I said. 'I'm waitin' for a call.'

'You gave somebody the room number?' he asked, testily.

'Relax,' I said. 'I checked with Jack first.' I hadn't, but I didn't want Billy to know that.

'Still . . .' he said.

'Relax, Billy,' I said. 'Everything's OK.'

Billy stepped away from me, but did not relax. He turned his attention back to the game . . .

When the phone finally rang the bartender answered it, then waved to get my attention.

'For you, Eddie,' he said as I approached, keeping his voice down.

'Thanks, Vinny.' I took the receiver. 'Hello?'

'Mr G.?'

'Hey, Jerry. You OK?'

'I'm fine, Mr G.,' he said, 'and so are Penny and the shamus.'

'Where's he been?'

'Workin',' Jerry said. 'He found out some stuff you should know about.'

'Can it wait til morning?'

'Oh, yeah,' Jerry said, 'it can wait a while. In fact, I told him we'd meet at the Horseshoe coffee shop in the morning. Nine a.m.'

'That's fine,' I said. That Danny and Jerry had chosen the Horseshoe was no surprise. 'I'm just glad he's OK, and not missing.'

'Not missing,' Jerry said, then added, 'but he took a few lumps.'

'What? Bad?'

'He's been worse,' Jerry said. 'You'll see, and you'll hear about it tomorrow.'

'Where are you?'

'I'm in my suite.'

'OK,' I said. 'Get some rest, and thanks for going out tonight.'

'Sure, Mr G.'

Neither of us hung up.

'Jerry?'

'Yeah?'

'Are you sure you're OK?'

'Oh yeah, I'm fine,' he said. 'There was some stuff . . . but you'll hear all about it in the morning. How's Mr R. doin' at the game?'

'He's watching,' I said, 'very closely.'

'Well, I'll see you in the mornin',' he said, and hung up. I hung up, too, deciding not to call him back and press him for more.

'Everything OK, Eddie G.?'

Robinson had come up to my elbow, holding his smoldering cigar aloft in one hand, his eyebrows up.

'Everything's good, Eddie,' I said. If it wasn't, apparently I'd find out in the morning.

Thirty-Six

Robinson grew tired long before the game ended. In fact, the game could have gone on for days. There was no way to know. When he and I left it made Billy much happier.

I spent the night in a room at the Sands and was knocking on the door to Jerry's suite early the next morning.

'Hey, Mr G.,' he said, fully dressed and ready to go. He also had a bruise on the left side of his face.

'That part of what happened last night?'

'Oh, uh, yeah,' he said, touching his face.

'Should I see the other guy?'

'I don't think anybody's gonna see the other guy again any time soon,' he replied.

'This somethin' I should hear about?'

'Yes, sir,' he said, 'but Danny wants to tell it at breakfast.'

'Then I guess we better go,' I said, 'because I'm real curious.'

'I'm ready.'

In the elevator he asked, 'How'd things go for Mr R.?'

'He got tired and I took him to his suite,' I said. 'I'm assuming he got some of what he needed.'

'That's good.'

'I'll check in with him when we get back,' I said. 'Right now I just want to find out what's goin' on.'

Jerry got behind the wheel of the Caddy and we headed for Fremont Street.

Danny was waiting for us in a back booth, sitting over a cup of coffee. As we approached he raised his head and I saw the lumps and bruises on his face.

'This should be a good story,' I said, sliding

125

into the booth next to him. Jerry needed one whole side for himself.

'It is,' Danny said. 'Jerry tell you much?'

'Not even where he got that bruise on his face.'

'Good. I asked him to let me tell it.'

'So, tell it.'

'Can we order?' Jerry asked.

'Sure,' I said. 'We can talk while we eat – or rather, Danny will talk, and I'll listen.'

The waitress came to the table and Jerry said to her, 'Pancakes.'

That was the only thing I heard over the next half hour that wasn't a surprise . . .

First, Danny hadn't told me everything he'd found in Helen's apartment, and her desk at the office.

'I found two matchbooks, one in each place,' he said, 'both from the same club.'

'What club?'

'It's called The Happy Devil.'

'Wait, that's a—'

'Sex club.'

'What?'

Danny took one of the matchbooks from his pocket and handed it to me. On the cover was a scantily clad woman with horns, a pitchfork and huge breasts.

'Is that like a swingers' club?' Jerry asked.

Swingers' clubs had come into vogue in the 60s, and were a precursor to some of the fetish clubs of later years. At the time, though, the Happy Devil was not advertised as a 'sex' club, but simply a 'hot' club. But people in the know were aware of what they peddled: sex.

126

Brothels were a legal business in Nevada for many years, since 1949 efforts were made to close them as a 'public nuisance', an action that was upheld by the Nevada Supreme Court. They still, however, continued to do business outside the city limits.

The Happy Devil was probably an attempt to run such a club inside the city limits, but they didn't call what went on there 'prostitution'.

'Kind of,' Danny said, answering Jerry's question. 'Swingers' clubs are usually for couples. Single people can go to the Happy Devil and find willing partners for the night. It's basically for people who don't want to deal with the emotional attachments that stem from sex.'

I looked at Jerry. By that definition it might be the kind of place that would interest him.

But Helen?

'Why didn't you tell me this when we talked last time?' I asked.

'I wanted to look into it first,' he said. 'For one thing, if Helen really did frequent the club – if she really did have a fetish – why would she keep a matchbook in her desk for anybody to see? I don't think she'd want that to be general knowledge.'

'You think somebody put it there?'

'Maybe,' Danny said. 'I did find one in her apartment.'

'Somebody could've put that one there, too,' Jerry said.

'Yeah,' Danny said, 'or it could have been hers.'

'What are you saying?' I asked.

'Maybe,' Danny said, 'somebody put the

127

matchbook in her desk to send us – or the cops – to the Happy Devil.'

'For what reason?' I asked. 'To put us on the wrong track?'

'Or the right one,' he said. 'I decided to go there and find out.'

Thirty-Seven

Over my ham and eggs and his own steak and eggs Danny told me the story . . .

Danny had talked with Jack Entratter and Marcy at the Sands, and briefly with some of the other office staff. He keyed on the names that Marcy had given him, but half-heartedly since Marcy was as much of a suspect as they were.

From his questions, though, he determined that Marcy had steered him right. Helen was not well liked at work, and some of the people – the names Marcy had given him – seemed to either intensely dislike or hate her.

And then there was the matchbook. The thing he found odd about both books was that there were no matches missing from either. It left him wondering if they were both plants.

At her apartment he found evidence that her place had been searched before him, but that could have been the police, probably hoping to find a suicide note. Her desk had also been rifled, likely by the cops. If the matchbooks were in place at the time they were either overlooked, or not considered to be of importance. Danny pocketed both.

After finishing up his interviews at the Sands Danny decided he better check out the Happy Devil, which was something he couldn't do until later that night. He had a few more Sands employees to see at their homes til then, and wanted to tell me about two of them specifically, as a small sample of what he'd been hearing . . .

Debra Runnels had an apartment in a residential motel that catered to singles. The apartments surrounded a center court which boasted a large swimming pool. During the day he knew he would have found single men and women in bathing suits lounging around the pool, but at dinner time there was only one man chatting up two girls who seemed bored. They perked up when they saw Danny, though that could have just been Danny's ego talking.

He had Debra's apartment number, on the second level. He knocked, and exchanged glances with the two girls while the man glared at him. He could tell they were flirting with him the way they kicked at the water and leaned back on their hands, thrusting their bikini-covered breasts forward. (OK, maybe not his ego.)

The door was opened by a pretty girl in her late twenties, who worked in the accounting department at the Sands. She had red hair, and was wearing a green, spaghetti-strapped cocktail dress.

'Yes?'

'Miss Runnels?'

'That's right.'

'My name's Danny Bardini,' he said. 'I'm investigating the death of Helen Simms, at the Sands?'

'Oh, God,' she said, going pale. 'That was awful. You know, I coulda walked into that ladies room and found her?'

'That would have been terrible for you,' he said. 'I'm glad you didn't. Could I come in? I just need to ask you a few questions.'

'Well . . . I'm waiting for my date, but . . . I suppose so.'

'Thank you.'

She allowed him to enter, then peered out the door before closing it.

'I'm sorry,' she said, 'I don't have anything to offer you—'

'That's OK,' he said. 'I won't be here long.'

'I don't know what I can tell you.'

'Well, you can tell me why some of the people I spoke to at the Sands told me you didn't like Helen very much.'

'Oh.' The girl hugged herself, as if she'd suddenly grown cold. She was slender, with a lithe figure that showed the result of regular exercise. He figured she got a lot of use out of the swimming pool. She had small breasts and a tiny waist, probably looked great in a bikini.

He continued to watch her and wait.

'Well . . .' she said. 'Um . . . I talked to the other detectives when they came to the office.'

Once again, he had not claimed to be a police detective but he said, 'I'm doing some follow up

130

interviews.' He decided to take a shot. 'Besides, you didn't tell the other detectives that you didn't like her.'

'Well . . . I . . .' Suddenly, she got a pugnacious look on her face and he half expected her to stamp her foot. 'Nobody liked her!'

'Why is that?'

'She was a bitch!' She put her hands over her mouth, as if she couldn't believe she'd said that out loud. If it was an act, it was a good one.

'To everyone?'

'To most people,' she said.

'To you?'

'Oh yes,' Debra said, 'she was mean to me.'

'Why is that?'

'I think because I'm young and pretty. She was *old*, you know.'

Yes, he knew, she was just under forty. Terribly old.

'She didn't like pretty girls,' Debra said.

'What about men?'

'A couple of the men tried to chat her up, but she was awful to them. I don't even know why they tried. She was . . . well, *old*.'

'Right.'

'I mean if you're mean and bitchy to everybody you've got to expect them to dislike you.'

'Or hate?'

She made a face. 'Hate is such an ugly word. I was brought up not to hate anyone, but . . .'

'But?'

'She tested me,' she said.

'She was mean.'

'Very.'

'Was she good at her job?'

'Oh,' she said, 'very. As much as you might dislike her, nobody could say she didn't do her job. Mr Entratter trusted her completely.'

Danny fingered the matchbook in his pocket.

'What do you know about a club called the Happy Devil?'

'The what? A club?' The girl looked confused. 'What's that got to do with anything?'

'Never heard of it?'

'Wha— well, no, I haven't. Is that in town?'

'Don't worry,' he said. 'It doesn't matter.'

She checked her watch.

'Your date?'

'He's late.'

'First date?'

'Yes,' she said. 'He's not making a good impression.'

'One more question,' he said. 'Did Helen ever do anything to you? I mean, anything specific that might have hurt you?'

'She treated me like dirt,' Debra said, 'and I'm not the only one. She showed no respect for anyone at the Sands – except for Mr Entratter. But she never did anything particularly mean to hurt me, personally.'

'Did she do anything specific to anyone you know?'

'You said one last question.'

'I'll make this the last one,' he said, 'depending on your answer.'

'Well . . .'

He continued to wait.

'She got Walter fired.'

132

'Walter?'

'Walter Spires,' she said. 'He used to . . . make fun of her. I mean, it was funny to the rest of us, but she didn't like it. So she got Mr Entratter to fire him.'

'How?'

'She told him that Walter . . . approached her . . . you know . . . sexually.'

'And that was a lie?'

'Oh, yes,' she said. 'Walter was funny, and nice. He wouldn't do anything like that.'

'How did Walter take getting fired?'

'Not well. Badly, actually. He said—'

'What did he say?'

'He said he was gonna make her pay.'

'When was this?'

'A couple of months ago.'

'Have you seen Walter since then?' Danny asked.

'Just once,' she said.

'Where?'

'On the street. He was . . . different.'

'In what way?'

'He used to dress nice, neat, you know? And he was funny. When I saw him he was wearing old clothes, you know, military green? Like he got them from a . . . a . . .'

'Army surplus?'

'That's it. And he wasn't funny, at all. He was . . . bitter. Mad. He still talked about getting even with Helen.' She bit her pretty lower lip and then said, 'To be honest, he scared me.'

'Do you know where Walter lives?'

'No.'

Danny knew Walter's name was not on his list, so he'd have to get the address from the personnel department the next day.

'OK,' he said. 'Thanks for talking to me. I hope your date shows up.'

She checked her watch, again.

'He's fifteen minutes late, now,' she said. She eyed Danny. 'Maybe I should go to dinner with somebody else.'

But he didn't bite.

'I'm sure he'll be here,' he said, and left.

Thirty-Eight

The second stop for Danny was a man named Ted Donnelly. I didn't know him, but according to Danny he worked on the fourth floor as a bookkeeper. He lived in the downstairs portion of a two family house on Decatur Street in north Las Vegas.

Danny parked in front and rang the downstairs bell. The door was opened by a bland looking man with a small mustache and thinning hair, both of which gave the impression of being color-less. That is, it was hard to say if they were sandy, blonde, brown; nothing seemed to fit.

'Yes?' he asked, looking a good six inches up at Danny.

'Mr Donnelly?'

'That's right.'

'My name is Danny Bardini,' Danny said. 'I'm

134

looking into the death of Helen Simms at the Sands.'

Donnelly frowned.

'Are you a policeman?'

Ah, somebody had finally asked.

'No,' Danny said, 'I'm private.'

'Who are you working for?'

'Jack Entratter.'

Donnelly hesitated.

'You can call him and check.'

'Come in, then,' Donnelly said. 'Close the door behind you.'

Danny obeyed and followed the man into an equally non-descript living room.

'Do you have identification?' Donnelly asked.

'Sure.' Danny produced his license and handed it to the man, who studied it closely then returned it.

'I've already talked to the police detectives,' he said.

'I understand that,' Danny said, 'but the police are kind of limited in their scope when it comes to this case.'

'Meaning what, exactly?' Donnelly asked, folding his arms. Not as mild mannered as he appeared.

'They believe Helen Simms killed herself.'

'And you don't?'

'No.'

'Why?'

'There are reasons,' Danny said. 'I need to know why you disliked her so much.'

'Who said I did?'

Danny smiled. 'Everyone.'

135

'Yes, well, I certainly wasn't alone,' Donnelly said.

'Because?'

'She was a queen bitch.'

'Lots of women wear that crown,' Danny said.

'Well, she wore it better than most. I seemed to be a pet project of hers,' he said. 'She was never happy with anything I did.'

'But she wasn't your boss.'

'No, but she had Mr Entratter's ear.'

'Do you think she could have gotten you fired if she wanted to?'

Donnelly snorted and said, 'Yes. She did it to Walter Spires.'

'Walter?'

'Lied about him to Mr Entratter, who fired him.'

'How did Walter feel about that?'

'He wasn't happy,' Donnelly said. 'Swore to get even.' His eyes went wide. 'You don't think Walter killed her, do you?'

'Maybe,' Danny said. 'Would anyone have thought it as odd to see Walter on the fourth floor?'

'Could be,' Donnelly said. 'But he could've been there trying to get his job back.'

'Have you seen Walter since he was fired?'

'No.'

'Do you know where he lives?'

'No. We weren't friends outside of work.'

'Mr Donnelly, do you know anyone else who might have had it in for Helen?'

'Lots of people,' he said, 'but nobody who would kill her.'

Again, Danny put his hand in his pocket to touch the matches.

'Have you ever heard of a club called the Happy Devil?'

'No,' he said. 'Is that important?'

'Not right now. Thanks for talking to me, Mr Donnelly.'

'You make sure Mr Entratter knows I cooperated with you?' he asked.

'Definitely,' Danny said.

Walking back to his car he thought about Walter Spires, but he wouldn't be able to check on him until the next day. On this night he still had to check out the Happy Devil . . .

'They both brought up Spires,' Danny said. 'Did you know him, Eddie?'

We had finished our breakfast and were lingering over coffee.

'No,' I said, 'never did.'

'Well, I need to know where he lives. Or where he lived when he worked at the Sands.'

'I can do that tomorrow,' I said. 'What about the club? Is that where you guys got your lumps?'

Danny sat back and waved at the waitress for more coffee.

'Let me tell it . . . this is where Jerry came in.'

Thirty-Nine

Jerry couldn't find Danny, but from the last time he was in town he remembered where Penny lived. After checking the office on Fremont Street and finding it locked up, he drove the Caddy to Penny's apartment house.

'Oh!' she said, surprised as she opened the door and saw the big man standing there. She recovered quickly, though. 'Jerry! How nice.'

'I hope I ain't botherin' ya,' he said.

'No, no, of course not.' She glanced out into the hall. 'Where's Eddie?'

'Back at the Sands,' he said. 'He was worried when we couldn't find Danny. Called you but didn't get an answer.'

'Come in,' she said.

Jerry entered, shut the door.

'I just got back,' she said. 'I had dinner with Danny. He's fine.'

'That's good. Do you know where he is?'

'He said he was going to check out some club tonight. The Happy Devil?'

'I don't know it.'

'Well, it's a . . . sex club. He thinks maybe the dead woman went there a lot.'

'Well,' he said, 'since I'm out, do you know where it is? Maybe I can back him up.'

'Oh, that would be great. Yes, I can tell you where it is . . .'

Danny parked down the street from the club, which was located in an area near the city's strip clubs, along Industrial Road. Obviously, the people running the club hoped to hide it there.

He had to pay a cover charge to get in. The man taking the money looked like a typical bouncer, but passed him in fairly easily, once he paid. He was surprised until he got inside. There was a second door manned by two bouncers. Apparently, they could still turn you away once you'd paid to get into the building. Slick.

One of them put his hand on Danny's chest and said, 'Members only.'

'How do I become a member?' Danny asked. He wondered if they knew he wasn't already a member, or they just assumed it.

'Gotta be sponsored,' the other man said.

'By a member,' the first man said.

'In writing?' Danny asked.

'Naw,' the first one said.

Danny thought a moment, then said, 'How about Helen Simms?'

The second man looked at the first who said, 'Yeah, I know Helen.'

'Actually,' Danny went on, 'she told me to meet her here. She inside?'

'Naw, she ain't been here tonight,' first one said. 'In fact, I ain't seen 'er in a week or so. Not since—' He stopped short.

'Not since what?'

'Never mind,' the first one said. 'Before we let you in we gotta frisk you.'

'For what?'

'Don't want nobody goin' in with a gun, or any other weapon.'

'Wow,' Danny said, lifting his arms, 'people try to get in here with guns?'

'It's been known to happen,' the second man said, as the first one checked him. He'd left his gun in the glove compartment of his car.

'OK,' the first man said. 'Go ahead in. Have a good time.'

'There's some hot bitches in there tonight,' the second man said and winked.

Danny started through the curtained doorway, then stopped and said, 'You fellas ever get to, uh, dip your wicks?'

The second man grinned. 'Once in a while . . .'

'Shut up, Manny,' the first man said. 'Go ahead in, sport.'

'Sure,' Danny said. 'Thanks.'

He went inside, having learned something, already. One, Helen was a member; two, she hadn't been there in at least a week; and three, the last time she was there, something happened.

Now all he had to do was find out what.

Danny had spent an hour at the Happy Devil, talking to some of the ladies, fending off a few of them – aged from twenty to fifty, who wanted to take him into a back room – and talking to the bartenders. He keyed on the fact that something had happened about a week ago, pretended to have heard 'something' about it, which made him curious.

While he didn't go into any of the back rooms, he did peek into a few. Lots of naked limbs, acres of flesh. And he didn't have to go into back rooms to see that. There were booths in the main section of the club that were being used, as well.

But he had apparently asked too many questions, because while he was sitting at the bar, nursing the same beer, three of the bouncers approached him, the one who had admitted him to the building, and the two who had frisked him.

140

'Time to go, champ,' the first one who frisked him said.

The second one, Manny, grabbed his arm around the bicep.

'Hey, ease up, fella,' Danny said. 'Can I finish my beer?'

The third man picked up the beer and moved it beyond his reach.

'Beer's finished.'

Danny had a bad feeling, got to his feet. Manny tightened his hold.

'What's this about?'

'Outside,' the first one said, 'or we'll make a scene right here.'

'That's OK with me,' Danny said. 'Make a scene here and maybe somebody will call the cops.'

'We make a scene here,' the first man said, leaning in close, 'and you won't last long enough for the cops to find you.'

The bouncer who let him into the building – number three – grabbed his other arm.

'Let's walk,' number one said.

They walked him across the club floor, and nobody even paid attention. Some very odd things must have gone on in that club in the past, including something a week ago that included Helen Simms.

'Listen,' Danny said, 'can we talk? I just need to ask a few questions.'

'No more questions.'

Forty

Instead of walking him out of the building, they took him down a hall, stopped in front of a door and knocked.

'Come,' someone said.

They pushed Danny into an office, and a beefy man in his forties, wearing a decent but not expensive suit, was standing behind a desk.

'Sit him down.'

They planted him in a chair in front of the desk. The two bouncers took their hands from his arms, and planted them on his shoulders. He couldn't have gotten to his feet if he tried.

'Get his wallet,' the man said.

'Hey, listen, are you the manager?' he asked.

'Manager, owner,' the man said, as the first bouncer took Danny's wallet from his pocket. The manager snapped his fingers and was handed the wallet. He opened it to check Danny's ID.

'Private dick,' he said, dropping the wallet on his desk. 'What are you doing in my club?'

Danny decided to be honest.

'Asking questions.'

'That I know,' the man said. 'Why?'

'It's my job,' Danny said. 'It's what I do.'

'For who?'

'Ah, now *that* I can't answer,' Danny said. 'Ask me another one.'

The manager nodded to the first bouncer, who

142

stepped in front of Danny and backhanded him. Danny's head rocked back and his lip split.

'Who are you asking questions for?' the manager demanded.

Danny licked his lip, said, 'Can't tell you that, no matter how much you beat on me. Ask me something else.'

The bouncer looked at the manager, who thought a moment, then shook his head.

'OK,' he said, 'let's try this. Who or what are you asking questions about?'

'That I can answer,' Danny said. 'Helen Simms.'

'Helen,' the man said. 'She's a member.'

'Right. I found that out.'

'What about her?'

'She's dead.'

'What? How?'

'Either she hanged herself in a ladies' room,' Danny said, 'or somebody did it and tried to make it look like suicide.'

The manager thought again, then shook his head as if to shake off some cobwebs and said, 'OK, so what's that got to do with me and my club?'

'I don't know,' Danny said. 'That's what I'm trying to find out. I found your matchbooks in her home and office, decided to check it out.'

'What about the cops. Why aren't they here?'

'Apparently,' Danny said, 'they think it was suicide.'

'And you don't.'

'No.'

The manager finally sat down, the leather of his chair creaking beneath his weight, which was considerable. Not tall, he was a wide man of considerable girth.

'What do we do, boss?' the first bouncer asked.

'I'm thinking,' the boss said. Up to this point no one had said his name.

'While you're thinking,' Danny said, 'can somebody tell me what happened here last week?'

'Last week?' the first bouncer asked.

'Or about a week ago?' Danny asked. 'I heard somebody mention it, and was wondering if it involved Helen?'

The three bouncers froze and the manager looked at him.

'Get him out of here,' he said.

'Where?'

'The alley.'

'What do you want us to do with him, boss?'

'Make sure he never wants to come back here.' He looked at Danny. 'We had you spotted the minute you came in, smart guy. You used Helen's real name. That's a no-no in our club.' He looked at his men again. 'Take him out and teach him a lesson.'

The first bouncer looked at the other two and said, 'We can do that,' with a smile that chilled Danny.

They half-walked half-dragged him back down the hall to another door, and then out into the alley that ran alongside the club. He could see the street, and wondered if he could break away and make it.

'Put him against the wall,' the first bouncer said.

The other two obeyed in spades. They slammed him so hard against the brick wall of the other building they knocked the air from his lungs. He wouldn't have a chance to defend himself if he couldn't breathe.

'Wait, wait, wait . . .' he squeaked out, trying to get a breath.

'Wait for what, Shamus?' the first man asked.

'This,' Danny said, and kicked him in the balls as hard as he could.

After that punches began to rain down on him until they drove him to his knees, and then the kicks came.

And then they suddenly stopped.

He looked up and, through a haze, saw Jerry tossing the bouncers around like rag dolls. One of them landed a lucky punch to his face, but it didn't seem to phase the big guy.

The first bouncer, still trying to recover from the kick in the balls, picked up a trash can lid and charged Jerry from behind.

'Jer—' Danny tried to warn him, but the word wouldn't come. He launched himself from the ground and tackled the man with the lid, taking him to the ground. He rolled away from him, still not really able to breathe.

Jerry came across and kicked the bouncer in the head. Now all three were down, out of the game.

'Come on, dick,' Jerry said, grabbing Danny. 'Let's get out of here.'

Forty-One

Jerry pointed to the side of his face and said, 'One of those bouncers had a fist like a ham, and got a lucky shot in.'

'Sounds to me like you saved each other's bacon,' I said.

'OK, sure,' Jerry said.

'No, Jerry saved my ass,' Danny said. 'And I thanked him profusely.'

'So let me get this straight,' I said. 'Something happened at the club sometime in the last week, week-and-a-half, that may or may not have involved Helen.'

'That's what I got,' Danny said.

'And nobody wanted to talk about it.'

'If I'd had a little more time I might have gotten something, but three apes came over and interrupted.'

'And took you to the manager's office. Do we know his name?'

'No,' Danny said, 'but we can find out.'

'Do you think those bouncers were just trying to persuade you not to come back, or were they gonna kill you?'

'I don't know,' he said. 'I think they might have gotten carried away and killed me. Thanks to Jerry, we didn't get that far.'

'Did you go to the hospital? See a doctor?'

'No, and no,' Danny said. 'I'm fine.'

'I wanted to take him to the hospital, but he wouldn't let me,' Jerry said.

'I've been beat up enough times to know when I'm seriously hurt,' Danny said. 'I've just got some bumps and bruises.'

'And a split lip,' I said.

Danny touched his bottom lip with his tongue and said, 'Yeah.'

'You really should be—'

'I get enough of that from Penny, Eddie,' Danny said. 'I don't need another mother hen.'

'OK, OK,' I said. 'I'm backing off.'

The waitress came and refilled our coffee cups without being asked.

'You know the thing I really can't accept?' I said. 'Or I guess process is the better word. Helen Simms being a member of a sex club.'

'Wasn't she attractive?' Danny asked.

'I suppose, to some men, she was.'

'Well, in that club, I don't think looks are even the most important thing,' Danny said. 'It's . . . the availability, I guess.'

'So what did you see in there?' Jerry asked. 'Good-lookin' broads, or available broads?'

'Both,' Danny said.

'Are you OK to go on with this?' I asked.

'After a day or two I should be fine,' Danny said, sitting up straight and wincing, 'but I wouldn't want to go back to that club just yet.'

'And we have to go back, right?' I asked. 'We have to find out what happened.'

'That's right,' Danny said.

'But you can't go back there,' Jerry said. 'They already know you.'

'He's got a point,' I said.

'Well,' Danny said, 'I still have to check into Walter Spires.'

'That leaves either me or Mr G. to go back to the club,' Jerry said.

'Those bouncers might know you, Jerry,' Danny told him. 'I mean, before you put their lights out one of them might have seen you.'

'Well, then,' I said, 'I guess that leaves me.'

'It might be smart,' Danny said, 'if you didn't do it the way I did.'

'You mean just walk in and start asking questions?' I said.

'Exactly.'

'Guess I could walk in and just listen.'

'And you'll have to have somebody's club name to get in.'

'We'll have to figure that out,' I said.

'And remember, a man alone in there is fair game,' Danny said. 'They were on me like locusts. Of course, I'm better lookin' than you are.'

I looked at his lumpy and bruised face and said, 'Not today.'

Forty-Two

After breakfast we agreed that Danny would go and talk to Walter Spires, but would not do much more than that. I would figure out an approach and go to the Happy Devil club. Jerry would

148

come along to cover me, but he'd have to stay outside.

When we got in the Caddy Jerry asked, 'When do you want to do this?'

'Probably tonight,' I said, 'but I've got to check in with Eddie Robinson and see what he wants to do.'

'What about Mr Hughes?'

That surprised me.

'What about him?'

'You gonna talk to him again?'

'I figure talking to his man, Maheu, is pretty much the same as talking to him,' I said. 'And I told Maheu I wasn't interested in Hughes' offer.'

'You think he's gonna accept that?'

'He doesn't have that much of a choice, Jerry.'

'He's a rich man, Mr G.,' Jerry said. 'They always got another choice.'

We went back to the Sands and split up.

'You sure you don't want me to stay with you, Mr G.?' Jerry asked.

'No, it's OK, Jerry,' I said. 'I just have some things to do here. I'm not gonna go out. Why don't you go into the casino?'

Jerry was a horse player, but recently had become interested in blackjack.

'I can do that,' he said. 'If you need me, I'll be around.'

'I appreciate it,' I said.

He nodded and went into the casino. I went up to the fourth floor to see Jack Entratter.

I filled Jack in on everything Danny had found out, and finished up by telling him about the club.

'Wait a minute,' he said, raising his hands. 'Hold the phone. Helen was a member of a sex club?'

'Apparently.'

'The . . . the what? Hungry Devil?'

'Happy Devil.'

'Wait,' Jack said, 'I know that name.'

'Yeah, you do?'

'Why haven't the cops closed that place down?'

'There's no prostitution going on there.'

'But there is sex.'

'There's sex going on everywhere in Vegas,' I said. 'You know that.'

'Yeah, OK,' Entratter said 'Sin city. I get it. So what happens next?'

'Danny talks to Walter, and I go back to the club to find out what happened. Maybe somebody there had something to do with killing Helen.'

'Walter,' Entratter said. 'Walter . . . Spires?'

'That's right.'

'Why don't I remember him?'

'He was a bookkeeper,' I said. 'Apparently, Helen dealt with him, not you.'

'One of the little people,' he said.

'Maybe he didn't like being one of "the little people",' I suggested.

'Yeah, well,' Entratter said, 'they never do.'

'Jack, did you have any idea how the other employees felt about Helen?'

'I knew she kept to herself,' he said. 'I didn't see anything wrong in that.'

'Nobody ever complained to you about her?'

'No.'

'They were probably afraid to,' I said. 'She

150

used the fact that she worked for you to her own advantage. Maybe to have a little power.'

'What kind of power?' he scoffed.

'Well, she got you to fire Walter, right?'

He pointed and said, 'That was him? She said he sexually assaulted one of the girls. She didn't want to press charges, but I fired him.'

'She probably lied.'

'Helen?' he asked. 'Lied?'

'Maybe more than once.'

He rubbed his face vigorously with both hands.

'I wonder what else she was lying about?' he said. 'Or if she was workin' for somebody.'

'I guess we're gonna find all that out,' I said, 'when we nail the guy who killed her.'

'Yeah,' he said nodding, 'yeah . . .'

'I'll continue to keep you updated, Jack,' I said, standing.

'Yeah, you do that,' he said.

I don't think he even noticed when I walked out of his office.

Forty-Three

I walked past the ladies' room on my way to the elevator, stopped and went in. There was yellow police tape hanging uselessly from the doorway.

Inside it was clean, and why not? Hanging is a clean death. No blood. I stood beneath the pipe that Helen had been found hanging from. From the looks of the pipe, it certainly would not have held Jerry, or Danny, or me. Probably not any man. But it held Helen. However, if she had stood on the edge of the sink and *leaped* into that noose – and she would have had to have leaped – the pipe would have come down. However, if someone had simply hanged her from it, it would have held. She probably weighed 110 or 120 pounds.

Somebody killed her.

She didn't like me, I didn't like her much, but she didn't deserve what she got. (I'm not nice enough to say nobody deserved that, because I knew a few people who did. But she didn't.)

I left the ladies' room and took the elevator down to the lobby. As soon as I got out, two men stepped up to me, one on either side. They were big; big as bouncers.

I thought, oh, no, not in my house.

'Take it easy, boys. Nobody needs to get hurt.'

'Our boss wants to talk to you.'

'Just talk?'

'That's what we were told.'

'So we're not goin' out back to pound on the smaller guy?' I asked.

They looked puzzled.

'Why would we do that?' the spokesman asked.

Hmm, I thought.

'OK. How we goin'?'

'We got a limo out front.'

'A limo?' I said, surprised. 'Wow.'

'Shall we go?' the spokesman asked.

These two seemed a step up from the three bouncers who had 'bounced' Danny around in the alley.

I couldn't tell if they were armed, and I didn't want to start anything in the lobby of the hotel. Maybe I could make a break for it outside.

'OK,' I said, 'let's go.'

We walked across the lobby to the front door, three abreast.

'Eddie—' one of the bellboys said, approaching, but I waved him away.

'Not now, Andy.'

Andy froze and frowned, but I'd apologize later for brushing him off.

We went through the front door and I saw the limo out front. As we started toward it Joey, the head valet, came running up to me.

'Eddie, you know anything about this limo? It's blocking traffic and I can't get anybody—'

'Relax, Joe,' I said. 'We're movin' it now.'

One of my escorts stepped to the back door and opened it for me. I was wondering when to make my break.

'In you go, man,' he said.

'After you,' I said.

'Oh, we're not getting in,' he said. 'Just you.'

'Just me?'

'That's the way Mr Hughes wants it.'

I froze.

'Mr Hughes? You guys work for Howard Hughes?'

'Yes, sir,' the spokesman said. 'Who did you think we worked for?'

'Never mind,' I said. 'You wouldn't like the answer.'

He let that go.

'Getting in?' he asked.

153

'Sure,' I said, 'why not.'

I slid into the back seat and got my second shock of the day.

Howard Hughes was there.

Forty-Four

'I told you,' Hughes said to me, 'I clean up good.'

And he did. The man in the back seat was impeccably dressed and styled. He bore no resemblance to the Hughes I had met in his hotel room at the Desert Inn.

'Yes, sir, you did. You told me.'

'Close the door, Eddie.'

I did, and started to move next to him, but he lifted a handkerchief to his face and said, 'No, not there. Across from me.'

'OK.'

'Drive on!' he snapped to his driver. 'And close that partition.'

He held the handkerchief to his mouth as the partition slid closed.

Hughes looked at me and lowered the cloth.

'You made me leave my room, Eddie.'

'And I did that . . . how?'

'By turning me down,' Hughes said. 'Nobody turns me down. I'm not used to that.'

'I'm sorry,' I said. 'I'm sorry I turned you down, and that you had to leave your room and get all dressed up for me.'

'And I had to overmedicate to do it,' he pointed out. 'This is not comfortable for me.'

'Well, Mr Hughes, that was my problem, too,' I said. 'I'm just not comfortable with doing what you asked me to do. I can't be your stalking horse.'

'All I asked you to do was give me some advice, Eddie,' Hughes said. 'A way to go.'

'It just seemed to me you were askin' me to find a weakness in somebody and expose it to you. I can't do that. I can't help you with a takeover.' I reached behind me and banged on the partition. 'Let me out anywhere along here!'

'Eddie,' he said, from behind the cloth, 'this doesn't make me happy.'

'I'm sorry, Mr Hughes. You have my answer.'

'No,' he said, 'you don't understand what I mean when I say I'm not happy.' He paused, as if for effect, then added, 'But you will.'

'Is that a threat?'

'Just know,' Hughes said, 'that I'm not leaving Vegas without getting what I want.'

I banged on the partition again and the car pulled to the curb.

'I'll be seeing you, Eddie,' Hughes said.

I was tempted to grab that handkerchief from his hand and give him a stroke, but instead I just said, 'No, you won't,' and got out.

I had no sooner slammed the door than the limo pulled away from the curb, peeling rubber. Hughes had probably told the driver to get him back to the Desert Inn as quickly as possible.

I started walking back to the Sands when Jerry pulled to the curb in my Caddy.

'What are you doin' here?' I asked, leaning in.

'I saw those two overdressed goons take you out of the hotel, and I saw you get into the limo. I grabbed the Caddy. Thought I'd cut the car off. What happened? Who was it?'

'I thought it was the bouncers from the Happy Devil, which was stupid, because I was never at the club. Anyway, it turned out to be Howard Hughes.'

'Hughes? Really? In the limo?'

'Yeah,' I said. 'He looked like he wanted to jump out of his skin, but he was there.'

'What'd he want?'

I hopped over the door into the passenger seat and said, 'Drive, brother. Back to the Sands.'

Jerry made an illegal U-turn, with style.

'What'd he want?' I said. 'I guess he was threatening me.'

'Because you won't work for him?'

'Exactly. He's not used to being turned down.'

'Well,' Jerry said, 'you're the man, Mr G. Everybody in Vegas knows it, and now maybe Howard Hughes knows it.'

'I don't think he does, Jerry.'

'Well, mark my words,' Jerry said, giving me a look, 'before he leaves Vegas, he will.'

Forty-Five

Back at the Sands Jerry parked the car and said, 'Whatever you're doin' next, Mr G., I'm gonna be with you.'

I didn't argue with him. All the way out to the limo I was planning my escape. If it hadn't been Hughes inside I might have still been running.

'I feel like a piece of pie,' Jerry said.

'That's all?'

'Well, I'm just a bit peckish.'

'I'll have some coffee,' I said. 'I need to catch my breath.'

We went into the Garden Café and Lily was working again.

She came over and turned the full wattage of those green eyes on Jerry.

'Hey, big guy, couldn't stay away, huh?'

'Uh, no, I guess not.'

'Hi, Eddie.'

'Lily. My big friend wants a big hunk of pie.'

'Really?' She looked at him, again. 'Just what kinda hunk of something sweet do you need?'

'I think, uh, cherry,' he said, keeping his eyes down.

'And you, Mr Eddie?' she asked.

'Just coffee.'

'Coffee with your pie, Big Jerry?'

'Yeah . . . uh, please.'

'Comin' up.'

When she walked away Jerry lifted his eyes and watched her.

'What's with the shy act, Jerry?'

'Huh?'

'It's like you can't even look at her.'

'She's . . . different.'

'How?'

'I don't know,' Jerry said. 'She ain't a whore, but she ain't . . .'

'. . . an angel, either?'

'That's it!'

I reached into my pocket and took out the matchbook from the Happy Devil that Danny had given me. I put it on the table between us.

'I'll have to go in there tonight,' I said. 'There's no point in waiting.'

'I don't know how you're gonna find out anything without askin' questions.'

'I don't either, but if I ask too many I'll get the same treatment Danny got.'

'And I'll be there to bail you out.'

'Let's hope it doesn't come to that.'

Lily came back with the pie and two coffees and set them down, then stopped short.

'Who's is that?' she asked, pointing at the matchbook.

'Why?' I asked. 'Do you know that place?'

'I do.'

'Are you a member?'

'Do you know what kind of place it is?'

'We do.'

She eyed us for a few moments, then said, 'Well, yeah, I've been there a few times, and yes, I'm a member.'

I slid over, 'Lily, sit down for a minute, will you?'

She looked around. It wasn't busy, so she sat next to me. I could feel the heat from her body.

'Did you know Helen Simms?'

'The girl who hanged herself in the fourth floor ladies' room?'

'Yes, only she didn't hang herself.'

Her eyes widened and she said, 'She was murdered?'

158

'Yes, by someone who wanted it to look like she did it to herself.'

'I knew her on sight,' Lily said, 'but we weren't friends. I don't think we ever even spoke.'

'You never saw her at the club.'

'This club?' She touched the matchbook. 'She was a member?'

'Yes.'

She shook her head. 'I never saw her there, but it's a big place, lots of people, and . . .'

'And what?'

'Well . . . I was going to say you don't really look at people's faces while you're there, if you know what I mean.'

'I think I do,' I said.

'Also,' she said, 'you don't use your real name.'

'You don't?'

'No,' she said. 'You need to come up with one just for the club.'

I decided not to ask her what hers was. At that point it really wasn't my business.

'Are you thinking of joining?' she asked.

'No,' I said, 'but we know something happened there within the past week that involved Helen. I need to go there and find out what it was.'

'How are you going to get in?'

'I don't know,' I said. 'I can't use Helen's name. I don't want them to know that I'm there because of her.'

'You can use mine,' she offered. 'I mean, you only need to mention a member's name to get in.'

'That would be great,' I said, 'thanks. Uh, I'd be using what name?'

159

'Sasha,' she said. 'Tell them you were sponsored by Sasha.'

'Sasha?' Jerry said.

She looked at him. 'Don't you like it?'

'I like Lily better.'

'You're sweet.' She stood up. 'Would you want me to go with you and get you in?'

'Well,' I said, 'that would probably be help—'

'No,' Jerry said.

'Why not?' Lily asked.

'It'd be too dangerous.'

'Aw, you're worried about me?' she asked.

'A friend of ours got beat up there,' he said. 'I don't want anything to happen to you.'

'He's right,' I said, feeling foolish that I had even considered it.

'Well,' she said, 'use my club name, and let me know if you change your mind.' She stepped to Jerry's side of the booth and stroked his face. 'You're cute,' she said, and walked away.

'I told you,' I said, 'she's a little wild – maybe wilder than I thought.'

'I like 'er,' Jerry said, and cut into his pie.

Forty-Six

I had to check in with Edward G. Robinson, see what he wanted to do. Even with trying to find out who killed Helen I couldn't lose sight of the fact that I was supposed to be taking care of

Eddie. I had Lily bring me a phone and called his room.

'Hey, Eddie G.,' he said, happily. 'I was just thinking about you and Jerry.'

'Eddie,' I asked, 'what did you have in mind for later tonight?'

'I was just going to call you,' he said. 'Frank wants to have dinner. Do you want to join us? You and Big Jerry?'

'Actually, this works out good,' I said. 'We've got something to do tonight, so I think you should have a good dinner with Frank and catch up.'

'Well, all right,' Eddie said. 'Will I see you fellas tomorrow?'

'Definitely,' I said. 'We'll call on you in the morning for breakfast.'

'Swell.'

'By the way, what's happening with you and the studio lady?'

'Oh, I gave in and agreed to have lunch with her today,' he said. 'She's a nice kid. I really don't want to give her a hard time.'

'That's good,' I said. 'Bring her down to the Garden Café. I'll make sure they make a fuss.'

'Thanks, Eddie G.,' he said. 'I'll do that.'

'OK, then. Tell Frank we're sorry we missed him, and I'll talk to you tomorrow.'

'Be careful, Eddie G.'

'About what?'

'Whatever you and Big Jerry are doing tonight,' Robinson said. 'Just be careful.'

'We will,' I promised.

'Sounds like there's no problem,' Jerry said, as I hung up.

161

'Nope,' I said, 'he's having lunch with the studio girl and dinner with Frank.'

'Then we're free until tomorrow?'

'Free as can be.'

'So what now?'

'Now,' I said, 'I guess I'll have to come up with a new name for the Happy Devil.'

'A new name?'

'Yeah,' I said, 'something that would go along with . . . Sasha.'

When Lily came by again Jerry said, 'That was a really good meal.'

'Glad you liked it,' Lily said. 'I'll tell the cook.' She looked at me. 'So, you goin' to the club tonight?'

'Yes, the sooner the better.'

'Well,' she said, 'I guess I don't know what it's all about, but if I was you I'd go at midnight. That's when things start jumpin'.'

'Midnight,' I said. 'Thanks, Lily. Or should I say . . . Sasha.'

'Call yourself . . . Errol.'

'Like Errol Flynn?'

'Exactly. Or Tyrone,' she added, 'after Tyrone Power. He's real dreamy.'

'Tyrone,' I said. 'I like that.'

Somebody called out, 'Hey, waitress!'

'I gotta go to work, Eddie,' Lily said. 'Come back and see me, Jerry.'

'Sure thing, Lily.'

As she flounced away he asked, 'Do you think she likes me, Mr G.?'

'I do, Jerry,' I said. 'I think she likes you a lot.'

162

'You wouldn't kid me, would you, Mr G.?'
'No, Jerry,' I said. 'I wouldn't ever kid you.'

Forty-Seven

At a quarter-to-midnight Jerry pulled the Caddy in to the curb down the street from the club.

'Sure you don't want me to come in with you?' he asked.

'No,' I said, 'somebody might recognize you. Besides, it would look strange, the two of us going into a sex club together.'

'Oh, yeah, right.'

'Just keep your eyes on the front door,' I said. 'If I get in trouble I'll try to find some way to let you know.'

'We need a time limit, Mr G.'

'Can't do that, Jerry,' I said, getting out of the car and leaning on the door as I closed it. 'I don't have any idea how long it'll take me to find out something. Just be patient, big guy.'

'Be careful, Mr G.'

'Right.'

I walked down the block to the club, paid the cover charge and was allowed inside after the bouncers checked out my sports jacket and sweater. I figured a tie was optional for sex clubs.

'Darling, there you are!'

I was surprised as a heavily made-up Lily came rushing toward me. She was wearing a dress that was very short, and very deeply cut

163

– so much so that her breasts were threatening to spill out. She looked a helluva lot different than the other times I'd seen her at work in her uniform.

She kissed me deeply, pushing her tongue into my mouth, and then hugged me and said into my ear, 'Go along . . . Tyrone.'

I struggled to remember her club name.

'OK, boys, my date's here,' she said to the two bouncers.

'OK, Sasha,' one of them said, opening an inner door, 'have fun.'

'Come on, Tyrone,' she said.

'Yeah,' the other bouncer said, 'have a good time, Tyrone.'

The two men laughed as they closed the door behind us.

'What are you doing here?' I demanded.

'Keep your voice down, Tyrone,' she hissed. 'I'm here to help.'

'Lily—'

'Sasha!' she said. 'My name's Sasha, remember?'

'OK, Sasha. You have to leave.'

'Leave?' she asked. 'I haven't even gotten started, yet.'

'Listen, Jerry is down the block in my Caddy,' I said. 'He'll take you home.'

'Oooh,' she said, 'goin' home with Jerry. Now that appeals to me.'

'It'll appeal to him, too.'

'Really? What did he say?'

'Never mind,' I said. I looked around. It was fairly dark, and there was a crush of bodies. 'Give me the lay of the land before you leave.'

'I'll do better than that,' she said, sliding her arm into mine. 'I'll show you around, big boy.'

'Lil— Sasha,' I said, 'this isn't a game.'

'Is this about Helen getting killed?'

'Yes.'

'Well,' she said. 'I didn't know her, but she worked at the Sands. That makes her family, right?'

'Right.'

'So I'll give you a quick once around,' she said, 'and then I'll go play with Jerry.'

'All right,' I said. 'Once around. And then you're gone.'

She kissed me on the cheek, then pulled me forward.

Lily/Sasha took me to the bar where we got drinks, and then showed me the various rooms that were available for use. Also some booths on the main floor that supplied a small bit of privacy for those who didn't want to use the rooms.

'Oh,' she said, 'one more thing. Let me show you the Jungle Room.'

'OK, I've got the lay of the land, Sasha. Time for you to go.'

'Sasha!'

We both turned to see who had said her name. A man came walking toward us, with a beautiful woman on each arm. Both were statuesque, one blonde, one brunette, both spilling out of their tops. And both very young. I wondered if they were showgirls, and where they worked.

'Hello, Derek,' Sasha said. 'Who are your friends?'

'This is Petal,' he said, indicating the blonde, 'and this is Storm.' Derek himself was well over six feet tall, rangy, handsome, wearing a black suit and no tie.

'Meet my friend,' she said, 'Tyrone.'

'Tyrone,' Derek said, 'haven't seen you here before.'

'That's because it's my first time.'

'Really?' Derek said. 'That's so groovy, man. Hey, why not let my ladies show you a good time? Ladies?'

On cue they detached themselves from him and attached themselves to me, one on either side. I'm no prude. Under normal circumstances I would have welcomed their attention, but I wasn't there for sex games.

'I'd love to take you up on that, Derek, man,' I said, gently disengaging the ladies, 'but I think for my first time I'll stick with Sasha, here.'

'Well, I can't blame you for that,' he said. 'She'll show you a good time.'

I put my arm around Sasha and walked her away.

I later realized that 'Derek' was really John Holmes, who went on to be a famous porn star named 'Johnny Wadd', also known as 'the Sultan of Smut'. In 1965 he was just starting to become involved in the industry. One of the girls with him was his girlfriend, Sandy Dempsey, who appeared in some of his movies with him.

'This ain't the only time you're gonna get hit on, Eddie,' she said to me.

'It's Tyrone,' I corrected her, 'and I don't have time for this kind of nonsense tonight, so Sasha, don't you dare leave me alone.'

166

'Don't worry, Tyrone,' she said, sliding her arm around my waist, 'I'll protect you.'

Forty-Eight

I didn't think I was putting Lily in any real danger. If anything, she was protecting me from being dragged into the Jungle Room by some sweet, wild young thing. Yeah, I said it. *Protecting me.*

Of course, I'm sure Danny felt the same way when he was there. He was just asking questions, and got bounced around the alley for it. If not for Jerry, he might have been seriously hurt.

In the end I decided that Sasha/Lily had to get out of there.

I walked her to the front door.

'Are you sure?' she asked. 'The women in here are gonna be on you like bears on honey.'

'I'll fend for myself,' I said. 'I want you in the car with Jerry, safe and sound.'

'Yeah,' she said, with a lascivious grin, 'but will Jerry be safe in the car with me?'

I patted her fanny and said, 'Go.'

She went.

I turned and surveyed the room. I decided since I'd been introduced to Derek and his two honeys that maybe that was where I should be concentrating my efforts – even if it meant letting Petal and Storm violate my body.

I found them at the bar, the two ladies still hanging on their escort, who seemed to be working on a busty, older brunette.

'Tyrone, my man!' he exclaimed when he saw me. 'Get on in here, man. I want you to meet Jewel. Jewel, this is my friend Tyrone.'

'Tyrone,' she said, turning the full wattage of her deep blue eyes on me. At thirty-five or six she was at least ten years older than Storm and Petal, but to my mind she trumped them, easily. She had packed a lot of curves into a tight fitting jumpsuit, and was obviously not wearing a bra. It was cold in the club and she was nipping out to beat the band.

'Tyrone,' she said, running her hand up my arm and then placing it on my neck. Her skin was warm – no, hot. 'What are your plans for the evening?'

'How long have you been a member here?' I asked.

'Years,' she said. 'It's my second home.' She stroked my neck and my pulse quickened. I moved in closer, stood next to her at the bar. She pressed her hip against mine. I could feel the heat through our clothes.

'So, you come here every week?' I asked.

'Almost.' She wore blood red lipstick, licked her lips so that they glistened.

'Were you here a week or so ago when something happened?'

'You wanna talk about all the fuss?'

'I'm curious,' I said.

'Kinky,' she said. She took hold of my tie and pulled. 'Come with me.'

168

'Where?'
'The talking room.'

She lied.
The talking room was not for talking.

I woke up the next morning with a headache and a vague recollection of the things we did in that room. Or rather, the things she did to me.

Like I said, I'm no prude. I've been with many women: showgirls, singers, dancers, hell, I had sex with Judith Campbell . . . with Ava Gardner. But the things that this girl did . . .

'Mmmmm,' somebody next to me moaned.

I sat up in bed. Not my bed. Not my bedroom. I was wishing it wasn't my head.

'Mmm,' she said again, and rolled over. As beautiful in the morning as she had been the night before in the club, even with the red lipstick gone – kissed off, I assumed, by me.

She opened her eyes, looked up and smiled at me. Her hair was fanned out on the pillow behind her.

'Wow,' she said.

'That's what I was thinking,' I said, although maybe for different reasons.

'Tyrone, right?' she asked. 'Your club name?'

'Uh, yeah.'

'What's your real name?'

I hesitated.

'Hey,' she said, propping herself up on her elbow. One full breast popped into view from beneath the sheet, like a big, pink-tipped melon. 'I've never brought anybody home from the

169

club before. I think I deserve to know your name.'

'Eddie,' I said, 'it's Eddie . . . Gianelli.'

'My real name is Emily,' she said, making a face. 'I know, ordinary. That's why I picked Jewel.'

'There's nothing ordinary about you, Emily,' I said. 'As far as I can remember.'

'And just how much do you remember, handsome?' she asked.

'More now than a few minutes ago,' I said, 'probably more later than now.'

She reached out and put her hand on my chest. The heat of her skin was familiar.

'You hungry?'

I thought about it and said, with surprise, 'I'm starving.'

'Well,' she said, 'I can cook.'

She got out of bed quickly, showing me acres of beautiful, smooth pale flesh as she grabbed a robe and pulled it on.

'Bathroom's there,' she said, pointing. 'Have a shower. We'll talk over breakfast.'

'Talk?'

She turned at the door and looked at me, cocked her head. Without all the make-up and lipstick, she looked younger.

'You want to know about the fight, right?'

'We . . . didn't talk about that, yet?'

'Honey,' she said, 'we really haven't had much time for talking.'

Forty-Nine

I soaked in Emily's shower, trying to shake the cobwebs loose and the night before back into focus. I remembered her tugging on my tie and taking me to the 'talking room', and not much after that. Apparently we never got around to talking about what had happened at the club, and that was what I'd gone there for. So maybe over breakfast I could salvage the trip.

I put on the clothes I'd worn the night before, sans jacket, and went into the kitchen.

'I hope you like burnt toast and burnt bacon,' she said, putting plates on the table.

I looked at the blackened toast and bacon and the wondrous, fluffy scrambled eggs that sat next to them.

'Oh yeah,' she said, 'I'm a whiz with eggs.'

'That's OK,' I said. 'I like bacon any way I can get it.'

We sat down across from each other and she said, 'Don't be too nice to scrape the burnt part off that toast.'

'Hey,' I said, 'that's how I grew up eating toast.'

I used a butter knife to scrape off as much of the black as I could, and then covered it with butter. I really did like bacon any old way, and the eggs were like eating clouds.

And the coffee was hot.

While we ate I learned her name was Emily

171

Marcus, and she was a legal secretary at a law firm in town, Denby & Sloane. I told her what I did and where, and she thought it was very exciting.

She ate with a hearty appetite. Jerry would have been proud.

'OK,' she said, halfway through our plates, 'so you wanted to know about the fight.'

'I came to the club because I heard something had happened a week or so ago, and it involved Helen Simms.'

'Who?'

'Helen – you know, I don't know her club name.'

'Well, there was a fight in the club,' she said, 'and it did involve a woman.'

'Describe her to me.'

She did. It was Helen to a T.

'That's her,' I said. 'What was the fight about?'

'I saw and heard some of it. They were thrown off the club floor.'

'By who?'

The bouncers.'

'And taken where?'

'The manager's office, I assumed.'

'OK,' I asked, 'what did you hear? What was the fight about?'

'Well, it seemed to be about . . . drugs.'

'Wait,' I said, 'drugs?'

She nodded.

'And Helen was in the fight?'

'She was one of the two people fighting,' Emily said. 'The other one was named Dante.'

'Dante?'

She nodded. 'Club name.'

'What did he look like?'

'Tall, sandy-haired, thirties.'

'Is he a regular at the club?'

'That was the first time I'd seen him.'

'OK,' I said, 'so the fight was about drugs, but . . . what, specifically?'

'Well, he seemed to think she was moving in on his, uh, turf?'

'Helen was selling drugs?'

'Tina,' Emily said, 'that was her name – her club name. Tina. And yeah, that's the impression I got.'

Helen Simms was not only a member of a sex club, but she was selling drugs? As hard as that was to believe, it certainly supplied a motive for murder. Even that dim-wit Hargrove would have to admit that.

If I told him.

'More coffee?' she asked.

'Yes, please.'

She went to the stove for the pot, filled my cup and hers, and then set it down on a metal tray on the table.

'Tell me,' she asked, 'what is this about?'

I realized she still didn't know that Helen was dead.

'Well . . . Helen . . . I mean Tina . . . worked at the Sands, for my boss,' I said. 'She was his secretary.'

'Yes,' she said, 'lots of secretaries go to that club.'

'Four days ago Tina was killed.'

'What?'

173

'It looked like she hung herself, but I think it was murder. And now you've given me a motive.'

'You mean . . . Dante killed her?'

'Maybe. I've been looking for someone who might have a motive.'

'My God,' she said, 'what are you going to do? Tell the police?'

'Well, that's a problem – see, the police believe she killed herself.'

'But . . . they're the experts. If they say she killed herself . . . wouldn't they be right?' She looked confused about why I'd question the experts.

'Yeah, you'd think they were the experts and they'd be right, but . . . not so much.'

She sat back in her chair and stared at me.

'This is amazing,' she said.

'Kinda, yeah,' I said. 'Listen, when we left the club last night did you see a Cadillac outside with a great big guy in it?'

'No,' she said, 'but then . . . I wasn't really looking, you know?'

'And how'd we get here? Did you drive?'

'Oh, no, I never drive to the club,' she said. 'I'm never in any shape to drive home. We took a cab.'

'OK,' I said, 'then I'll have to call Jerry to pick me up.'

'Jerry?'

'The really big guy.'

'Oh.'

'Can I use your phone?'

'Why not?' she said, with a smile. 'You've used everything else I have.'

174

Fifty

Jerry got there half an hour after I called. During that time I was tempted to use everything Emily had again, just so I'd remember doing it, but she said she had to get ready for work.

'Maybe another night,' she said, patting my cheek.

She moved around her apartment as if I wasn't there, most of the time in a bra and slip. I felt like a piece of the furniture. She got dressed faster than any woman I'd ever known before. Certainly quicker than any woman I'd ever watched before.

When she was ready to leave she stood at the door in a blouse, a tight skirt, holding her purse and her keys.

'Gotta go,' she said, looking at me expectantly. She even jingled her keys at me.

I was sitting on the sofa, waiting, when suddenly I realized what she was saying. She had to leave and she wasn't about to leave me in her home, alone.

'Oh,' I said, getting to my feet, 'OK. I'll wait for Jerry downstairs.'

'OK,' she said, opening the door.

We stepped into the hall and I waited while she locked her door. We took the elevator from her floor – the fourth – to the lobby, where I walked her to the front door. There was no doorman, no guard in the lobby.

175

She hastily kissed me on the cheek and said, 'Maybe we'll see each other again.'

If I needed to go to that club to do that, I doubted it, but I said, 'Sure, maybe. Thanks, Emily.'

'For what?'

I smiled.

'Best burnt bacon I ever had.'

She laughed and walked off, I assumed, to get her car. I waited in front of the building – a block of apartment buildings not far from Fremont Street – until Jerry pulled up in front, in the Caddy.

He leaped over the door into the passenger seat.

'Good morning,' I said.

'Yeah.' He pulled away from the curb.

'What? You're mad at me?' I said, instantly detecting a chill.

He didn't answer.

'What did I do?'

He intended to give me the cold shoulder, but he couldn't.

'You shoulda sent Lily home last night, right away.'

'Oh, that,' I said. 'I tried. As soon as I saw her I tried to get her to leave. But she wanted to show me around first. I got her out of there as soon as I could.'

'And I had to drive her home,' he said. 'By the time I got back, I didn't know what happened to you. You never came out.'

'You didn't try to go in, did you?'

'I thought about it,' he said, 'but no, I didn't.'

'Good. I was fine, Jerry. I . . . left with someone.'

'Who?'

'A woman.'

'Mr G.,' he said, 'that ain't exactly what you went there to do.'

'I know that,' I said, 'but it turns out she gave me the information I was looking for.'

'Which is?'

'Helen Simms had a fight at the club with a man who might have been a drug dealer.'

'So he killed her?'

'Apparently, she was moving in on his territory.'

'Wait, she was dealin'?'

'She was, or she intended to,' I said. 'At least, that's the feeling Emily got.'

'Emily's the broad you left with? Who lived in that building?'

'That's right.'

'How do you know she was tellin' you the truth?' A very simple question from a very simple man. One I should have asked myself.

'What reason would she have to lie?' I asked. 'I only met her last night.'

'Did she know Helen?'

'She says no, just that she saw her there. At least, that's what she said when I asked her.'

'We should have a picture of her to show people.'

'You're right,' I said. 'I'll try to find one. We might have to go to her apartment.'

'Maybe the dick took one when he was there.'

'I'll ask him. Did you hear from him this morning?' I asked.

'No.'

'OK,' I said. 'Take me home. I'll change, and then call him.'

'And then we eat?'

'You haven't had breakfast?'

'No. I was worried about you.'

'And it affected your appetite?'

He didn't answer. Instead he said, 'Did you eat?'

'I had some burnt bacon.'

'I like burnt bacon,' he said. 'Do you want to eat again?'

'I could eat,' I said.

Fifty-One

Jerry took me to my house and waited while I changed into a more casual sport coat, this time with a blue T-shirt underneath, and grey slacks. Then we drove to a nearby diner for breakfast. I decided not to call Danny to join us.

'We'll see him in his office,' I said to Jerry, 'if we can find him.'

Jerry was carving his way through a stack of pancakes, slathered with butter and syrup. I never ate pancakes when I was with him. I tried it once, and felt inadequate. So I stuck to eggs and ham, or bacon, with home fries and toast.

'If the lady was killed by this drug dealer,' Jerry said, 'why would he do it in the Sands? And how would he get in and out?'

'That's what we have to find out.'

'So how do we find out who the drug dealer is?'

'I have his club name,' I said.

'But we can't walk into that place and ask what his real name is.'

'Maybe not,' I said, 'but that doesn't mean we can't ask outside the club.'

'Ask who?'

'The manager.'

'Outside the club?'

'He's got to leave the building sometime, right?'

'Right,' Jerry said, 'and when he does, we grab him.'

'Unless you have a better idea.'

'Nope,' he said, spearing a huge hunk of pancakes with his fork, 'I like that one. We can squeeze him for what he did to the shamus.'

'You can do the squeezing.'

'That's what I figured.'

After we left the diner I called Danny's office from a pay phone, Penny answered, said he was in his office. I told her to keep him there, we'd be right over.

On the way Jerry asked, 'Are you gonna tell the cop about this drug dealer?'

'Maybe,' I said, 'but not yet. Not until we know more.'

'That's what I was thinkin'.'

'I've also got to check in with Robinson,' I said, 'see what he wants to do today.'

'Ain't he done?' Jerry asked. 'He watched a game, right?'

'I'm sure he didn't come to Vegas just to watch

179

once,' I said. 'I might have to set him up with another one.'

'What if he actually wants to play?'

I thought about that and said, 'Yeah, what if he does.'

'He's still in his office,' Penny said, as we entered the offices of Bardini Investigations.

'Thanks, doll,' I said.

'Hello, Jerry.'

'Hi, Penny,' he mumbled, still shy around her even though he'd known her for a few years, now. I always thought it was because she was such a nice girl.

'Hey, guys,' Danny said, as we entered. 'Got something?'

'We do,' I said. 'You?'

'Well,' he said, 'I talked with the guy, Walter Spires.'

'And?'

'The guy's a nerd, Eddie,' Danny said. 'The kind of guy we used to beat up in school every day, remember?'

'What did he have to say?'

'He said Helen Simms was a mean, nasty bitch who got him fired for no reason at all.'

'I don't know if that's a motive for murder,' I said, 'but it would explain how he got in and out.'

'Anybody seeing him there might assume he still worked there,' Danny said.

'Right.'

'Well, what did you guys get from the sex club?'

'Mr G. got laid,' Jerry said.

180

'Is that a fact?' Danny asked, gleefully. 'Couldn't stay out of those rooms, huh?'

'There was a woman who had some information,' I said.

'So you had to sleep with her to get it?'

'It was a dirty job . . .' I said.

'How'd you get in?' Danny asked. 'I mean, into the club. Did you use somebody's club name?'

'Actually,' I said, 'somebody was there to help me.' I told him about Lily, the waitress at the Sands.

'Whoa,' he said.

'What?' I asked.

'Did she have anything against Helen?'

'She said she hardly knew her,' I said.

'Eddie,' he said, 'what are the chances that two people from the Sands would belong to that club?'

'I didn't think of that.'

'She didn't lie,' Jerry said.

We both looked at him.

'How do you know?' Danny asked.

'I just do,' Jerry said.

I tried to give Danny the high sign so he'd leave the subject alone. Jerry was obviously sensitive when it came to Lily.

'OK, big guy,' Danny said, getting my message. 'Whatever you say.' He looked at me. 'So we've got to find this drug dealer.'

'Right.'

'For that we need his name.'

'Jerry and I have a plan for that.'

'Lemme hear it,' Danny said, sitting back. He

181

listened without saying a word, then commented, 'That'll work. And I'll come along.'

'For a little revenge?' Jerry asked.

'Nah,' Danny said, 'I can point him out. I don't need revenge. I'm a pro, I can take my lumps. When do we wanna do this?'

'I need some time,' I said, 'to get things at the Sands straightened out. What about tomorrow night?'

'Why don't you both meet me here?' Danny said.

'OK,' I said. 'We'll need someplace to take him once we snatch him.'

'Leave that to me,' Danny said. 'You go and take care of your business at the Sands.'

Jerry and I headed for the door, but Danny piped up and we stopped.

'Whoa!'

'What?' I asked.

'I forgot to ask,' he said. 'What's happening with Howard Hughes?'

'Oh yeah, that,' I said, turning, 'I took a limo ride with him.'

'He came out of the Desert Inn?'

'All perfumed and pretty.' I told Danny about my conversation with Hughes.

'It doesn't sound like he's gonna take your refusal lying down.'

'He's gonna have to,' I said. 'I'm not working for him, period. No matter how much money he throws at me, my loyalty is to Vegas.'

'Attaboy, Mr G.,' Jerry said.

'Stick to your guns, buddy,' Danny said. 'Just watch your back.'

'That's my job,' Jerry said.

Danny grinned at the big guy and said, 'I feel better, already.'

Fifty-Two

We headed back to the Sands so I could check in with Entratter, Frank, and Edward G. Robinson. I also thought I'd have a word with Billy Pulaski about security. If it wasn't Walter Spires who got into the Sands to kill Helen, and then got out without being challenged because he used to work there, then who was it? And how did they get in?

'I'm gonna talk to Jack,' I said, as we entered the lobby. 'Why don't you—'

'Come with you. I'm stickin' with you, Mr G.'

'OK,' I said. 'Let's go.'

As we entered Jack's outer office Helen's desk looked very empty. When we went into Entratter's office, he was sitting behind his desk, staring off into space. It was a rare moment when he wasn't busy.

'Jack!'

He started, then focused his eyes on us.

'Oh, hey,' he said. 'Eddie. Jerry.'

'What's going on?' I asked.

'Nothin',' he said. 'I was just thinkin'. What's goin' on with you?'

'I want to update you on what we know about Helen's death.'

'Go.'

Jerry and I both remained standing as I related our activities and discoveries to Jack. By the time I was done he was reeling.

'Jesus Christ!' he said. 'I really didn't know nothin' about this woman, did I? Drugs?'

'That's what we heard,' I said. 'But we didn't find anything in her apartment or her desk.'

'Then how do you plan to confirm that rumor?'

'We're going to find the drug dealer she argued with at the club.'

'And how are you gonna do that?'

'You don't wanna know, Jack.'

He held his hand out and said, 'You're right, I don't. What's happenin' with Eddie Robinson?'

'I have an idea, but I wanted to check it with you first.'

'What is it?'

I told him, and he listened, nodded.

'Hey,' he said, 'if Eddie will go for that, it's fine with me. Set it up.'

'OK.'

'Now, what about Hughes?'

'Well,' I said, 'after I saw you last time, he took me for a ride.'

'Whataya mean?'

Again, Jerry stood by, silent and solid as a rock, while I told Jack about Hughes and the limo ride.

'Did he threaten you?'

'Not exactly,' I said, 'but he let me know he wasn't happy.'

'Watch your ass, Eddie,' he said. 'With

184

everything you're involved in, that might be where you get hurt the most.'

'I haven't heard that Hughes uses muscle, Jack.'

'Howard Hughes will do anything to get what he wants,' Entratter said. 'Remember that. He didn't get where he is by goin' easy.' Entratter addressed Jerry for the first time since we'd entered the room. He pointed at him and said, 'You better have his back, Jerry.'

'I always do,' Jerry said.

'Well, just keep an eye out in every direction,' Entratter said. 'There's no tellin' where hell is gonna come from this time.'

'Don't worry, Jack,' I said. 'We're on it.'

'OK, then,' he said. 'Just be careful. I don't need any more surprises.'

'Jack, I'm going to talk to Billy Pulaski about security.'

'What about it?'

'A killer shouldn't have been able to walk in here, kill Helen, and just walk out.'

'Security in the casino and hotel business usually don't involve murder, Eddie.'

'I know,' I said. 'Still, he might not like my questions. Billy's got an ego.'

'Yeah, who doesn't,' Entratter said. 'Ask your questions. I'll take care of Billy.'

'OK.'

'Eddie,' he called as we reached the door.

'Yeah?'

'You've got a free pass around here,' Jack said. 'Whether it's got to do with Helen's murder, Eddie Robinson, or Howard Hughes. Whatever you want, you got it.'

185

'Thanks, Jack.'

'And when this is done,' he went on, 'we're gonna talk about a new position for you.'

'Whatever you say, Jack.'

On the way to the elevator Jerry asked, 'What new position, Mr G.?'

'I guess when this is all over,' I said, 'we'll find out.'

'I hope it means a raise.'

'You and me both.'

Fifty-Three

Billy was in the security office, dressing down one of his men for losing a cheater.

'Once we identify a cheat,' he was saying as we entered, 'we don't let him leave the premises without having a little talk. Understand?'

'Yes, sir.'

Billy looked over at me. 'Somethin' I can do for you, Eddie?'

'Yeah, we need to talk, Billy,' I said. 'You can finish rippin' this guy a new one later.'

'Listen—' Billy started, but Jerry cut him off by stepping between him and the other guy, his broad back to Billy.

'Out!' Jerry said to the worker in trouble.

'Yessir!' The guy ran away, and I closed the door to the office.

'What the fuck, Eddie,' Billy said. 'That guy had potential, and your big gorilla probably scared it out of him.'

186

'I don't care, Billy,' I said. 'I want to know how somebody waltzed onto the property, killed Helen – took the time to hang her up in the ladies' room – and then walked out.'

'You don't have the authority to ask me that.'

'Yes, I do,' I said. 'Go ahead. Check with Entratter.'

He stared at me, put his hand on his phone, then relaxed it.

'You know,' he said, 'I left the Chicago PD to get away from brown nosers.'

'Fine,' I said, 'you think I'm a brown noser. Now answer my question.'

He sat down behind his desk and leaned back. All in one moment his manner changed. His shoulders slumped, and he looked defeated.

'You know,' he said, 'casino security was supposed to be a cushy job for me. Catch cheaters, teach 'em a lesson. Mr Entratter even told me I could do it the Chicago way. But this – murder? That wasn't supposed to be on the cards – no pun intended.'

I sat across from him. Jerry leaned against the door.

'The robbery, yeah,' he said, 'I fucked up there, and you cleaned up the mess. But the murder – if it was a murder . . .'

'It was.'

'. . . that ain't my fault. So why does it feel like it was?'

'Look, Billy,' I said, 'the murder wasn't your fault, all right? I'm just wondering how somebody walked in, did it and walked out – like he was invisible.'

'Maybe he was known,' Billy offered.

'An employee?' I said.

'Or an ex-employee.'

'We checked out Walter Spires,' I said.

'Spires?' Billy said. 'That name sounds familiar.'

'Helen had Entratter fire him,' I said. 'He could have walked in here and if some of the employees didn't know about the firing, they would have assumed he still worked here.'

'That's possible.'

'But we checked him out,' I went on. 'He's a nerd. A wimp. I don't know if he had it in him to kill her, let alone string her up that way.'

'Could be some other ex-employee, then.'

'OK,' I said, 'why don't you check that out for me? See who's been fired in the past month or so, who might have had a grudge against Helen Simms.'

'I can do that,' Billy said. 'OK, I'll do that.'

I stood up.

'What was your position when you left the Chicago PD?' I asked.

'Detective.'

'Homicide?'

'Sorry,' Billy said, 'Bunco. That's why Mr Entratter hired me.'

'OK.'

I started toward the door. Jerry opened it and waited. I turned back to Billy Pulaski when another question occurred to me.

'Billy, how did Entratter find you?'

'I was recommended to him for the job.'

'By who?'

'I think that's somethin' you'll have to ask Entratter, Eddie.'

I nodded and went out, Jerry right behind me.

When we got back to the lobby Jerry asked, 'Who do you think recommended him, Mr G.?'

'I don't know,' I said, 'but it would have to be somebody who's word Jack put a lot of stock in.'

'In Chicago?' Jerry said. 'Gee, I wonder who that could be?'

We both had an idea but we kept it to ourselves.

Fifty-Four

I called Eddie Robinson's room and he said to come right up. When we got there the studio girl – I forgot her name – opened the door. Her eyes widened when she saw Jerry, but then she held her finger to her lips.

'Wha—' I started.

'Shh,' she hissed. 'Mr Robinson is being interviewed. You can come in and listen, but you have to keep quiet.'

'OK,' I mouthed.

The three of us walked into the suite. Robinson was sitting on the sofa. A man with a pad of paper in his lap was across from him, asking questions and jotting down Robinson's answers.

'Rico, Rico,' I heard Robinson saying as we entered. 'Everybody wants to know about Rico.'

'What would you like to talk about, sir?' the interviewer asked.

'Lancey Howard.'

'That's the part you're playing in *The Cincinnati Kid*, right?' the man asked.

'That's right. He's a very complex, interesting man.'

We stood and listened while Robinson regaled the reporter with Lancey's virtues and faults. The man wrote feverishly while the actor spoke, until the interview was over and the two men stood up and shook hands. The studio girl walked the reporter out of the room.

'Was he from a magazine or a newspaper?' Jerry asked.

'I don't even know,' Robinson said. 'The girl showed up with him this morning, without warning. She and I are going to have a talk. How are you boys?'

'Good,' I said, 'we're good. How was your dinner with Frank?'

'Great,' Robinson said. 'Frank's a wonderful guy, and I can see that the people in this town treat him like royalty.'

'Pretty much,' I said. 'What are your plans for more research?'

'I figured you'd get me in to watch another game,' Robinson said.

'We could do that,' I said, 'or . . .'

'Or what?' he asked, raising his eyebrows.

'Well, I could bring a dealer up here to work with you, teach you the game the way it should be played. Then maybe later we could actually get you into a game.'

'High stakes?'

'Well, I wouldn't think you'd want to play too high, but yeah, if that's what you want.'

'Could the dealer be a female?'

'Why Eddie, you dirty dog,' I said.

'No, no,' he said, 'there's a female dealer in the film. The character's name is Lady Fingers. Do you have anyone like that?'

'Sure,' I said, 'but her name's Madge.'

He sighed and said, 'I guess that'll have to do.'

'Madge?' Jerry asked, as we left Robinson's room.

'What can I tell you?'

'I like Lady Fingers better.'

'It's a movie, Jerry,' I said. 'Nobody has a name like that in real life.'

'I know a guy in Brooklyn they call Twinkletoes,' he argued.

'That's Brooklyn,' I said, as if that said it all.

We went downstairs and into the casino to see if Madge was working. She was, at her regular table. I talked to her point boss, and then pulled her out.

Madge had been dealing at the Sands for a long time. She was about fifty, and while Jack Entratter liked hiring pretty young things as not only waitresses but dealers, Madge was just too good at her job to let go now that she was no longer sweet or young.

She was, however, a handsome woman who still had to fend off passes during the course of the day.

'What gives these guys the idea I'm just waitin'

for them to take me away from all this?' she demanded.

'I guess they just can't believe their luck that you're their dealer, Madge.'

'Yeah, bite me,' she said. She eyed Jerry but didn't say anything to him. 'So what's on your mind, Eddie?'

'I've got a special client who wants to learn how to play poker.'

'Now I'm supposed to be a teacher?'

'It's a little more than that, Madge,' I said. 'This is somebody who's researching a role for a movie. It's a poker movie, and there's a female dealer in it. They might be looking for someone to base her on.'

She touched her dark hair, which was streaked with just enough gray to look fashionable.

'We ain't talkin' about Paul Newman, are we? Maybe Rock Hudson?'

'No.'

'Who then?'

'He's a special friend of Jack Entratter's, and Frank Sinatra's.'

'OK, I'm curious,' she said. 'Who?'

'Edward G. Robinson.'

'No shit?'

'No shit.'

'Holy cow,' she said. 'He's like . . . major.'

'Yeah, he is. And it's for a movie he's doing with Steve McQueen.'

'Jeez – do I get to meet him?'

'Who knows?' I said. 'You up for this?'

'You know it,' she said. 'When does he want to start?'

'Right away,' I said. 'He's in his suite now, waiting.'

'Now?' She touched her hair, again. 'Jeez, Eddie, I gotta freshen up.'

'Well, you go ahead,' I said. 'I'll call and tell him you're on your way.'

'OK,' she said. 'Hey, thanks, Eddie. I'm so tired of playin' grab-ass with these jamokes down here.'

'I don't think Edward G. Robinson is going to play grab-ass with you, Madge, but he may want to buy you dinner.'

'That's cool,' she said.

'OK,' I said. I gave her his suite number and she ran off to the ladies' room.

'She's all excited,' Jerry said, as we walked to the lobby to a house phone.

'Why shouldn't she be?' I asked. 'She gets to spend time with a movie star in his suite rather than down here with grab-ass gamblers.'

'Jeez, a woman her age and they're still tryin' to grab her ass?'

'I think she has a nice one,' I said.

'Hey, sure, I'm just sayin' . . .'

I called Robinson and told him to expect Madge any minute. I also told him if he wanted to buy her dinner at the Sands I'd arrange for it to be on the house.

'Eddie G.,' he said. 'I think I can afford to buy a young lady dinner.'

I almost told him she wasn't exactly a young lady, but maybe at his age she was.

When I hung up I said to Jerry, 'OK, he's taken care of for a while.'

'You ain't gonna put him in a high-stakes game tonight?' he asked.

'Too soon,' I said. 'Let's see what kind of student Madge says he is.'

'So whatta we do now?'

'Back to work on Helen's murder. Let's plan our snatch of the manager of the Happy Devil.'

Fifty-Five

It wasn't hard to find out that the listed manager of the Happy Devil was named Francis D'Auria. I was able to do that with a quick phone call.

Out in the Caddy Jerry said, 'You know what I'm thinkin'?'

'Yeah,' I said, 'we need to find out if this club is connected.'

'That's what I'm thinkin'.'

'Let's go to Fremont Street,' I said. 'I think I know who to ask.'

'The dick?'

'No,' I said. 'I'll tell you when we get there.'

Jerry shrugged and gunned the engine.

We parked behind the Horseshoe and walked up to Fremont Street. Across from Danny's office was an arcade. Jerry and I had used it a few months before to do some surveillance. Its clientele was less than desirable, as was its owner, but the place was connected.

'Angie Vadala owns this place,' I explained as

we entered. 'He knows who and what's connected in Vegas, especially when it comes to sleaze.'

A hooker was off in a corner making a deal with a john. She was young and overly made-up. Everything was for sale here except drugs. The 'boys' weren't into the drug trade in Vegas, but I suspected Angie had his way of getting around that.

Even though Dutch Schultz and Meyer Lansky were involved in drug trafficking early on, the Italians stayed out of it. The Mafia was, after all, about 'family', and the bosses hated to think of their own kids being able to buy drugs. But that had changed to some extent. Lucky Luciano was one of the first Mafia bosses to get involved with drugs, and after he was deported Genovese and Gambino took over. But Genovese was sent to prison in 1959 on drug charges. Some thought that Luciano had engineered this from exile in Italy. This left Gambino in power. Luciano died of a heart attack in 1962, when he was meeting with a movie producer in Naples International Airport to discuss a possible film biography. (A film did eventually get made about Luciano, but not until 1973.)

But as far as I knew then, Vegas was still off limits when it came to drugs.

We walked through the arcade, careful not to touch anything – that included skittle tables, pinball machines, and people.

In the back was a door with OFFICE written on it. No plate or fancy lettering, just OFFICE scrawled on the door itself. Classy.

I knocked, and then opened it. A painfully thin hooker, probably younger than the one outside, leaped to her feet, her hand going to her heavily lipsticked mouth.

'Jesus Christ – oh, hey, Eddie,' Angie said, hastily doing up his pants. 'Hey, bud, ya gotta knock, ya know?'

'Sure, Angie.'

'I'll see you later, babe,' he said to the girl.

'My money,' she said.

'We didn't finish—'

'That ain't my fault!' she whined.

'I said later!' Angie growled, trying to sound tough. It wasn't easy. He had a weak chin, a receding hairline and a distinctive pot belly.

'Pay the girl, Angie,' I said.

'Hey, Eddie, come on,' he said. 'This is my business, ya know?'

'Jerry . . .' I said.

Jerry moved in on Angie, whose weak chin began to quiver.

'Pay her!' Jerry said.

Hastily, Angie went into his pocket, came out with some crumpled bills and offered them to the girl. The girl took the money, then turned to me.

'Thanks, mister,' she said, her wide eyes ringed by so much mascara she looked like a raccoon. I doubted she was fifteen. 'If ya wanna do somethin' later—'

'Go home, sweetie,' I said.

'Sure, but—'

'Go home!' Jerry said.

She looked up at Jerry with wide eyes, then hurried from the room.

196

'Who's the gorilla, Eddie?' Angie asked, still trying to be tough.

'Don't get him mad, Angie,' I said. 'He'll tear off your arms.'

Angie self-consciously folded his arms.

'Whataya want, Eddie?'

'The Happy Devil.'

'A sex club,' he said. 'Kinda high end. What about it?'

'Is it connected?'

'Well, sure.'

'What about the manager? A guy named D'Auria.'

'Frankie D.,' he said. 'He's connected, but he ain't much of nothin'.'

'Chicago?' I asked.

'Cleveland.'

Well, at last I knew he wasn't working for Momo Giancana.

'You gonna do 'im?' Angie asked. 'Nobody'll care. They'll just put somebody else in his place.'

'Nobody's doin' nobody, Angie,' I said. 'I'm just interested in knowing who I'm dealing with.'

'What's your beef with him?'

'Never mind,' I said. 'Just go back to work and don't worry about it.'

We turned to leave, but I stopped short.

'Angie.'

'Yeah?'

'If you should think about callin' Frankie D., don't. I wouldn't like it.'

'Mr G. wouldn't like it,' Jerry said, moving close to Angie. 'And neither would I!'

'Yeah, s-sure, OK,' Angie said, holding his hands out in front of him. 'No problem.' He was speaking directly to Jerry. 'Me and Mr G. – I mean, Eddie – we're pals, ya know?'

'Yeah,' I said, 'pals.'

As we walked through the arcade we saw the girl from the office in a corner with a middle-aged man. She was on her knees in front of him, her head bobbing up and down.

'Want me to scare her away?' Jerry asked.

'No,' I said, 'she knows what she's doing, I guess. Forget it.'

Fifty-Six

We decided we needed to change our clothes, something more appropriate to what Jerry called 'a snatch'.

First we drove to my house, because it was the furthest away from Fremont Street.

Jerry waited in the kitchen while I pulled on a black sweater, dark blue jeans and black shoes and socks. I came out and grabbed a black wind-breaker from the closet.

'Mr G.,' Jerry said, coming out of the kitchen, 'you got nothing in your fridge to eat.'

'Well, I haven't been able to do much shopping, lately.'

'We're gonna have to eat before we make this snatch.'

'OK,' I promised, 'after we go back so you can change, we'll get something to eat.'

'You know,' he said, as we left the house and walked to the Caddy, 'I learned a long time ago I don't do so well on an empty stomach.'

'How do you know?' I asked.

'Huh?'

'Come on, Jerry,' I said, as we got into the car, 'when is your stomach ever empty?'

Jerry changed into clothes similar to mine, all dark. We still had time before we were to meet Danny, so we went down to the Garden Café to fill his stomach. And I had to admit, I was hungry, too.

'You two look like twins,' Lily said, 'except for, you know, the size difference.'

'Lily,' I said, 'I'm glad to see you're OK.'

'Didn't Jerry tell you? He took me home and saw me to my door, like a gentleman.'

'No, we really haven't had time to discuss last night in depth,' I said.

'Speaking of which, what happened to you after I left?' she asked.

'Mr G. hooked up.'

'Well, well . . .'

'I met a woman who had helpful information,' I said, hoping Jerry would let it go at that.

No such luck.

'And he went home with her.'

'Wow,' she said, 'that's a rare occurrence. All the hook-ups take place in the club. We don't usually see each other outside. Outside those walls we're all very different people. She must have really liked you. Who was it?'

'Her club name was Jewel.'

'Jewel,' Lily said, 'I don't think I know her.'

'What do you know about drugs being dealt in the club?'

'I know it's done, but that's not my scene, man.' She gave us a saucy grin and added, 'Sex is my drug of choice.'

Jerry blushed.

'Was I helpful to you, Eddie?' she asked.

'You were, Lily,' I said. 'We got some information we can act on. Thank you.'

'No sweat,' she said. 'You guys gonna order?'

I said the first thing that came to mind.

'Burger platter for me.'

'Same for me,' Jerry said. 'Extra fries.'

She put her hand on Jerry's shoulder, squeezed it and said, 'I'll even add a second burger, on me.'

As she walked away and Jerry watched her I said, 'I forgot to ask what happened when you drove her home last night.'

'Like she said, I took her to her door.' He gave me a pointed look. 'I had to get back to the club to see what you were doin'.'

'I know,' I said. 'Sorry.'

Lily brought our platters and we plowed through them. I don't know why, but whenever I was around Jerry it seemed to affect my appetite. When he stayed in Vegas for any extended period of time, I gained weight.

'Where do you think the shamus is gonna have us take D'Auria.'

'I don't know,' I said, 'but it'll be someplace out of the way.'

'Good,' Jerry said. 'I don't like askin' people questions quietly. So we can be as loud as we want – and so can he.'

Jerry was obviously looking forward to this.

Fifty-Seven

When we walked into Danny's office he said, 'Holy shit.'

He was dressed the same way we were.

'I guess black is in,' he said. 'Are we ready?'

'Ready,' I said. 'Where are we taking him?'

'A house I've used before,' he said. 'It's in a rundown neighborhood and there's really nothing around it.'

'Good,' Jerry said.

'Are we going to use the Caddy?' I asked.

'Why not? We'll blindfold him.'

'OK, then,' I said. 'Jerry, you wanna pull the Caddy up front?'

'Sure, Mr G.'

Jerry left and I looked at Danny.

'The big guy seems ready,' he said.

'Maybe too ready,' I said. 'Could be this guy'll tell us what we want to know willingly.'

'You find out if the place is connected?'

'Supposedly.'

'Then he'll act tough, at least at the beginning,' Danny said. 'We may just have to let Jerry do what Jerry does.'

'We'll see.'

We went downstairs, where Jerry sat in the Caddy with the motor running.

It was late when we left Danny's, about one a.m. We knew that the club stayed open late, but we didn't know if the manager stayed the whole time. We needed to find out if he was still there.

We should have done it before we left Danny's office, but we stopped along the way at a pay phone and I called the club.

'Yeah?' somebody said.

'Is Frankie there?'

'The manager?'

'You got another Frankie there?'

'Hold on.'

The guy put the phone down. In a few moments it was picked up again.

'Yeah, this is Frankie.'

'Wrong number.' I hung up and went back to the car. 'He's there.'

'What if the call makes him nervous and he runs?' Jerry asked.

'We'll be there before that happens,' I said. 'Drive.'

We pulled up across the street from the club, a few doors down. It was only minutes since the phone call. I doubted Frankie had left by then.

'What about another way out?' I asked.

'The alley,' Danny said. 'If he has a car in the alley he still has to drive it out this way. I'm thinkin' his car is one of these on the street.'

'OK,' I said, 'so we wait. Maybe the call will drive him out.'

'Only if he's got something to hide,' Danny said.

'Well, if he's connected,' I said, 'and he's selling drugs in the club, or letting somebody sell drugs there, he just might.'

And that must have been the case, because we only waited half an hour when the front door opened and a beefy guy came out.

'That's him,' Danny said. 'Let's go.'

Danny and I leaped over the seats while Jerry opened his door and got out. Danny rushed ahead of us to face Frankie D.

'Hey! Remember me?'

Frankie turned, frowned at Danny, and then recognition dawned.

'You!' he said. 'What the fuck—'

He stopped when he was grabbed from behind by Jerry's strong hands. The big guy pinned Frankie's arms behind him.

'Ow! Hey, what the fuck?'

I stood in front of Frankie.

'You've got one chance to end this right here on the street,' I told him. 'Who's selling drugs in your place?'

'What? Drugs? I don't allow no drugs in my place.' I might have believed him if he hadn't immediately started to sweat. I looked at Danny, who shook his head. He didn't believe him, either.

'OK,' I said, 'I gave you a chance.' I took out a cloth Danny had supplied and tied it around his eyes.

'Hey, wha . . . help!' he started, but Jerry clamped a big hand over his mouth and dragged him across the street to the Caddy. I unlocked the trunk and Jerry lifted him up and dumped him inside. Before closing it we tied his hands behind him and bound his feet. He immediately began beating on the inside with his feet, but he wasn't getting out.

'OK,' Danny said, 'let's remember when we get there, no names, right?'

'Right,' I said.

Jerry nodded.

'OK, let's go,' Danny said. 'Jerry, I'll give you directions.'

We hopped into the Caddy and got away without anyone seeing us.

Fifty-Eight

The house was a small, dilapidated A-frame exactly as Danny had described it. There was nothing else around.

We dragged Frankie D. out of the trunk and Jerry pretty much drag-carried him into the house. There was a sturdy wooden chair in the middle of an empty living room. Danny had obviously spent time setting the place up. All the windows were covered with brown paper.

Jerry pushed the protesting Frankie into the chair and tied him there. We left the blindfold on. He'd seen Danny, but not me and Jerry. We wanted to keep it that way.

We also decided that I'd do the talking. Jerry finished tying him and then stood aside. When and if it came time to squeeze, he'd take over. We also had masks, which we'd only wear if we decided that Jerry's bulk would come in handy.

'OK, Frankie,' I said, 'here's the deal.'

'You sonsofbitches don't know who you're dealin' with.'

'Yeah, we do,' I said, 'and we don't give a rat's ass.'

'You better—'

Without a signal from either me or Danny, Jerry stepped forward and clubbed Frankie once. It was a love tap, really, but Frankie's head rocked back, and his bottom lip split.

'Now shut up until I've asked a question,' I said.

He licked the blood off his lip and kept quiet.

'Somebody's dealing drugs in your club,' I said. 'I don't care if he's doin' it on his own, or workin' for you. I just want to know who he is.'

'Look,' he said, 'I don't know what you're talk—'

Bam! Jerry hit him, again. It wasn't in the plan, but Danny and I decided to just go with it.

'In a minute I'm gonna take off your blindfold so you can see who's hitting you; and so you can see it comin'. Wanna try this again . . .?'

Well, he held out for a while – over an hour, really. Then we found out why.

'Look,' he said, 'if my bosses find out I'm peddlin' drugs in my club they'll kill me.'

'Well, if it turns out your dealer killed Helen Simms,' I told him, 'it's all gonna come out in the wash and they'll find out, anyway.'

'Jesus . . .' he said, with a sob.

'Come on, Frankie,' I said. 'Your dealer had a fight with Helen in the club, right?'

'Right.'

'And now she's dead. Do you think he killed her?'

'I don't know,' he said, meekly.

'Well, we want to ask him,' I said. 'So we need his name, and address. Then we'll take you back to your car.'

'Y-you're not gonna squeal on me?'

'We don't care about you or your club,' I said. 'We just want the name and address.'

'OK, OK,' he said, 'his name's Joey Rigoletti. Uh, they call him Joey Rigatoni.'

'Is Joey connected?'

'He's just a kid who wants to be a wise guy,' Frankie said. 'He knows I'm connected, and thinks he's gonna ride my coattails to bein' a made man.'

'And he doesn't even know you're not a made man, right?' I asked. 'Doesn't know you're just an errand boy.'

'N-no, he don't.'

I looked at Danny and Jerry and they each, in turn, nodded, indicating they believed him.

'Tell us where to find Joey Rigatoni and we'll take you back to your car.'

He gave us an address, and I signaled Jerry to untie him from the chair.

We took him outside and put him back in the trunk. Jerry made sure he banged his head getting in. We tied his hands and feet again, and closed the lid.

Before I closed the door I said, 'Frankie, if it turns out you lied to us, you won't even see us comin', next time. Got it?'

'Yeah, I got it.'

'And the same goes for calling Joey.'

'Fuck Joey!' Frankie swore.

I slammed the trunk closed.

'What now?' Jerry asked.

'I suggest we all get some sleep. We can pick up Rigatoni tomorrow,' Danny said.

'What if he warns him?' Jerry asked.

'I don't think he will,' Danny said. 'He's scared enough to let Joey fend for himself. He probably feels this is all Joey's fault, anyway.'

'OK then,' I said. 'Jerry, you drive.'

We left him off in front of his club, still tied and blindfolded. Let him get himself free. We drove off and, at Jerry's urging, went to get something to eat.

Fifty-Nine

'What about the cops?' Danny asked, when we dropped him off at his place.

'Fuck 'em,' I said. 'Let Hargrove do his own job.'

'What if we find out Rigatoni did kill Helen?' Danny asked. 'What do we do with him then?'

'I'll think about calling Hargrove if we get a confession.'

'Well, come and get me if you want me there when you grab him.'

'Thanks, Danny, for all your help.'

Danny pointed at Jerry and then at me, saying, 'And you watch his back.'

'I always do,' Jerry said. He sounded annoyed. This was not the first time somebody had told him that, and he probably thought he didn't need to be told.

'You goin' home?' Jerry asked, as he pulled away from the curb.

'No, just driving to the Sands; I can spend the night there. I have a change of clothes. Tomorrow morning we can decide what to do about Joey Rigatoni.'

'I say we grab him and squeeze.'

'If he killed Helen he's not gonna crack as fast as Frankie did. He's got a lot more to lose.'

'So how do you want to play it?'

'That's what we have to talk about,' I said, 'and think about.'

'You gonna tell Mr Entratter what's happenin'?'

'Not yet.'

'Is he gonna be pissed?'

'Maybe,' I said, 'but even though he wants Helen's killer caught, he may not approve of how we're doing it.'

'So better he don't know, huh?'

'Much better,' I said. 'When we have more information, we'll clue him in.'

'OK with me,' he said. 'I'll think on it too and we can talk at breakfast.'

I looked at my watch. It was 4 a.m.

'Let's meet in the Garden Café at nine a.m.'

Jerry nodded and headed down the strip. I watched the marquees go by, Alan King at the

Riviera, Della Reese at the Desert Inn and, as we approached the Sands marquee, Nat King Cole. When we passed the Sahara I saw Dino's name all lit up, and it reminded me that he was in town doing a show.

Things were changing in Vegas. Howard Hughes wasn't the only person with money who was trying to move in. The mob's hold on the casinos was not as strong as it had once been. The Rat Pack was not as close knit a group as it once was. Peter Lawford was on the outs, Joey Bishop was busy with his TV show, Sammy and Frank were on shaky ground. The only thing that was certain in their world was that Frank and Dino were friends – each other's friend, and mine.

But the marquees went on, the neon lights shone brighter than ever, and I was on the verge of some sort of new position. All I had to do was find a killer, and ward off Howard Hughes' clutches.

Life used to be easier. What happened to those days?

Sixty

I spend a lot of time with a table between Jerry and me. And the table was usually covered – I mean covered – with food. Maybe Jerry and I should start having our discussions while walking, instead of eating. No, I'd never be able to convince the big guy of that.

When he came down to the café at nine a.m. he was wearing the houndstooth sport coat I'd first seen earlier in the year. I had on jeans, a T-shirt and light windbreaker kept in a locker at the Sands for emergencies.

''mornin', Mr G.' He sat down, looked around, probably for Lily. I'd already determined that she wasn't working that shift. Instead Nell came over to take our orders.

We'd eaten after returning Frankie D. to his club, but we were both hungry again and ordered eggs.

Over coffee Jerry asked, 'You come up with a way to go?'

'Maybe.'

'Good,' Jerry said, ''cause all I got is to grab 'im and squeeze 'im.'

'Well,' I said, 'that may be the way to go.'

After breakfast I called Robinson to make sure he was in his suite, and then we went up. He was alone and answered the door himself.

'How did it go with Madge?' I asked.

'She was marvelous,' he said, happily. 'I learned more about the game, and the strategies, than I ever thought I could.'

'Do you think you're ready to play?'

'Oh, no,' Robinson said, 'no, no, Madge is coming back this afternoon. I don't think I'll be ready to play until she says so.'

'I see,' I said. 'Well, that's good. I'm glad she's taking care of you.'

'How are things going for you fellas?'

'I think we're getting close, Eddie,' I said.

210

'That's fine,' he said. 'I think you boys can leave me in Madge's hands and take care of your business.'

'You're OK with that?' I asked.

He put his hand on my shoulder and said, 'I know both Frank and Jack Entratter have put pressure on you to squire me around, Eddie G., but yes, leaving me with Madge is very all right with me. Perhaps by the time she says I'm ready to play, your business will be concluded.'

'I hope so,' I said, 'I sincerely hope so.'

We made one more stop before leaving the Sands.

'Come on in,' Frank said. 'You get my message?'

'I didn't, Frank,' I said. 'Sorry.'

'I left it at the front desk. Ah, it's OK, kid,' he said. 'I just wanted you to know that you, me, Eddie Robinson, and Big Jerry here are going to see Dino when he opens tonight at the Sahara.'

'That's great, Frank.'

'Yeah – Smokey's comin', too. He's flying in for the show.' Smokey was Frank's pet name for Sammy, not because he was black, but because he smoked so much. I was glad to hear that Sammy was coming in. He'd said something on the radio a while back that pissed Frank off. Maybe they were over it.

'I just wanted to let you know what's goin' on with Eddie.'

'He told me,' Frank said, 'you got some broad showin' him how to play poker. He loves it! I appreciate you doin' what you can for him, Eddie G.'

'Sure, Frank, sure,' I said. 'Happy to do it, you know that.'

'You guys be ready tonight about six,' he said. 'I'll have a limo out front. We're gonna have dinner and see the show, give Dago a hard time, eh?' Dago was Frank's nickname for Dean.

'You got it, Frank,' I said, and we left. I was satisfied that both Eddie Robinson and Frank were taken care of, for the time being.

'Sonofabitch,' Jerry said.

We were in the Caddy, watching for the address that we had for Joey Rigatoni. It was a small house in a residential neighborhood of almost identical houses.

'Not where I'd expect a drug peddler to live,' Jerry said, when we pulled into the block.

We watched the house for an hour before the front door opened and a young man stepped out. He was tall, skinny, wearing worn jeans and a jacket. His hair was long and unkempt, and even at a distance I could see it needed washing. I couldn't imagine him in the Happy Devil.

'Fits the description Frankie D. gave us,' Jerry observed.

'Yeah.'

When a white-haired woman came out behind him Jerry said, 'Sonofabitch.' The boy and woman hugged, he kissed her on the cheek and started down the cracked concrete walkway. 'Looks like he lives with his mother.'

'Yeah,' I said, 'or aunt.'

'Landlady, maybe?'

'No,' I said. 'I don't think he'd be renting a

212

room in this neighborhood. I think he lives here. Probably grew up here.'

'And he's dealin' drugs to try and get out?' Jerry asked.

He walked in the opposite direction from us. The woman stood on the porch and watched.

'We can't grab him in front of her.'

'If we try to grab him in this neighborhood we might be seen,' Jerry observed.

'OK, then,' I said, 'let's see where he goes.'

We tailed Rigatoni in the Caddy, which Jerry was very good at, despite the size of the car and him. We watched as Joey met with some friends, stood on a corner for a few minutes, then moved on and did the same thing a few blocks away. When he stopped at a bus stop I said, 'Did I see right?'

'Yeah,' Jerry said. 'He's dealin'. He was passing some bags to his buddies and getting paid in with all that hand shakin'.'

'Let's grab him before he gets on the bus.'

'Gotcha, Mr G. When I jump out, you slide in behind the wheel.'

'Gotcha,' I said, letting him call the play because he was the experienced one.

Jerry screeched up to the bus stop. Joey was standing there with an older man who was sitting on a bench, eating a bagel. He jumped out of the car and I slid behind the wheel.

Joey saw him coming, knew something was up and said, 'Hey, wait—'

'Let's go, Joey!' Jerry said and literally picked Joey up and threw him into the back seat of the Caddy.

The old man watched, his eyes wide, a bite of bagel half in, half out of his mouth.

'Sorry, sir,' Jerry said to him. 'Hope we didn't interrupt your breakfast.'

'What'd he do?' the man asked.

'He's been dealin' drugs.'

The old man said, 'Fuck 'im up, then,' around the bagel, and went on chewing.

Jerry got into the back seat with Joey, who was just scrambling up to try and climb out. Jerry clubbed him and Joey Rigatoni fell back onto the seat, glassy-eyed.

'Go, Mr G.!' Jerry said.

I peeled out, burning rubber. Helluva way to treat a Cadillac.

Sixty-One

OK, so we hadn't planned this snatch as well as Danny had planned out the snatch of Frankie D. So for want of a place to take him and question him, I just drove to Industrial Road, found a deserted stretch, and stopped.

'Hey, what the fuck—' Joey started, but Jerry pushed him into one corner of the Caddy's back seat and then planted his massive foot on his chest.

'Jesus!' Joey said.

'Listen to this man's questions,' Jerry said, 'and answer them, truthfully. If I think you're lying, I'm gonna grind my heel into your chest.'

'But wait—'

Jerry cut him off by pushing his heel into Joey's ribs.

'OK, OK!' Joey yelled. 'Take it easy.'

Jerry looked at me.

'Joey, you're dealin' drugs.'

'Hey, what—' he started but Jerry dug his heel in, then leaned forward, stuck his hand into Joey's jacket pocket and came out with some nickel bags.

'This is a fact, Joey,' I said. 'You're a drug dealer. Don't deny it, or my friend will put his foot right into your heart.'

'Yeah, OK,' Joey said, as Jerry let up on the pressure. 'So what, I'm tryin' to make a livin'. Who ain't?'

'You're right, everybody is trying to make a living, but not by hooking other people on drugs.'

'Hey,' Joey argued, 'I don't hook people on drugs, I just help 'em when they're sick.'

'Right, right,' I said, 'they hook themselves. Well, I tell you what, Joey. We're really not concerned with you dealing drugs. We have a problem with something else you did.'

'Like what?'

'Murder.'

'What?' He tried to come up out of his seat, but Jerry slammed him back with his foot. 'What the hell? I didn't murder nobody.'

'You know a woman named Helen Simms?'

'Never heard of the lady.'

'How do you know she was a lady?' I asked.

'It's just a sayin', man,' he said. 'I don't know the broad.'

215

'Well, how about a woman named Tina?' I asked. 'How about her . . . Dante?'

Joey Rigatoni deflated at the sound of his club name. Or maybe it was hers.

'Aw, jeez, man,' he said, 'you ain't gonna tell my mom about that, are you?'

'I don't know, Joey,' I said. 'Am I?'

'Look,' he said, 'I didn't kill nobody; I don't know about nobody bein' killed. Just tell me what you wanna know.'

'You had a fight with Tina – Helen Simms – in the club a while back.'

'Yeah, so? She was tryin' to muscle in on my turf.'

'She was selling drugs?'

'Yeah, why's that so hard to believe, because she's a woman?'

'Was a woman.'

'What?'

'She *was* a woman,' I said. 'Somebody killed her.'

He was stunned – or he was a very good actor. My heart sank, because I had thought we had our guy.

'Oh, man,' he said, 'oh, man, I didn't do that, man. I ain't never killed nobody.'

'Really . . . Rigatoni?' Jerry asked.

'Hey,' Joey said, 'that's just a stupid name, OK? I ain't connected, I ain't no made guy, and I probably never will be.' He hesitated, then said, 'I just ain't got the balls.'

It must have killed him to admit that.

'OK,' I said, 'then tell me who you think did it.'

'I got no idea,' he said. Jerry pressed with his

boot, but this time the kid fought it. 'Hey! Cut it out! I didn't even know the woman until I saw her dealin' in the club.'

'What about the manager? Frankie D.?'

'What about him?'

'Does he know you're dealing in his club?'

'Well, yeah,' Joey said, 'he takes a percentage.'

'What did he think of Tina trying to sell in his club?'

'His bouncers pulled us apart. They put me outside, and that was it.'

'And what happened to her?'

'I don't know, man,' he said. 'I don't know where they took her. Maybe to see Frankie. Why didn't you ask him about it?'

'I will.'

'You better watch it, though,' he said. 'Frankie D. got connections.'

'Turns out, not so much, really,' Jerry said. He took his foot off Joey's chest.

'Get out of the car, Joey,' I said.

He brushed at the front of his chest and said, 'You gonna dump me off here?'

'Want us to drive you home and tell your mama what you been up to?'

'No!' he snapped. He leaped up and out of the car like a gymnast. 'You ain't gonna talk to her, are you? Look, the money I make I give to her.'

'And where does she think you get it?'

'Odd jobs,' he said, with a shrug.

I wondered if the woman could really be that stupid, to think that Joey would take home that much money from odd jobs?

217

'Don't skip town, Joey,' I said, 'or we will talk to her. And to the police.'

'Oh, man, don't bring the fuzz into this.'

'You better hope I don't find out you were lying to me.'

'I ain't lyin', man.'

'That better be true,' I said, 'because if you are, first I'll give you to my friend here, and then we'll give what's left to the cops. And believe me, they'll call your mother.'

'Fuck, man!'

'Take my advice,' I said. 'Get yourself into another business.'

He started walking, his shoulders slumped, and we drove the other way.

Sixty-Two

'You believe 'im?' Jerry asked when we stopped to switch places.

'Damn it, I do,' I said. 'He was just too stunned when we told him she was dead, and he was a suspect.'

'Suspect,' Jerry said. 'That's a cop word.'

'Sorry.'

'Speaking of cops, should we give him to them?'

'No,' I said, 'I'm not looking to be a narc.'

'Maybe we should have asked him for his source?'

'No,' I said, 'same reason.'

218

'What about these?' He took his hand out of his pocket, holding the small bags.

'We've got enough to do.'

'Yeah, we do.' He waited a beat. 'So what do we do?'

'Let's talk to Danny,' I said. 'Maybe he'll have some ideas.'

'I've got no idea,' Danny said.

We were in his office, all seated with coffee in our hands, supplied by Penny.

'Come on, Danny,' I said, 'what do you do when your best suspect turns out to be innocent?'

'I go back to square one,' he said. 'Start all over again.'

'That means the Sands,' I said. 'Back to the ladies' room.'

'Yes.'

'Danny?' Penny stuck her head in the door.

'Yeah, sweetie?'

'The police are here to see you.' Hargrove barged past her into the room. 'Detective Hargrove?' she finished, sarcastically.

'OK, honey,' Hargrove said, as his partner, Martin, came in behind him. 'We'll take it from here.'

Martin looked at Penny, mouthed, 'Sorry,' and she just shrugged and backed out.

'Hail, hail,' Hargrove said, 'the gang's all here, huh?'

'What can we do for you, detective?'

'Well, I could use some coffee.'

Danny drained his mug and put it on the desk.

219

'Fresh out.'

'Yeah, OK,' Hargrove said.

Martin leaned against the wall and kept quiet. I still didn't understand why he hadn't tried to get another partner. Nobody liked working with Hargrove because he was such a dick – and not the detective kind.

'Again,' Danny said, 'what can we do for you?'

'You can tell me what this little gabfest is all about.'

'Sports . . .' Danny said.

'Broads . . .' Jerry said.

'Art . . .' I said.

'Art?' Hargrove asked.

'It could happen,' I argued.

'Yeah, right,' Hargrove said. 'Look, I'm actually glad you're all here. Saves me the trouble of having to look for you.'

'We'd love to help, detective,' I said. 'Just tell us what you need.'

'I need to know what you three have been up to.'

'What do you mean?'

'You,' he said, pointing at Danny, 'were askin' questions in the dead woman's building. And you,' he went on, pointing at me, 'I'm bettin' he's workin' for you.'

'What about me?' Jerry asked.

Hargrove looked at Jerry and said, 'It won't be long before you're in a cell for something.'

'Hope it's a nice one,' Jerry said.

'I'll make sure you've got a big, fluffy pillow.' He looked at Danny again. 'Listen, Shamus, I don't want you botherin' my suspects.'

'Suspects?' I asked. 'What kind of suspects do you have in a suicide case? Or don't you really think it was suicide?'

'I think any broad who had to deal with you and your boss day in, day out had to be suicidal. Just keep your trained private dick away from my case, Eddie. You don't want to piss me off.'

I thought of a few comebacks for that, but decided to leave it alone.

'Don't make me come lookin' for you bums again.'

'No problem, detective,' Danny said. 'Now you have a nice day.'

Hargrove looked over at Martin, who shrugged.

'Let's get out of here, Henry,' Hargrove told his partner.

He went past Martin, out of the room first. Martin actually looked at me and raised his eyebrows, then turned and left.

'What's goin' on?' Danny asked.

'Seems to me they don't think it's a suicide,' I said, 'they just told Jack Entratter that.'

'Why?' Danny asked.

'I don't know,' I said, 'but I think I know how to find out.'

'How?' Danny asked.

'Martin,' I said. 'He's not a happy camper.'

'You think he'll talk to you?' Danny asked.

'Well, we've got something in common.'

'What's that?' Jerry asked.

'Neither one of us likes Hargrove.'

Sixty-Three

I had time to try to collar Detective Henry Martin and get him to talk to me before we had to get ready to go to Dino's show.

I gave the detectives a couple of hours to get back to their desks, and then called from the Sands, using the phone in Jerry's room.

'Detective Martin,' he said, answering his phone.

'Martin, this is Eddie Gianelli. Can we talk?'

'About what?'

'Things that are mutually beneficial.'

'And I assume you want this talk to be between you and me?' he asked.

'That's right.'

'Without my partner, and without any of your buddies?'

'That's right.'

'Why should I do this?'

'Maybe because you've got a case you can't solve or you need help,' I said, 'or maybe just because your partner's a prick.'

He hesitated, then said, 'All good reasons. Where and when?'

'Tomorrow afternoon,' I said. 'Some place neutral.'

'You know where Grabstein's is?'

That surprised me. Grabstein's was a Jewish Deli I had been introduced to by Danny's lawyer, Kaminsky, just a few months ago.

'I know it.'

'Meet me there at one.'

'OK,' I said, 'see you then.'

'And Eddie?'

'Yeah?'

'Have something for me,' he said. 'Don't make me waste my time.'

'Eating at Grabstein's?' I asked. 'When has that ever been a waste of time?'

I hung up. Jerry had been standing at the bar, listening.

'Hey,' he said, 'you were supposed to take me to Grabstein's next time I was here. That's now.'

He was right. After I ate at Grabstein's with Kaminsky, without Jerry, and told him about it, he'd pouted until I promised to take him.

'Well, you can't come tomorrow,' I said. 'I told him I'd come alone. But before you go home, definitely.'

'Hmph,' he said, unconvinced.

I decided to change the subject.

'You got a suit to wear to the show tonight?'

'No.'

I picked up the phone.

'I'll get you one, and me, too, so I don't have to go home to change.'

I called the concierge desk, talked to a man named Ted, told him what I needed. I gave him both our sizes and he said he'd have two suits up to us pronto. Pronto turned out to be an hour, which was OK.

Jerry was just starting to talk about getting room service when the suits arrived.

'We're gonna eat dinner out,' I said. 'Let's just get dressed and not ruin our appetites.'

223

Jerry frowned. 'I don't understand? Ruin our appetites?' Obviously, this was not a concept he'd ever had to deal with before.

'Get dressed!' I said.

He humphed again, and took the suit into the bedroom.

Sixty-Four

We met Frank, Sammy and Edward G. Robinson at the limo, in front of the Sands.

'Hey, Eddie G.!' Sammy said gleefully, shaking my hand. It was always one of the oddest sights to see Sammy shaking hands with Jerry. The difference in size was staggering.

We all piled into the back which, even with Jerry in the group, was big and spacious enough to hold us. Frank had made sure of that.

Sammy chattered the whole way, his body vibrating with energy. I think he was just happy to be around Frank, again. I knew Frank liked Sammy a lot, which was why I expected him to forgive him, eventually. Not so with Peter Lawford. That was a rift I didn't think would ever mend.

At the Sahara we filed out of the limo and into the Moroccan themed Congo Room. Because Frank was Frank we got a table up front, where Dean would be sure to see us. Buddy Hackett came over to say hello. He played the Sahara so often he had the honorary title of vice-president of entertainment. I was sure it was he who got Dean to play there.

Seated around us at some of the other tables were the likes of Steve and Eydie, Tony Curtis and Janet Leigh, Red Skelton – I assumed he hadn't lost his shirt at the Sands after I increased his limit – George Burns, and other stars who had come out to support Dino. He was very popular because he was not only a fabulous entertainer, but a great guy. And if you didn't believe me, you could have asked Frank. He loved the guy.

We had dinner – Sammy and Edward G. Robinson doing most of the talking – and were all well lubricated by the time the house lights went down and a spot hit the stage. He did one quick song – 'Ain't That a Kick in the Head', a song he did in *Ocean's Eleven*, which had been filmed right there in the Sahara – and then asked for the house lights to be brought up, 'So I can see if any of my friends showed up.'

He spotted us right away and pointed at Frank, the ever present cigarette between his fingers. 'Everybody slugs somebody sometime,' he sang. 'Hey Frank, hit anybody on the way in?'

'I'm gonna hit you in a minute, ya dago,' Frank fired back good-naturedly.

'And ladies and gentlemen, sitting with Frank is my other buddy, Sammy Davis Jr. Hey Sam, stand on somebody's shoulders so the people can see you!'

Sammy cracked up, and so did the crowd. The Rat Pack magic was alive, even though Dean was the only one on stage.

'And look there, with Frank and Sammy, is that

Edward G. Robinson? Ya know, Eddie did *Robin and the Seven Hoods* with us and he was a blast. Hey Eddie, where's your Messiah now?'

Eddie Robinson laughed and applauded.

He pointed out a few other stars – specifically thanking Buddy for booking him in the room – and then went on with the show.

He sang a bunch of his songs, did a few more jokes, then finished up with 'Everybody Loves Somebody Sometime', which had been a huge hit for him just that summer of 1964.

'Damn, he puts on a great show!' Frank said, enthusiastically.

'He sure does,' Robinson said. 'How come you fellas didn't jump up there and do some songs with him?'

'Because this is Dino's show,' Sammy said.

'That's right,' Frank said. 'You know, people come to the Sands to see the Summit. This was all Dean. Come on, let's order some more drinks. Dino'll be out here soon.'

Dean did come out after about twenty minutes, wearing a different tux, looking fresh and rested. He worked the room for a few minutes, pumping men's hands and kissing women, before joining us at the table.

He slapped me on the back and pumped my hand, said hello to Jerry, then pulled up a chair between Frank and Sammy.

Jerry leaned over and asked, 'How come he didn't say hello to you from the stage, Mr G.?'

'Me?' I said. 'Why should he say hello to me? I'm nobody.'

226

'That ain't true, Mr G.,' Jerry said. 'You're the man in Vegas. Everybody knows that.'

Robinson heard what Jerry was saying and leaned over.

'He's right, Eddie G.,' he said, waving a hand that held a cigar. 'All these entertainers should acknowledge you from the stage.'

'That's nice of you, Eddie,' I said, 'but I'm afraid that, in this room and rooms like it, I just don't cut it.'

A waitress came over and we ordered another round of drinks. Frank stuck with martinis – and ordered one for Robinson – I had bourbon, and Dino ordered a coke. Sammy went with bourbon, and Jerry had a beer.

Everybody was happy and having a good time. Even Jerry was laughing at the interplay between the three friends, Frank, Dino and Sammy. But it was Dean who called an end to it, saying he had to go back to his room to call Jeannie and then turn in early. Dean was not the drunken swinger he was purported to be.

So we paid the bill – somebody paid the bill, I think it was Frank – and made our way back out to the limo. Because he was playing the Sahara, Dean had a room there. When he said goodnight, he grabbed my arm and pulled me aside before I could get into the car.

'Let's have a quiet dinner while I'm here and catch up,' he said.

'Sure, Dean,' I said. 'Say when.'

'Tomorrow night, before the show,' he said. 'Come to my room at five. We'll do it early.'

'You got it.'

His handsome face broke into a huge smile and he gave me a hug before going back inside. I hoped I wouldn't be up to my eyeballs in something tomorrow night, and that I'd be able to make it.

I got into the limo and we headed back to the Sands.

Sixty-Five

I stayed overnight in a room at the Sands, but I had to go home the next morning. I had no fresh clothes, and wanted to use my own shower. I rose early, didn't bother waking Jerry, got dressed, and went downstairs. I checked at the front desk for messages. The only one they had was the one Frank said he'd left me. I left a message for Jerry, telling him I'd gone home and would be back in the afternoon.

I went out, got into the Caddy and drove to my house.

I came out of the shower, grabbed a towel and started to dry off. Then I pulled on a terry cloth robe and walked out of the bathroom into the bedroom. I was going through my closet when there was a knock at my door. Still in my robe, I went to see who it was.

I was surprised to find Emily Marcus standing on my doorstep. I thought about pulling on some pants first, but finally just opened the door. She was dressed for work in a gray suit, and matching heels, make-up perfectly applied.

'Well, hello,' I said.

'Good morning,' she said. 'I hope you don't mind . . . I tracked you down.'

'How?'

'Well, I could say that I checked your wallet while you were in the shower and got your address off your license,' she said. 'Or I could say that I work for a law firm and used my contacts there.' She winced and asked, 'Which do you prefer?'

'I really don't care,' I said. 'Both showed initiative. Come on in.'

'Thanks.'

I closed the door after she entered and said, 'Ah, I just got out of the shower, so I should put something on.'

'Why?' she asked. 'I've seen you naked, remember?'

'Some of it,' I said, 'still not all of it. How much did I drink in that club?'

'It might not have been what you drank,' she said.

'OK,' I said, waving the information off, 'don't tell me if I took something. I don't want to know. What brings you here? Why did you track me down?'

'Can't it be that I just wanted to see you again?'

'It could be,' I said, 'but if you found out my address, I'm sure you also managed to discover my phone number.'

'That's true,' she said. 'OK, here it is. My memory of that night wasn't really much clearer than yours. But I finally remembered something that was bothering me.'

'And what's that?' I asked. 'Wait, can I get you something? No, wait again. I have nothing.'

'Why don't you get dressed and buy me some coffee?' she asked.

'OK,' I said. I went into the bedroom and, while I dressed, called out, 'How did you get here? Do you have a car? I can drive you and then come back here if you do. Emily?'

It only takes a minute to pull on jeans and a T-shirt, slide your feet into some loafers. 'Emily?' I called, coming back into the living room.

Emily wasn't there.

But two guys were, and they had the look of a couple of knuckle-dusters.

'The lady was nice enough to let us in,' one of them said.

'I guess I should be more careful about who I let in,' I commented.

'Yeah, that's probably a good idea,' the other one said.

I looked them up and down, searching for weapons, bulges, in their jackets.

'What can I do for you fellas?' I asked.

'We've been sent here to deliver a message,' the first one said.

'And let me guess,' I said, 'this isn't the kind of message you could have slid under the door, or just put in the mail box.'

''fraid not,' the second one said, shaking his head. He had a thick neck and a head like a block of cement; they both did.

'Who's the message from?'

They looked at each other. Could it be they were instructed to deliver a message, but weren't told how to handle this question?

'Come on, you guys are messengers, right?'

'We're convincers,' the first one said.

'Is that what you're called now?' I asked.

'Convincers,' the second man said. 'We're here to convince you to change your mind.'

'Take a new course of action,' the first one said.

'Do the right thing.'

All of sudden I was thinking, Tweedle-dee and Tweedle-dum.

'Yeah,' I said, 'but who's the message from? Just so I know what the right thing is.'

'We're not supposed to say,' Dee said.

'Not til after, anyway,' Dum said.

'So,' Dee said, 'make this easy on all of us.'

'Take it like a man,' Dum said.

They started toward me and I thought, fuck me if I'm gonna take a beating just to make it easy for them.

I broke for the door, knowing there wasn't a chance I was going to make it.

Sixty-Six

I tried not to feel the pain.

I tried to withdraw, crawl inside myself, deny the pain and look at the situation dispassionately. Were these guys sent by Frankie D., to prove he was a tough guy? Or by Howard Hughes, to convince me to work for him? Those were the only two situations I was dealing with. Frankie had been blindfolded, but maybe Rigatoni went back to him as soon as we let him go.

Boy, I thought, Jerry's gonna be disappointed that he hadn't scared Frankie enough – or maybe even Joey Rigatoni – to avoid this.

Unless they were working for Howard Hughes, the businessman, the corporate raider, the Hollywood producer. Had he decided to turn to violence to make his point? Was that the way he thought it was done in Vegas?

These guys were good. Their punches were well-placed for maximum effect. At one point I thought, Man, if they keep this up they could kill me.

I got a shot in once in a while, but eventually I just tried to cover up, roll myself up into a ball . . . and then it stopped.

I uncovered my head, uncoiled my body to take a look, and saw them being pummeled by Jerry. His big fists landed telling blows, convincing the convincers that their job was done and they better get out. He actually lifted one of them off his feet and tossed him across the room. I think it was Dee. Dum ran over, picked his friend up, and they ran into the kitchen, presumably looking for a back way out.

Jerry bent over me, saying, 'Mr G., Mr G., are you OK?'

I opened my mouth to speak, but nothing came out. I tried again. 'Catch one,' I croaked. 'N-need to know who sent them.'

'Are you OK?'

'Go!'

He got up, ran into the kitchen, following them out the back door.

I staggered to my feet and took stock. Bruises, pain, all my teeth were still there, no permanent damage – probably thanks to Jerry.

By the time he returned I was sitting on my sofa with a glass of bourbon. The bottle was on the coffee table in front of me.

'I couldn't catch 'em,' he said, mournfully. 'I'm sorry, Mr G.—'

'Don't be sorry, Jerry,' I said. 'If you didn't save my life, you saved me from a lot more pain.'

'You're bleeding.'

'I am? Where?'

'Your head.' He touched his forehead at the hair line.

I touched myself in roughly the same place, came away with some blood.

'I'll get a wet cloth,' Jerry said.

When he returned I was on my second glass. I sat still and allowed him to clean the scalp wound, which bled worse than it was. My jaw hurt, as did my ribs, probably from kicks that had made it through my defenses.

'Do you wanna go to the hospital?' he asked.

'Not so far,' I said. 'Let's see what happens when I try to stand up again.' I pushed the bottle towards him. 'Have a drink and a seat.'

'I'll sit,' he said, 'but bourbon ain't my drink, and you got no beer. Mr G., what was you thinkin', comin' here alone?'

'I thought I was going to change my clothes and come back to the Sands.'

'And what happened?'

'A woman.'

'Always a broad,' he said.

'Emily,' I said, 'the girl I met at the club. She showed up at my door. I was going to take her for coffee, and when I stepped into the bedroom to get dressed, she apparently opened the door to those two and took off.'

'Bitch!'

'Yes,' I said, 'but now I wanna find her.'

'And make her pay.'

'First,' I said, 'I want to know who sent her.'

'You think it was Frankie D.? That Rigatoni told him what happened?'

'Maybe,' I said, 'but remember, Howard Hughes isn't happy with me.'

'You think Hughes would send two mugs to work ya over? Does he do business that way?'

'Maybe that's the way he thinks it gets done in Vegas,' I said. 'Before we can do anything, we have to find out.'

'Suppose she'd go back home?'

'No,' I said, 'she'd go where there are people, thinking she'll be safe.'

'Where's that?'

I put the empty glass down, didn't refill it. 'She works at a law firm. She'll go there.' I checked my watch. 'But I have a lunch date with Detective Martin, at Grabstein's. I'll have to do that first. That'll give her time to think she's safe.'

'I'll go with you to Grabstein's,' he said.

'Yeah, you will,' I said. 'I'll explain your presence to Martin. You can sit at another table and eat. Are you heeled?'

'I am,' he said, 'I have been since we snatched Frankie D.'

'OK,' I said, 'but leave it in the Caddy when we go into the deli. I don't want Martin to notice it.'

'I ain't comfortable with that, but OK,' he said. 'If those two mugs come back, I can handle.'

'They didn't look armed to me,' I said. 'I guess they figured they didn't need to be. But after going up against you, my guess is they won't come back without guns.'

'What happens if they try for you – for us – at the deli?'

'I'm sure Detective Martin will have his gun on him.'

'Hey, that's right,' he said. 'OK, then. Did you have breakfast?'

'No.'

'Me, neither.'

I still had three hours before I had to meet Martin. I stood up. 'I'm gonna clean up, stretch, see what kind of shape I'm in. If I don't have to go to the hospital, I'll buy you breakfast.'

As I stood up, he stood with me, ready to catch me if I fell over.

I didn't.

Sixty-Seven

Martin was already in a booth when we entered Grabstein's. I was moving OK, if a little stiff, as

I approached. Jerry had eaten a full breakfast, while I had gone with coffee and toast. We were both ready for some good deli.

'You brought your friend,' Martin said. 'That have anything to do with how stiff you're moving?'

'It has everything to do with it.' I sat across from him, lowering myself gingerly into the booth. I told him about the company I'd had that morning. 'So you can see why I wouldn't want to be walking around alone the rest of today.'

'I do see,' he agreed. 'Did they say who sent them?'

'They were gonna tell me after – if I was in any condition to hear them.'

'Are you going to report this?'

'Not until I find out who sent them,' I said. 'Until then, Jerry can sit over there and enjoy some deli. He's never been here.'

'OK,' Martin said, 'I'll go along with that. He's not heeled, is he?'

'No,' I said. 'We figured you would be.'

'Would I be disappointed if I searched him?'

'No,' I said, 'but I'll make him stand still for a frisk if you want.'

Martin took only a second to make up his mind. 'That's fine. He can sit and enjoy.'

'Thank you.' I waved at Jerry, who nodded and sat in another booth, about twenty feet from us. From there he could see me, and keep an eye out the window. I knew that, across the street, was the building the lawyer, Kaminsky, had his office in. I thought I might stop in on him, after. I had an idea.

The elderly waitress came over to take our order, acted like she knew Martin.

'How are you, boychick?' she asked.

'I'm fine, Sima. Tell Manny I'll have my usual.'

'Of course.' She looked at me, then, and raised her eyebrows. 'You I don't know so well.'

'I've been here with Kaminsky.'

'Of course,' she said, 'Kaminsky's friend. What will you have, Kaminsky's friend?'

'Pastrami on rye,' I said.

'Good choice.'

She walked away and, before putting in our order, stopped at Jerry's table. She was there for quite a while, and before long she was laughing. When she walked away she was still laughing and shaking her head.

'OK,' Detective Martin said, 'so what's on your mind, Eddie?'

'You don't like Hargrove any more than I do, right?' I asked.

He frowned and said, 'He's my partner.'

'But that wasn't your choice.'

'No.'

'Why is he so dead set on calling Helen's death a suicide?' I asked.

Martin didn't answer right away.

'He isn't, is he?' I asked. 'You guys are investigating it as a murder and he doesn't want me and Jack Entratter to know it.'

'Let's suppose you're right,' Martin said, 'and we are investigating it as a murder. Would you have anything that would be helpful to us?'

'Is that what Hargrove wants?' I asked. 'He

237

wants us to solve it for him? He's been warning us off knowing that we'd go ahead?'

'You guys may not like each other,' Martin said, 'but you know each other pretty well.'

'Sonofabitch,' I said.

'What've you got, Eddie?'

'Man,' I said, 'I would love to give you something and have you solve it right under his nose . . . and take all the credit.'

'I can't do that,' Martin said. 'He's my partner. Whatever you give me, I'll have to share.'

'And tell him you got it from me?' I asked. 'I hate to give him that satisfaction.'

Martin sat back and regarded me for a minute. 'I don't have to do that.'

'What?'

'I don't have to tell him I got it from you,' he said. 'I'll tell him I got it from a source. We each have our own sources.'

'That's good,' I said. 'That's very good.'

'It's even better if you've got something,' he said.

'Maybe I've got something,' I said, 'and maybe I don't know what to do with it.'

'Could be I'll make sense of it, then,' he said. 'Let me have it.'

I wouldn't have been there if I wasn't willing to take a chance on him. If I gave him what we had and he told Hargrove, well, that was his choice.

'OK,' I said, 'OK,' and I started talking . . .

Sixty-Eight

Our food came while I was talking, so I continued as we ate. When Sima came out with Jerry's order she had three times as many plates as she did for us, but I couldn't see what was on them.

Martin was a good listener, which probably made him a good detective. It was just one of many ways he was different from his partner.

'And you don't think this kid, Joey, is on the lam now?' he asked, when I was done.

'I don't think he did it,' I said. 'Why go on the lam?'

'But you think he might have talked to Frankie D., given you guys up? And that's why you got worked over this morning?'

'It's a possibility.'

'You piss anybody else off?'

'Maybe.'

'Who?'

'It doesn't have anything to do with the murder.' I looked at him. 'Murder, right?'

He signed and said, 'Right.'

'The key, right?' I asked. 'And the fact that she couldn't have hanged herself without something to stand on.'

'Do you know why Hargrove hates you?' he asked.

'There must be more than one reason,' I said. 'Because I work for the Sands, and the mob owns it, so he thinks I'm connected.'

'That's one reason,' Martin said. 'The other is that you seem to be a natural.'

'Natural what?'

'Detective. He struggles, and it seems to come easy to you.'

'Nothing comes easy to me,' I said. 'I'm not a detective, Danny's the detective. And a good one.'

'Well, it must've rubbed off on you, then,' he said. 'There was also the fact of the two ligature marks on her neck.'

'Two?'

'Only one from the hanging.'

'She was strangled first?'

He nodded. 'Somebody didn't know that the two marks would be a dead giveaway – no pun intended.'

We pushed our plates to the other end of the table until Sima came to refill our coffee cups.

'So you managed to find a couple of suspects,' Martin said, 'but now you don't think they did it. Why not?'

'It's all about where it happened,' I said. 'They couldn't have gotten in and out of the Sands so easily.'

'So you're saying it's an inside job.'

'Gotta be.'

Martin sat back and lit a cigarette.

'Come on,' I said, 'you guys must have been looking at employees this whole time.'

'We have.'

'And?'

'She got on the wrong side of some, but not enough for them to kill her.'

'What about Walter Spires?'

'He got fired.'

'So? Haven't you looked into ex-employees?'

He didn't answer.

'He was fired recently,' I said. 'He could've walked in and out with a lot of employees who didn't know he was fired.'

'We talked to him,' Martin said. 'He's a wimp.'

'That's what Bardini said, but I haven't talked to him myself.'

'Maybe you should.'

We sat in silence for a few minutes. I'd learned what I wanted to. They actually were working the case as a murder. Hargrove had lied to Entratter about calling it a suicide.

'OK,' Martin said, 'I'm gonna tell you one more thing. And if Hargrove finds out, he'll kill me.'

'He won't find out from me.'

'The belt.'

'The one she hung herself with?'

He nodded.

'It was too big.'

'What do you mean, too big?'

'It was too big for her,' Martin said. 'She wasn't a big woman, and the belt was sizes too big for her. It wasn't her belt.'

'So . . . it was the killer's.'

Martin nodded.

'Then the killer is a woman.'

'Maybe,' Martin said, 'and maybe she had help, but a woman was definitely there.'

'And you've checked all the female employees?'

'Talked to all of them,' he said. 'No confessions, yet.'

This confirmed what I had been thinking about the club, and the drugs. No connection.

'Well,' Martin said, 'we've compared notes and haven't come up with much, have we?'

'Have we compared notes?' I asked. 'You haven't told me much, beyond the belt.'

'Frankly,' Martin said, 'that's because we've got nothing but the belt.'

'What about the drug angle?' I asked. 'You knew about that, right? I mean, you knew she was a member of the Happy Devil club?'

He didn't answer.

'Why do I feel like I got the raw end of this deal?' I asked.

Sixty-Nine

Martin stood up and left. I thought I was going to get stuck with the bill, but Sima didn't bring one. I stood up and moved to Jerry's table and took my coffee cup with me.

His table was covered with food – pastrami, knishes, lox, soup; I wondered if Jerry had sampled almost everything on the menu.

'Hey, Mr G.,' he said, 'this place is pretty good. Not like a Brooklyn deli, but pretty good.'

'I know.'

'So, what happened?'

'We got took,' I said. 'Turns out we had more information than they do.'

'What about the drugs?'

'They didn't have it,' I said. 'They didn't even have the club.'

'They got anythin'?'

'They've mostly been checking out employees, and coming up empty.' I told him about the belt.

'Well, that's something, but it sure sounds like we got fucked.'

'At least we know they never really believed the suicide angle,' I said. 'But in the end that doesn't help us much.'

'So whatta we do now?'

'Well,' I said, 'you're gonna finish eating and I'm going to have some more coffee.'

'I'm going to need a piece of cheesecake for dessert,' he said. 'You might as well have one, too. You know, to keep up your strength.'

'Why not?' I said.

When we left the deli, Sima gave Jerry a big hug and told him to come back next time he was in town.

'I might even be back this visit, before I go home,' he told her.

'Good. *Mazel tov.*'

Out front I stared at the building across the street.

'What's up, Mr G.?'

'That's where Danny's lawyer, Kaminsky, has his office,' I said. 'I was thinking about dropping in and seeing if I can catch him.'

'What for?'

'Kaminsky knows everybody,' I said. 'I thought I'd talk to him about Howard Hughes. See what

243

he thinks about the man maybe sending a couple of knuckledusters after me.'

'Well, why not?' he asked. 'After all, we're here.'

'Right,' I said. 'Let's see if he's in.'

He was in.

Kaminsky ran a one-man shop, didn't even have a girl working for him. When we walked in we could see through to his office, and he was behind his desk.

'Hey, Kaminsky,' I called.

He looked up, frowned, then brightened.

'Boychicks!' he yelled, 'Come in, come in.'

We walked into his office and he came around his desk to give us each a hug – a pretty powerful hug for a forty-five-year-old, five-foot-four Jewish lawyer.

'Kaminsky is glad to see you,' he said. 'Sit, sit. What brings you here?'

'Well, we were eating across the street and thought we'd drop in.'

He seated himself behind his desk and said, 'Nobody just drops in on Kaminsky unless they've got a problem. Come on, bubuluh, give.'

'Kaminsky, how much do you know about Howard Hughes?' I asked.

'A lot,' he said but he didn't say how.

I told him that Hughes had come to town and was looking to buy a casino.

'Take one over, you mean.'

'Exactly, and he wanted me to help him.'

'And you refused.'

'I did, yes.'

'Good for you. I'll bet he wasn't happy.'

'He was not, and that's what I wanted to ask you,' I said. 'Would he send a couple of mugs to work me over to get me to change my mind?'

'I thought you flinched when I hugged you,' he said. 'From what I know about Howard I would say no, he wouldn't do that.'

'Really?' He was talking like he knew Howard Hughes really well.

'No,' he said, 'but now Maheu, that is the kind of thing he would do. He's a snake.'

'He'd take it upon himself to do that without the word from Hughes?'

'Oh hell, yes,' Kaminsky said. 'He works for Howard, and does what he's told, but he is not without initiative.'

I looked at Jerry, who shrugged.

'Well, OK,' I said, 'that's what I was wondering.'

'Well, you came to the right place for the answer.' He spread his arms. 'Kaminsky knows everybody, right?'

'That's what I told Jerry,' I agreed. 'Kaminsky knows everybody.'

We got up to leave when the import of what we had just said hit me.

'Wait a minute,' I said. 'Kaminsky, what do you know about a law firm called Denby & Sloane?'

'Big business,' he said. 'If Howard Hughes was comin' to town to buy, he'd need somebody local to work with. They'd be one of the firms he'd look into.'

'That's good to know,' I said.

'You want the name of some others?' he asked.

'Nope,' I said, 'Denby & Sloane will do. Where are their offices located?'

Outside Jerry asked as we got into the Caddy, 'So where we headed now?'

'Denby & Sloane,' I said. 'The address Kaminsky gave us.'

'The broad?'

I nodded.

'We've got some questions for Miss Emily Marcus, if that's even her name.'

Seventy

The offices of Denby & Sloane were in a high-priced neighborhood, a long way off from where Kaminsky – by choice, mind you – had his offices. More and more I had to believe that Kaminsky kept his low rent location because it was across the street from his favorite deli.

We had to stop in at a security desk in the lobby to announce ourself. That made getting in a problem, unless we came up with the right name to reference.

The blue-suited security man with a name tag that said BELMONT stared at Jerry, but spoke to me. He looked like an ex-cop gone to seed.

'Help ya?'

I took out my business card – which I hardly ever used – and handed it to him.

'Eddie Gianelli?' he said. 'The Sands Hotel and Casino?'

'That's right.'

'Who are you here to see?'

'Either Mr Denby or Mr Sloane.'

'Denby & Sloane,' he said to himself. He looked down at the phone, which had lots of lights on it, some lit, some dark. He found the one he wanted, picked up the handset and pressed the button.

'Yeah, I got a Eddie Gianelli here from the Sands Hotel? He wants to see Mr Denby or Mr Sloane.' He listened for a moment, then covered the mouthpiece and asked me, 'What's it about?'

Here came the tricky part.

'I'm here representing Frank Sinatra.'

That made the guard raise his eyebrows. He didn't know me from Adam, but he knew Frank's name.

'He says he represents Frank Sinatra. Yeah, OK.' He hung up. 'You can go up. Nineteenth floor. Somebody will meet you at the door. Here, put these on.' He handed us each a visitor's badge. He was still giving Jerry looks, but didn't ask any questions about him.

'Thanks,' I said.

As we walked to the elevator court Jerry said, 'That was too easy.'

'Yeah.'

According to the directory Denby & Sloane occupied several floors in the building. We found the proper elevator – the one that went to floors fifteen thru twenty-four – and took it to nineteen. As the doors opened a smartly dressed young woman in high heels and a short skirt was standing there.

'Are you Mr Gianelli?' she asked. She was slightly breathless, and her eyes were bright. She looked past me at Jerry, then past him, probably hoping to see Frank.

'That's right.'

When she didn't see Frank she lost some of her brightness.

'Follow me, please.'

We followed her, which was a pleasant enough experience, but all-in-all I didn't think she'd cut it at the Sands as a waitress on the floor. She walked us past many desks and offices, where a lot of activity was taking place. Obviously, Kaminsky was right, Denby & Sloane was big business.

'Are we going to see Mr Denby or Mr Sloane?' I asked.

'Mr Sloane is away on business,' she said. I guessed that meant we were seeing Mr Denby.

I looked for Emily along the way, but didn't see her. However, when we finally got to Mr Denby's door the woman sitting at the desk outside it *was* Emily. She was wearing the same clothes she'd had on at my house that morning.

Three cherries!

Jackpot!

'Here are the gentlemen to see Mr Denby,' she said. 'They represent Frank Sinatra.'

'What?' Emily lifted her head and when she saw us her crest fell. (I've always wanted to say that.)

'What are you doing here?' she asked me.

'Came to see your boss.'

Emily gave the other girl a murderous look. I assumed that, at the mention of Frank's name, the young girl had neglected to check with Emily before she allowed us to come up.

'That'll be all, Nancy,' she said, icicles hanging from every word. Nancy skulked away, knowing that she was in trouble.

'You can't see Mr Denby,' Emily said.

'Why not?' I asked, pointing. 'Isn't he right behind that door?'

'Eddie,' she said, 'I can explain—'

'You mean why you came to my house this morning and let a couple of goons in to beat the crap out of me? Yeah, I'd kinda like to hear an explanation for that, but why don't we do it in front of your boss.'

'Eddie—'

'Announce us, Emily,' I said, leaning my palms on the desk, 'or my friend Jerry, here, will pick up this desk and use it to knock down the door.'

She looked at Jerry and immediately knew he was capable of doing it. She picked up her phone and pressed one button.

'Mr Denby? Eddie Gianelli and . . .'

'. . . Jerry Epstein,' I supplied.

'. . . Jerry Epstein are here to see you. They're from, uh, the Sands Hotel and Casino. Yes, sir.' She hung up. 'I'll take you in.'

'Thank you.'

Seventy-One

We followed her through the door to her boss' office. When she closed the door we were all inside.

'Mr Gianelli? I'm Howard Denby.'

Denby was a tall, handsome man in his fifties who was in pretty good shape. He extended his hand to me, which I shook.

'And this is Mr . . . Epstein, was it?'

'It is,' Jerry said. He ignored the man's hand and Denby finally dropped it.

The fact that Emily was still in the room told me that we all knew why we were there, but he played confused, anyway.

'I understand you represent the Sands? What can I do for Jack Entratter?'

'Come on, Denby,' I said. 'You know I'm not here for the Sands or Mr Entratter. This is about Howard Hughes. No, this is really about the two goons somebody – I'm guessing you – sent to my house this morning to work me over, probably to convince me to take the job Mr Hughes had offered me.'

'Howard Hughes,' Denby said, getting back behind his desk. 'I'm afraid I don't understand.'

Emily moved around to stand next to her boss, her hands behind her back, her eyes worried.

'I tell you what,' I said. 'Why don't I have Jerry, here, explain it to you?'

250

Denby looked at Jerry and I'll give him this, he was pretty cool. Emily started to hyperventilate, though.

'I can have security in here in two minutes,' he said.

'Jerry only needs one to break an arm or a leg,' I said. 'He's really good at it.'

Denby looked at Jerry, who smiled at him.

'Maybe we've managed to jog your memory a bit?' I said.

'Perhaps . . .'

I looked at Emily, who looked away. So I wasn't as irresistible as I thought. I figured we'd met in the club by coincidence, and she had recognized my name because she'd heard it from Denby, who had heard it from his client. She decided to try to advance her career by taking an active part in convincing me to work for Hughes – a very active part. Still, the information she'd given me about Helen/Tina had been good, so the time hadn't been a total loss. I just didn't like the coincidence of Helen's murder and Hughes' business suddenly intersecting. It smacked of bad mystery fiction.

'All right,' Denby said. 'Emily, you can go.'

'Yes, sir.'

He looked at me. 'Is that all right with you?'

She gave us a wide berth as she walked to the door and left.

'Will you have a seat?' he asked.

'No,' I said, 'I want Jerry on his feet, in case he has to get to you before Emily sends security in here. Believe me, he's faster than he looks.'

He studied us for a moment, then picked up

the phone, pressed one button, and said to Emily, 'Don't call security. It's fine.'

He hung up and glared up at us.

'What do you want?'

'I don't want any more muscle boys sent after me,' I said. 'I don't want any more attempts to try to convince me to work for Mr Hughes.'

'Mr Hughes doesn't know anything about this.'

'I don't care if you got your orders from Hughes or Maheu,' I said. 'I want it to stop. Tell both of them they can get a lot of bad press out of this, and on top of that Vegas will hear that Hughes is coming. Believe me, they'll close ranks in town.' I paused, then added, 'That will cause you to lose a lot of business.'

Denby hesitated, then said, 'I will deliver your message.'

'Add this to it,' I said, with a sudden thought. 'Tell Hughes it's not time for him in Vegas. We don't want him here. Tell him to try again in a few years.'

'I will tell him,' Denby said, obviously not happy.

'And if he wants to see me again,' I said, with finality, 'tell him to call for an appointment.'

Seventy-Two

On the way out we ignored Emily, walking right past her desk without giving her a look.

Outside, in the car, Jerry said, 'Do you think

that did it? Hughes gonna leave you alone now?'

'I hope so,' I said, 'because I meant what I said. I can rally Vegas against him.'

'I know you can, Mr G.,' he said. 'I keep sayin' you're the man.' He started the car. 'Where to?'

'Back to where it all started,' I said. 'I think I gave Martin enough so that he and Hargrove can clean up the club.'

'The drugs, you mean?'

'Yeah,' I said, 'without meaning to, I think we gave up Frankie D. and Joey. His mom's gonna be real disappointed, after all.'

'We told him we wouldn't tell her.'

'We won't,' I said. 'The cops will.'

'So what do we do now?'

'Like I said,' I told him. 'Let's go back to where it all started.'

'The Sands?'

I nodded.

'It started there,' I said, 'and I think maybe it'll end there.'

The Sands.

The answer had to be there.

Helen's killer had to be someone who knew her, someone who could move about in the hotel and without being questioned. That meant an employee, or a past – but recent – employee.

'We should have been thinking this way from the beginning,' I said to Danny on the lobby phone. Jerry was standing nearby, listening to my end of the conversation.

'Eddie, remember,' Danny said, 'I was able to move around freely.'

'Yeah, but you had permission.'

'So you need to add someone who had permission to your list,' he said. 'Employees, recent employees, and people with permission.'

'Like workmen,' I said, 'delivery men, like that.'

'I'm on my way,' Danny said. 'You're gonna need another set of hands.'

'See you soon,' I said, and hung up.

'Is he comin'?'

'He is.'

'Where do we start?'

'Fourth floor.'

Entratter was not in his office when we got there, so Jerry and I stayed in the outer office, where Helen used to work. I sat behind her desk and absently started opening and closing drawers while giving the whole case some thought.

'I don't know if Danny's gonna agree with me or not,' I said, 'but we should have just concentrated our efforts here, at the Sands.'

'What about all that stuff about the club?' Jerry asked.

'It showed us a different side of Helen, for sure,' I said, 'but Frankie D. and Joey Rigatoni are lightweights. Not killers.' I looked up at him. 'Or don't you agree?'

'I do agree,' he said. 'Those guys would get chewed up and spat out in Brooklyn.'

'Frankie could have made a call to Cleveland for some real muscle, but then he would've had to admit to selling drugs in the club.'

'Cleveland could be in favor of that, Mr G.,'

254

Jerry said. 'Some of the bosses are considerin' it.'

'Well, I guess we could ask Jack to check up on that,' I said.

'Check on what?' Entratter asked, walking in. 'Come on inside.'

He entered his office without breaking stride. Walking behind him I noticed his shoulders slumping, which was unusual for him. He was a big man with wide shoulders, and always a commanding presence in his good suits. Today he seemed tired.

He dropped into his chair and stared at us. I told him about the meeting with Martin, about the drug thing being wrapped up, and about doubting that it had anything to do with Helen's death. He took special satisfaction in hearing that the cops didn't really think Helen had killed herself.

'Unless, like Jerry suggests,' I finished, 'Cleveland is getting into the drug business and sent somebody to take Helen out.'

'If they did,' he said, 'I doubt they would've done it this way. They would have put a bullet in her and planted her in the desert, but I'll check into it.'

'So my thought is that the answer is here, right here, in the Sands,' I said, 'and then there's the belt.'

'What belt?'

I told him what Detective Martin had told me about the belt not being hers.

'So all you have to do is find out who owned the belt,' he said, when I was finished.

255

'Well, the cops have it,' I said. 'It was cloth, so they won't find fingerprints.'

'Great.'

'Danny's coming over,' I said. 'We're gonna hash this out.'

'Don't forget about Robinson,' he warned.

'I won't. I'll call him and check in. And Dean wants to have dinner with me.'

'Don't stand him up,' Entratter said. 'I know you got a lot on your plate, Eddie, but I also know you can handle it.'

'Don't worry, Jack,' I said. 'I've got it all under control.'

I left his office wishing I felt as confident as I sounded.

Seventy-Three

I met Dean in the lobby for dinner. The only place Frank and Dean ate off the strip was the Bootlegger, so we went there. Over excellent lasagna and ravioli we caught up with each other's lives.

'You're Nobody Til Somebody Loves You' had been a huge hit for him during the summer, reaching number one. Dean had just made another movie with John Wayne, a western called *The Sons of Katy Elder*. *Rio Bravo* had been a big hit for them in 1959. He was planning to make some movies based on the Matt Helm spy novels of Donald Hamilton. And then next year, he was going to have his own variety TV series. He didn't know it at the time, but it would run successfully for nine years and make him an even bigger star than he already was.

While Frank was 'The Chairman of the Board', Dean was known as 'The King of Cool'. All of those endeavors would make him even cooler.

I told him stories of murder, sex, Edward G. Robinson and Howard Hughes.

'You have such an exciting life, Eddie,' he said. 'And a full one. Sometimes I think I'd trade with you.'

'You're kiddin'.'

'I'm not,' he said. 'Being me is hectic, and not always exciting or full.'

'You have a great family and a fabulous career,' I said. 'Jesus, you're Dean Martin.'

'Yes, I am.' He picked up his soft drink. 'I'll drink to that.'

I picked up my beer and drank with him.

'Tell me more about the murder.'

I did. I laid it all out for him. Maybe he'd have some insight, or a suggestion. Maybe I just needed to hear it all out loud . . .

Earlier Danny had come by the Sands and we had gone over the case again. We talked about the women who worked there and came up with a list of nine suspects. Since I had agreed to have dinner with Dean, Danny said he'd once again talk to them, and look into their lives.

I wanted Jerry to go with him, but he insisted on trailing Dean and me to the Bootlegger. I told him to eat with us, that Dino wouldn't mind, but he said no. He'd be outside, making sure we weren't disturbed. I told him I'd take him for something to eat after.

'I know you will, Mr G.'

So I listened to myself talk to Dean and in the end he asked, 'Would a woman alone have been able to lift her up and hang her from a pipe?'

Good point. That was why the cops thought there might be two of them.

But think about it, I told myself. What kind of a woman would it take to be able to do that alone?

'It could have been a strong, pissed off woman,' I said. 'Or a desperate one.'

'Desperate people can do amazing things, sometimes,' Dean said. 'Feats of strength they wouldn't ordinarily be able to accomplish.'

'That's true.'

'Well,' Dean said, 'I had something I wanted to talk to you about, but it seems like your time is well accounted for.'

'I'm never too busy for you, Dino,' I said. 'What's up?'

'It's not about me, really,' he said. 'It's Jerry.'

'Jerry . . . Lewis?'

He nodded.

'I thought you two weren't speaking?'

'Well, not every day.'

The animosity of their split had been played up in the press, but I knew that the two had briefly reunited on stage at the Sands in 1960, and later that year when Jerry was too exhausted from his schedule while filming *The Bellboy* to perform his act, Dean stood in for him.

'So what's up?'

'Jerry's got a problem he needs help with, and I think you're the guy,' he said. 'But finish up what you're working on – get things worked out with Eddie Robinson and Hughes – and then we can talk again. OK?'

'Sure, Dean,' I said. 'Whenever you say.'

After dinner we took the limo back to the Sands. Dean was quiet, and I realized I still had to call Eddie Robinson and set up a poker game for him.

I knew Big Jerry was on our tail – probably with the Caddy – but I didn't spot him. Jerry was good at that.

In the lobby Dean gave me a hug and said we'd see each other again before he finished his run at the Sahara and left Vegas. That suited me just fine.

It wasn't that late – Dean liked to turn in early when he could – so I called Eddie Robinson's room and was invited to come up.

When I knocked, the door was opened by Madge, who grinned crookedly at me and said, 'Hiya, Eddie.'

'Madge.'

'Come on in.'

Robinson was sitting at the bar on a stool, and Madge moved around behind it. There were cards on the bar, so I knew she was dealing from there.

'Hey, Eddie G.!' Robinson said, enthusiastically. 'I think I've got it!'

'It?' I asked, coming up alongside him.

'Actually, I should say I've got "him". Lancey Howard. Thanks to Madge I've got the character.

Now all I need to do is try him out in a real game.'

I looked at Madge and she shrugged. She was wearing her work clothes – black trousers, a white shirt and tie.

'He's as ready as he'll ever be.'

'For a high-stakes game?'

'I have the money,' Eddie said, 'but I think I can get the studio to back me so I don't have to use my own. It's all part of my research.'

'Well, always a good idea if you can get somebody else to back your play.'

'Can you set it up?' Robinson asked, excitedly. 'Maybe tonight?'

'That's cutting it a bit close,' I said. 'I think tomorrow night would work better.'

'All right,' Robinson said. 'I'll just keep on working with Madge tonight – that is, if you can stay?' He directed his question to her.

'As long as I'm still off the clock,' she answered, looking at me.

'You are.'

She smiled at the charming actor and said, 'Then I can stay.'

'Excellent!'

'I gotta go, Eddie,' I said, 'but I'll talk to you tomorrow.'

'I'll be waiting for your call, Eddie G.'

'I'll see you out.'

Madge walked me to the door, and when I stepped into the hall I found out why.

'Eddie, Mr Robinson insists on payin' me somethin' for these lessons,' she said. 'I know I'm still on salary, but . . . is it OK?'

260

'That's fine, Madge,' I said. 'No problem with you making a little extra cash.'

'Thanks, Eddie,' she said, 'and thanks for thinkin' of me. He's really a helluva nice guy.'

'Yeah, he is,' I said.

She smiled, backed up and closed the door. With my commitment to Eddie Robinson fulfilled, and my dinner with Dean finished, I could relax and turn my mind back to murder.

Seventy-Four

I got off the elevator on the fourth floor. The office staff had long since gone home, and it was dark and quiet. I went into Jack's outer office and turned on the lights, sat behind Helen's desk. I thought about what Detective Martin had told me about the belt that had been used to hang her. It was too big to have been hers, so it had to have belonged to the killer. That made the killer a woman. But a woman alone? Certainly a large enough woman could have lifted the slight Helen up to hang her. And Helen was light enough for that belt not to have snapped.

How many of the female staff in the Sands were large enough and strong enough to have done it? I knew of a few right off the top of my head, including Marcy, who had found the body.

Marcy. She had run into Jack's office in a panic. What had she been wearing? I couldn't remember. I hated to think of her as a suspect. She had been

261

working at the Sands for a long time. We had dated a few times, and she had even gone out with Danny.

For want of something better to do I got up and walked down the hall to the office where Marcy worked. I turned on the lights and sat behind her desk. There were other women I could think of who the belt might have fit, but they were a little older than she was, and heavier. Big women, for sure, but not fit. Even with Marcy's weight gain, she was fit and strong.

I started to sweat.

Could Marcy have killed Helen, hung her up, and then come running into Jack's office, play-acting at being in a panic? Was she that cold? In my experience, that didn't fit her character at all.

But look at how much we didn't know about Helen's character.

I started going through Marcy's drawers. One was filled with chocolate, and hard candies. Another with envelopes and paper. A third was stuffed with photos. I went through them. Most were of celebrities, and some with Marcy posing with celebrities. There was one of her and Dean, another of her and Sammy. A few of her and Jack Jones, who I knew she liked a lot.

The top center drawer had paper clips, various types of bulletin board pins, pens, pencils, a pack of cookies, some keys . . . I paused, and looked at the key. I knew that the ladies' room was kept locked and anyone needing to use it had to get a key, either from Marcy or Helen. The keys in the desk were loose. Marcy probably knew the restroom key on sight, but I didn't. I took the keys and went to the ladies' room door.

I had five keys in my hand. As I tried them the third key opened the door. I almost went back to the office at that point, but decided to try the other two keys, anyway. The last key opened the door, also.

What was Marcy doing with two keys to the ladies' room?

Was the other one Helen's missing key?

Why would Marcy have Helen's key?

My heart sank, I got a sick feeling in my stomach. Had all the investigating, all the surmise and effort been for nothing? The killer was right there the whole time?

I went back to the office and sat behind her desk again. I put the other keys back in the desk, held the two ladies' room keys in my hand. The fact that Marcy had two keys did not make her a killer. It wasn't even a sure thing that the second key had been Helen's. Maybe Marcy had had a second key made since the murder.

I jingled the keys in my hand for a few more minutes, then put them back in the drawer. If Marcy had killed Helen I needed to prove it, needed to draw her out, somehow.

An extra key, and a belt that would probably have fit Marcy. Not a lot to hang a theory on. And it really wasn't worth mentioning to anyone else – not Danny, not Jerry or Jack, and certainly not the cops.

I had to do this myself, because if I was wrong I was going to feel like a fool, and I was going to owe Marcy a huge apology.

Seventy-Five

I went home and spent a fitful night. I wasn't feeling good about what I was going to do, and hoped I was wrong – dead wrong.

I got two calls that morning. The first was from Jerry.

'Where are ya, Mr G.?'

'I'm home, Jerry.'

'Well, I know that. Why didn't ya tell me where you were goin'?'

'I was tired,' I said. 'I just decided to drive home and go to bed.'

'You remember what happened the last time?'

'I do,' I said. 'I'm gonna get dressed and come right back to the Sands this morning.'

'OK, then I'll wait for you to have breakfast.'

'I'll meet you in the café.'

I hung up, and it rang again even before I got my hand off of it.

'Eddie? Where you been?' Danny asked.

'I came home to go to sleep, Danny.'

'Jerry with you?'

'No.'

'Remember what happened last t—'

'I remember,' I said. 'I'm heading back to the Sands. What have you got?'

'Nothin',' he said. 'I checked out the female staff, there's a few women big enough to have done the job – even Marcy fits – but I don't see a motive. No secret lives for these women, either.'

264

Good, that meant Marcy wasn't a member of the Happy Devil club.

'OK, Danny,' I said.

'I figured I'd check out some of the male staff today, unless you got something else for me.'

'No, go ahead – but wait. Yeah. Maybe check out Walter Spires again.'

'The wimp?'

'Being a wimp doesn't mean he can't be a killer, Danny,' I said. 'Maybe he flipped out.'

'I'll take a look, Eddie,' he said.

'Good. I'll talk to you later. I should be at the Sands all day. I've got to set up a poker game for Edward G. Robinson tonight.'

'High stakes?'

'Yep.'

'Is he ready?'

'He and Madge say he is. I guess we'll find out.'

'I hope he does OK,' Danny said. 'See you later.'

I hung up, took my hand off the receiver quick, but it didn't ring again. I went to shower and get dressed.

Jerry was staring into a cup of coffee when I got to the café.

'You look like you lost your best friend,' I said, sitting across the booth from him.

'Huh? Oh, no, I'm OK.'

I looked around, didn't see Lily working. I figured that was what had Jerry down in the dumps.

The waitress who came over was Nell. Jerry and I both ordered bacon and eggs.

265

'What's the idea of goin' home without me, Mr G.?' he asked.

'I'm not gonna let anyone make me afraid to go to my own house, Jerry,' I said. 'Besides, I think we handled the Howard Hughes problem.'

'I hope you're right.'

'And I'm settin' Robinson up in a poker game tonight,' I went on. 'That leaves us only with the murder.'

'What's the shamus doin'?'

'Checking into some of the male employees who might have wanted Helen dead, but I don't think he's going to find anything.'

'So we're thinkin' it was a woman? Alone? Because of that belt?'

'It would seem so.'

'She'd have to be big, and strong – not like me, but bigger than the dead woman.'

'Right.'

He studied me for a minute then said, 'You got somebody in mind.'

'Am I that easy to read?'

'I know you pretty well, Mr G.'

'Yeah, I guess you do,' I said. 'OK, I wasn't going to share this with anyone, Jerry, but I'll share it with you. Not a word to Danny or Jack Entratter. Agreed?'

'Sure, Mr G., whatever you say.'

I told him about finding the second ladies' room door key in Marcy's desk.

'And the belt,' I said, 'it would fit her.'

'What about the clothes she was wearin' that day?' Jerry asked. 'Would they match the belt?'

'I don't know. To tell you the truth, I can't

remember what she was wearing. But if it did match she's probably gotten rid of it by now.'

'If she's smart.'

'I think Marcy's kind of smart.'

'Then what is she doin' with the second key in her desk?' Jerry asked.

'I don't know,' I said. 'Maybe she didn't think anybody would look. And even if somebody did, it's sitting there among all those other keys.'

'So what are you gonna do?'

We sat back at that moment and allowed Nell to put down our plates.

'I've got to figure out a way,' I said, 'to get her to move that key. Maybe even try to put it back in Helen's desk. Then if we catch her in the act, she'll have to explain. Maybe she'll break down and confess.'

'You and her are friends, ain'tcha?'

'We are,' I said, 'but that doesn't mean I can let her get away with murder.'

'I guess not.' He picked up a piece of bacon and popped it into his mouth. 'How you gonna get her to do it?'

'I don't know,' I said. 'Let's eat and try to figure it out.'

Seventy-Six

Marcy was at her desk when I entered the office. She was busy with something and didn't see me come in. I watched her for a few moments, wondering if I was doing the right thing. She must have finally sensed me there, for she looked up, saw me and smiled.

'Good morning, Eddie.'

'Morning, Marcy,' I said. 'How are you doing?'

'I'm fine, I guess,' she said. 'It's still hard . . . I'm trying to forget, but every time I go into that ladies' room . . .'

'I know,' I said. 'I understand.'

'Do you know . . . have the police finished with their investigation?'

'They're almost convinced that she committed suicide.'

'Almost?' she asked. 'W-what do they need to make up their minds?'

'Well, they're kind of hung up on her key.'

'Her key?' I saw her hand go to her desk drawer, but she pulled it back quickly. 'What key?'

'The key to the ladies' room,' I said. 'They're wondering how she got in there without her key.'

'Well . . . maybe she unlocked it, and then put her key back in her desk.'

I rubbed my jaw and said, 'That would work, but only if they managed to find it there. Yeah, I'm sure if they found her key in her desk, that might do it.'

'Well,' she said, without looking directly at me, 'maybe they should just try . . . looking again. Maybe it's tucked under something, or caught somewhere . . . I don't know?'

'Yeah,' I said, 'yeah, maybe it is. They should look again. Maybe I'll suggest it.'

I didn't leave right away. 'Is there . . . was there something else?'

'No,' I said, 'I was just checking to see how you're doin'. I have to go and talk to Jack. I'll see you around, huh?'

'Sure, Eddie,' she said. 'See you around.'

I walked down the hall to Entratter's office, having planted the seed.

'Did she bite?' Jerry asked.

He was waiting for me in Jack's outer office.

'I hope so,' I said, 'and then again, I hope not.'

'What's goin' on out there?' Jack yelled from inside.

Jerry looked at me. He knew I was trying to keep my suspicion of Marcy just between him and me.

'What are ya gonna tell 'im?'

'I'll tell him what I did,' I said, 'just not who I did it to.'

'You don't think he'll figure it out?'

'He might,' I said. 'Let's see.'

We went into his office and, as usual, Jerry left the talking to me.

'So you're expectin' this person to come to Helen's desk when they think nobody's lookin'?' he asked. 'That's gotta be after hours.'

'If they try it during the day,' I said, 'they could run into you, or somebody from one of the other offices. So yes, I think it'll be after closing.'

'How are you gonna catch 'em?'

'Jerry'll be here when I'm not,' I said.

'What else do you have to do?' Entratter asked.

269

'I need to set up a game for Eddie Robinson to play in, and be there when he starts.'

'You used Madge to coach him, didn't you?'

'I did.'

'How'd they get along.'

'Great! They really clicked,'

'Then use her again,' Jack suggested. 'Get the game started and leave her there with him so you can get down here.'

'Good idea.'

'What will you do after you catch Marcy?' Jack asked. 'What? Did you think I was stupid.'

'No, Jack,' I said, sighing. 'I just . . .'

'I understand,' he said. 'She's your friend. I'm disappointed, too. I was actually considering her as Helen's replacement.'

'If she shows up,' I said, 'I'll have to turn her over to the cops.'

'Hargrove?'

I shook my head. 'I'll call Martin.'

'Hargrove won't like that,' Jack said.

'Let him take it up with his partner.'

Jack sat back and shook his head.

'Having Helen killed is bad enough, but if Marcy did it . . . what's happenin'?'

'Let's hope we can find out soon.'

'Yeah, OK,' Jack said. 'Get it done, boys, get it done.'

'Go home early, Jack,' I said.

'Yeah,' he agreed. 'Call me when it's over, no matter what time.'

'Gotcha.'

Seventy-Seven

I was able to find five high-stakes gamblers who didn't mind playing poker with Edward G. Robinson.

'But no backsies, right?' one of them asked.

I grinned and said, 'No, definitely no backsies. If he loses his stake it's just part of his research.'

The five gamblers assembled in the private room at the Sands first, awaiting Robinson's arrival.

'One other thing,' I said to them, 'he's going to be playing as Lancey Howard. That's the character he's playing in the movie he's researching. Got it? Don't treat him like a movie star.'

'But we can still take his money, right?'

'Take it all, if you can,' I told them.

That made them happy. They thought 'Lancey Howard' was going to be easy pickings.

I walked over to the bar, where the well vetted bartender was standing with Billy Pulaski. The Sands head of security hadn't been very helpful when it came to Helen's case, so he volunteered to help with security for the 'Lancey Howard' game.

'Billy,' I said. 'I have to go, but I might be back.'

'I'll be here the whole time, Eddie.'

'Thanks.'

When Eddie Robinson arrived he was in full

'Lancey' mode, complete with cigar. Madge was with him. She was not wearing her uniform, but she was also not dressed to the nines. The Lancey character was not a womanizer, so Madge was dressed in slacks and a jacket over a powder blue blouse. Not exactly dressed down, she looked good and I told her so.

'Thank you, sir.'

I shook hands with 'Lancey'.

'Thank you for this, Eddie,' he said. 'The experience will be invaluable to me.'

'I hope you win.'

'That's not the point,' he said, with that smile and twinkle, 'but it would be nice. Will you be watching?'

'I have to leave to take care of something,' I said, 'but I may be back.' I slapped him on the shoulder. 'Good luck.'

It was almost midnight when I got down to Jack's office. Jerry was there, waiting.

'Nothin'?' I asked.

'Not yet.'

'OK,' I said, 'you can go.'

'I figured I'd stick around.'

'Get some sleep, Jerry,' I said. 'I'll call you if I need you.'

'Mr G.—'

'I think I can handle Marcy.'

He considered that, then said, 'OK, I get it. She's your friend.'

'Thanks.'

He started to leave, then turned and said, 'I hope she don't turn up.'

272

He left.

'So do I,' I said.

But I wouldn't get that lucky.

Marcy probably figured the later she showed up, the less chance she'd have of being caught. She'd attract no attention walking through the lobby to the elevators. Everybody knew she worked there.

I heard the elevator stop, and the door open. I stood off to the side, peering around the door frame. She must have crept down the hall slowly, just to be sure, but she finally appeared. She stepped into the room, dressed in a sweater, T-shirt, jeans and sneakers. When she got to Helen's desk she opened the top drawer, put her hand in her jeans pocket and came out with the key.

Helen's key.

As she opened the top drawer to put the key back I stepped out from hiding.

'Oh, Marcy.'

She caught her breath and turned her head quickly.

'Eddie!'

'Put the key down.'

She still had it in her hand, so she dropped it on top of the desk, then turned to face me.

'Y-you don't understand,' she said.

'I guess not,' I said. 'Why don't you tell me why you killed Helen?'

'I-I didn't mean to,' she said, her eyes filling with tears. 'She was just . . . such a bitch!'

'You killed her because she was a bitch?'

'N-no, not exactly,' Marcy said. 'She, uh, caught me.'

'Caught you doing what?'

She wet her lips, took off her glasses and wiped her eyes.

'I . . . I took some money from petty cash.'

'What?'

'I needed some extra cash,' she said.

'Why?'

'It doesn't matter, Eddie,' she said. She put her glasses back on. 'She saw me. We were in the ladies' room and she said she was going to tell Mr Entratter.'

'You would have been fired.'

'And arrested.'

'Probably not,' I said. 'Jack wouldn't have prosecuted you for petty cash, Marcy. In fact, he may not have fired you, if you had good reason to take it.'

'I didn't think of that,' she said. 'Helen's never liked me; we never liked each other. She laughed when she said she was going to tell Jack. She turned to leave the bathroom and I-I snapped.'

'You took off your belt and strangled her with it.'

She frowned.

'You knew that?'

'The belt left a mark where you strangled her, and another mark where you strung her up,' I said. 'The cops knew all along it wasn't a suicide. And I never believed it was.'

She laughed at herself and said, 'I'm a fool. It was late – Helen and I stayed late often – and none of the office staff was around. I thought I had gotten so lucky.'

'Marcy . . .'

'Eddie,' she said, 'you're not going to turn me in, are you?'

'I am, Marcy.'

'B-but . . . we're friends.'

'I know,' I said. 'That's why it hurts.'

Suddenly, she did something I never expected. She put her hand in her sweater pocket and took out a gun – a small one. I hadn't even noticed the weight of it in there.

'Oh, Marcy,' I said, 'don't be a bigger fool.'

'I-I don't know what else to do.'

'Why do you have a gun?'

'I've been carrying it since . . . since I killed Helen.'

'Where'd you get it?'

'I've always had it at home,' she said. 'A woman alone . . . you know.'

I didn't know. There was a lot I didn't know about Helen, and about Marcy. The other thing I didn't know was whether or not she'd really pull the trigger.

I got a cold feeling in the pit of my stomach.

'Are you gonna shoot me, Marcy?'

'Just let me go, Eddie,' she said. 'You-you won't see me again.'

Why not? I thought. Let her go, and then call Detective Martin. Let him worry about finding her, catching her.

'OK,' I said.

'W-what?'

'OK. Go.'

'D-do you mean it.'

'I do.'

'Eddie . . . thank you.'

'Just stop pointing the gun at me.'

She did, but only for a second. She aimed it, again.

'Marcy—'

'You're going to tell the cops,' she said. 'You'll let me go, and then you'll call the detectives and tell them. I can't let you do that, Eddie. They'll-they'll catch me.'

'Then turn yourself in,' I said. 'It'll go better for you.'

'I can't go to jail, Eddie!' she almost screamed. 'I can't.'

'Marcy, people know I'm here, waiting for you.'

'Who? You told?'

'Jack Entratter,' I said, 'and Jerry . . . they know. Danny Bardini, too,' I lied, figuring the more, the merrier. 'You can't kill all of them. If you kill me they'll know. The cops will find you, anyway.'

She frowned, trying to figure out her next move.

'It's over, Marcy. Take a rest. Give me the gun.'

'I-I didn't mean . . . I didn't mean it. Any of it.'

'I know you didn't,' I said. 'I know.'

She was just standing there, frozen, so I took a chance. I took a step, then another, and another. When I was close enough I took the gun from her hand, and then she collapsed into my arms.

My friend.

Epilogue

I turned off my VCR, took my glass into the kitchen and washed it out in the sink. Time for the old man to turn in.

While I got myself ready for bed I thought back some more . . .

Detective Martin came and took Marcy off my hands. He came without Hargrove.

'Solving this myself, I can get rid of him as a partner,' he said. 'Thanks, Eddie.'

'Sure.'

Eddie Robinson lost a bundle playing poker, but as he said, the experience was invaluable. He gave a bravura performance in *The Cincinnati Kid*, which was a big hit.

Jerry stayed around a few more days, then went home.

'Maybe I should just move here,' he said, at the airport.

'Leave Brooklyn?'

'You did.'

'Give it some thought, Jerry.'

'Sure, Mr G.'

Jack Entratter had to hire two new employees, one to replace Marcy, and the other to be his new girl. What was her name?

277

Oh yeah, I had one more visitor that week . . .

I was in my pit when he walked up.

'Can we talk?'

'Sure,' I said. I waved at somebody to take my pit for a few minutes, then walked Robert Maheu over to the lounge.

'What's on your mind?' I asked.

'Look,' he said, 'Mr Hughes had nothing to do with the men who . . . assaulted you.'

'Uh-huh.'

'In fact, I didn't, either,' Maheu said. 'That was all the attorneys. They were trying to impress Mr Hughes. Needless to say, they've been fired.'

'And?'

'And Mr Hughes has left Vegas,' he said. 'I'll be leaving today.'

'Good,' I said. 'Tell him not to come back.'

I started to walk away, but he grabbed my arm. I stopped and he took it away.

'You came out on top this time, Eddie,' Maheu said. 'Mr Hughes doesn't want to push it, but he'll be back. Maybe next year, maybe two.'

'So you're blaming the lawyers. You'll let some time go by, and then try again?'

'And you won't know a thing about it,' Maheu said.

I smiled at him.

'My town, Maheu,' I said. 'If you or Hughes put one foot into it, I'll know. Count on it.'

I walked away . . .

Howard Hughes did come back to Vegas in 1967, and he started buying. But that's another story.